THE DOGCATCHER

AND

THE FOX

J. D. Porter

To my dogs and the unconditional love they offered to me:

Mitsy & Tippy, who ran with me as a child,
a dog named Joy, who eased me into retirement,
and the dogs who shared my life in-between – Simba & Jana
and Chelsea & Bexley.

1

Raven Griffith was holding on for dear life. Her horses had panicked and were pulling the wagon at a frightening pace down Forty-First Street. People jumped out of the way, giving her dirty looks when she passed them, as though she were some juvenile troublemaker out for a joy ride on a dogcart.

"Whoa!" she shouted as she stood up and tugged on the reins with all her might.

Raven's problem had begun as soon as she turned off State Street. The horses had cocked their heads and raised their ears when they saw the angry mob milling around on a sidewalk with torches and clubs. She sensed the animals were about to go from nervous to all-out panic, and there was nothing she could do to stop it. The backfire of a truck engine had sounded like a gunshot. That was all it took.

She had been assigned to deliver the team of horses to Rondell Boyd's Livery Stable by her boss at the Animal Welfare Association. The animals had killed their previous owner when, in a panic just like this one, they had rounded a corner too fast and overturned their wagon. Raven wondered if she was about to suffer the same fate.

"Whoa, damn it!" The words jarred her, even as she said them. It was not her habit to curse, but the horses were not the only ones in a panic.

Pulling back on the reins seemed to have no effect, but the horses did respond to a tug left or right. She passed her destination and was fast approaching the busy Michigan Avenue intersection, where motor cars, people on foot, and street cars crossed her path. She was desperate. Instinct took over as she sat down and pulled on the left rein, steering the horses to the left side of the road. She then began what she hoped would be a gradual turn to the right—into an alley. The horses calmed as they came off the pavement and onto the quiet, dirt surface of the alley. When the wagon wheels hit the dirt, and the pulling became more difficult, they slowed even more. Raven eased off the reins and uttered a quiet, "Whoa". When they came to a full stop, she bent forward slightly and took a few deep breaths.

"That was a nice move."

She didn't need to look up to see who was moving up from behind the wagon. Rondell Boyd moved slowly and ran his hand along the left-side horse's flank, patting and talking as he moved to stand between their heads. He took each animal by the halter. They shied away from his touch, but he held on.

"You okay?" he asked.

She was out of breath, so she simply bobbed her head and allowed Rondell to take control. The horses were sweating and sucking air in deep breaths, but they calmed under his soothing voice. He led them in a wide circle that took them back toward the street.

"What set them off?" Rondell asked.

"A mob of people back at State and Forty-First," she said. She held the reins loosely and leaned back in her seat. "I thought the riots were over. Why are white people down here?"

"The troops stayed around for a couple of months," Rondell said over his shoulder, "but as soon as they left, the Irish started picking at us again."

He leaned into the horses, pushing them off the street and into the front yard of his stable. Raven dropped the reins and rose from her seat, but he stopped her. "Hold on." He looked up toward State Street, then pulled the wagon through the barn and out the back. He directed Raven to get down and take control of the horses as he went to close the front door to the barn.

"You don't think they'll come down this far into the Black Belt, do you?" she asked when he returned.

"I don't know what to think," he replied. "I just know that with the troops gone and the police back to looking the other way, we need to be careful."

Rondell Boyd and his wife Essie had moved north from Alabama a couple of years ago with two mules and a wagon. They had found work hauling manure out of the stockyard and sleeping under their wagon at night until they could scrape up enough to buy this barn from a Jew named Greenberg. Rondell had carefully restored the structure and, Raven knew from her experience during the riots that he would rather die than see it destroyed.

Raven had known Rondell back home in Thomasville before he abruptly left town and returned to his people in Alabama. When she learned he was in Chicago, she convinced her boss to work with him. The Association had placed numerous horses and mules into his care—some abandoned, some rescued from abusive owners—and all had thrived. He was a good man who looked after his animals, but she also knew him to be stubborn and opinionated.

"How did you get stuck with this delivery?" he asked as they each unhitched a horse and placed it in a stall.

"The Association is still looking for an officer to work with horses, so I volunteered for this," she replied. She smiled and continued, "I thought it would be an easy ride."

He laughed as he took the halter she handed him and hung it on a nail. She closed the gate and leaned on it to watch the horse nibble at the hay in the manger. Before he could say anything further, their attention was drawn to the loud thump of something heavy hitting the front door of the barn.

"Boyd!" a voice shouted from outside.

Raven and Rondell looked at each other. He picked up a pitchfork and made for the door.

"Wait," she said grabbing his arm. "Let me go out there."

"Hell no," he replied. "I ain't letting you fight my battles."

She took off her cap and shook her head to let her hair fall around her shoulders. "If I go, there won't be a battle to fight."

He turned back to the door, ignoring her plea.

"What's going on, here?" Rondell's wife Essie had appeared in the barn.

"Essie," Raven said. "There's a mob out front and he won't let me go out there to quiet things down. If they see him, there'll be trouble."

Essie looked from Raven to Rondell, weighing the options. A few minutes later, Raven stepped into the front yard of the stable to face the angry men. She deliberately closed the door and pressed her back against the barn, hoping she could keep Rondell inside.

The small crowd before her grew quiet. They were more like boys than men, not over seventeen or eighteen. They undoubtedly expected to see the Negro whose name was scrawled above the door. Instead they faced a white woman with wild black hair and slate-gray eyes—a woman in trousers holding a pitchfork.

Raven kept both hands on the implement so they would not see her shaking, and she swallowed hard, hoping to dislodge the lump in her throat. She also carefully avoided looking directly at the torch in the hands of one of the men. She unconsciously kept her pitchfork pointed in his direction as though it might ward off the flames.

"Where's Boyd?" one of the men demanded.

"He's not here," she lied. "You need to move on. There are animals inside, and I'm not letting you burn them up."

"Then get 'em out of there," shouted another man who rounded the corner of the building. He was squat with a square face and flaming red hair and he was followed by a dozen or so boisterous companions bearing torches, clubs, and rocks. They were laughing and jostling as though they had been drinking and they, too, came up short at the sight of a white woman in this neighborhood.

"I can't get them out. There's nowhere for them to go."

"What are you protecting that job-stealing nigger for? There should be a white man running this livery."

"Who you callin a nigger, boy?"

Raven was confused. That was Rondell's unmistakable baritone voice, but she was practically touching the barn door and it had not opened. Her eyes swung toward the voice as Rondell emerged from the shadows at the side of the building. The entire congregation of people shifted in his direction.

He stood holding an axe handle with his feet apart, ready for action—a slender man with smooth skin that defied any attempt to guess his age. His deep voice, clever mind, and defiant disposition made her think he was pushing forty. Rondell was one of those Negroes who clearly did not like white people telling him what to do. He would probably have been lynched, had he stayed in Alabama. Now he might be lynched here in Chicago.

As she moved to head off trouble, Raven raised the pitchfork and pointed it at her opponents. The flash of a camera momentarily blinded her and gave her hope that the mob would not harm a white woman in front of a news photographer.

The little red-headed man clenched his fists, rose up on the balls of his feet, and said, "Come on, boys. Let's burn this place down."

Raven gripped her pitchfork and felt Rondell move up beside her. She wanted to run away, but her feet were rooted to the spot. She was relieved to see the crowd hesitate and to hear another man speak for the first time.

"Danny," he mumbled to his red-headed companion, "Let's move on. We can't win a fight with a woman. The newspaper is here, and they will eat us alive. Mr. Sweeney won't like that."

At the mention of Sweeney's name, Danny's demeanor changed. His puffed-up presence deflated like air coming out of a tire. His fierce eyes became shifty, and he glanced over his shoulder at some invisible presence.

At that moment, Raven realized that this hateful mob—these men of violence—were not here on some noble mission. They were here at the behest of others. They were puppets whose strings were being pulled. Raven could not help but worry. Who were the puppeteers and what could motivate them to foment such hatred and violence? Raven planted the pitchfork handle in the dirt and let the man approach her. She towered over him, her black hair billowing in the evening breeze.

"This ain't over," Danny said. He backed away from her and said louder as he glared at Rondell and moved away. "We'll be back."

They never came back. Boyd's Livery stable and all the animals inside were spared, thanks to the courage of one woman—at least that's how the newspaper reported it. The photograph of Raven Griffith holding off a mob with a pitchfork would become iconic both for the strength of one woman, and for her fierce determination to protect helpless animals. Her boss, however, would not be impressed.

2

"What were you thinking?" Louis Hanson said as he confronted her in the office the next morning. He waved the morning edition of the *Chicago Herald and Examiner* at her.

Raven was relieved that Lou remained seated at his desk. It made her uncomfortable when they stood talking. She was nearly six feet tall, and she towered over Lou's slender, five-foot, six-inch frame.

She had been looking out for the welfare of Chicago's animals for over a year—hired by Lou at a time when America's participation in the Great War had made jobs for women more plentiful. She had a passion for animals and decidedly little patience for those who neglected or mistreated them.

"If I hadn't gone out there, they would have burned those animals alive," Raven replied with more anger than she intended. She turned and walked back toward her table, mumbling loud enough for him to hear, "I'm tired of serving coffee to teamsters."

"That's your job." He was practically shouting. "That's why I hired you!" He gave her a long, appraising look, then continued, "Why don't you put on a dress, clean yourself up, and find a man who'll marry you. You could be an attractive young woman if you'd put your mind to it."

He might have been genuinely worried about her, but Raven suspected the long-time Superintendent of the Animal Welfare Association simply did not like having a woman's photo in the newspaper representing his organization—especially, Raven suspected, this impertinent young woman who had a way of getting under his skin. In all the time she had worked for him, he had only used her in their workhorse relief program, giving out thousands of bags of oats, carrots, and chopped apples for horses; dog biscuits for dogs; and even coffee and doughnuts for drivers.

"This picture shows you pointing a pitchfork at Danny Malone and his brother Sean," Hanson continued, holding the front page in one hand, and pointing with the other. "Do you know who they are?"

Raven shook her head.

"They're Sweeney's Colts, that's who they are. They're gangsters and Brian Sweeney doesn't like being bested. Those Malone boys aren't going to forget you."

His telephone rang, so she took the opportunity to ease out of his office. She knew of the so-called athletic clubs that dotted the Irish territory in the south end of town and recalled the murderous look in Danny's eyes as she loomed over him in front of the stable. He and his friends would have burned that barn with the animals inside if she had let him. They were little more than a gang of bullies who liked to drink, fight, and assault outsiders. Their latest target was the thousands of blacks who had migrated up from the Deep South during the Great War and had taken up residence across Wentworth Avenue from their Canaryville neighborhood in what came to be known as the "Black Belt".

Many of the clubs were tied to important Irish politicians and Raven wondered if Lou was worried about the fallout that might affect his political standing. She didn't know much about Chicago politics, but she knew palms were greased and favors were called-in even, probably, in the world of animal welfare.

She was hanging up her coat when Lou approached her from behind. "Here," he handed her a slip of paper. "Make yourself useful and go see about this."

Opal Fassbender's kitchen made Raven uneasy. Yesterday's dishes were piled in the sink, pots and pans littered the stove, and Opal Fassbender herself—well, the term slovenly was as kind a term as Raven could conjure. It also reinforced her opinion as to why she was here. This untidy woman had misplaced her dog, and she expected Raven to find it for her.

Mrs. Fassbender placed two cups of coffee on the table and plopped down opposite Raven. Her eyes were still red from crying.

"Tell me about your dog," Raven said, trying to muster a tone of genuine concern. "Mr. Hanson's note said she is a golden retriever."

Mrs. Fassbender looked at Raven, and then said, "I let Molly outside to do her business yesterday afternoon, and when I went to call her in, she was gone—just gone." She began to cry and through her sobs said, "I went up and down the street calling her. I asked the neighbors, and no one saw her."

"Could she have just run off?" Raven asked.

"Oh no," Mrs. Fassbender exclaimed.

Raven let her cry for a minute then asked, "Mr. Hanson sent me out here because you said Molly was stolen. Why do you think that? Did you see something suspicious?"

She blew her nose. "Arthur, the man next door, did. He saw a green box truck with two men in it driving slowly up and down the street at the time she went missing. It's the only explanation."

"Could I have a look at your back yard?"

"Of course."

Raven slipped into her coat and wrapped a scarf around her neck. Mrs. Fassbender opened the door to the back porch and stood in the doorway as Raven walked the perimeter of the yard. The white picket fence had turned to gray, and some tops were broken off, but it appeared solid with no breaks or holes under it. The garden itself was not much of a garden. The leaves had not been raked and weeds had taken over the planted areas. Raven could see her breath in the frosty air as she stepped carefully to avoid Molly's frozen droppings. She tested the side-gate, which was held closed by a spring. Her first thought was that the dog would have had somehow to pull the gate open in order to let herself out, but it wasn't difficult to imagine the gate being held open by the mounds of leaves and sticks that littered the yard. The dog, Raven decided, had probably opened the gate with her nose and was gone thanks to the untidy habits of a careless owner.

As Raven concluded her walk-around and mounted the steps, Mrs. Fassbender seemed to be regaining some composure and said, "Lou's a sweetheart for sending you out here."

Raven had to repress a smile at the thought of Lou Hanson as a sweetheart. There was little to do here, but she didn't want to rush off, so she walked back into the kitchen and stood next to the table. "Have you known the Hansons long?" she asked.

"Mildred and I were in school together," she said. Then she caught Raven off guard. "She's dying you know—heart failure."

Mrs. Fassbender was looking down at her coffee and did not see the shock on Raven's face.

"No," Raven said quietly, "I didn't know."

Raven sat back down at the table, mildly embarrassed—not because she did not know about Mildred Hanson's terminal disease (why would she?)—but because she could not work up much sympathy for Lou or his wife. Even though he had offered her an opportunity to do something she had a passion for, she found him to be irritating to work for and difficult to be around.

They sat for a moment in silence, and then Raven said, "Do you suppose I could have a word with your neighbor?"

"He'll be at work," she said. "He's a switchman for the Illinois Central, the same railroad my husband works for."

Everyone in this neighborhood probably worked for the Illinois Central. The rail yard was at the end of the block, near enough that Raven could hear the banging of the cars as they were switched and coupled.

Raven sipped her coffee and eyed Mrs. Fassbender over her cup. Perhaps Molly had been stolen, but it was more likely that the dog had simply chased a cat onto the next block. It would not be unusual for a house dog, unaccustomed to life on the streets, to forget how to find her way home. It was also unlikely, although Raven would not voice this, that Molly would survive for long out there.

"We'll be on the lookout for any golden retrievers that are picked up," Raven rose to leave. "Are there any unusual characteristic that would help us identify Molly?"

She thought for a moment then said, "Not really, except for the red bandana that I keep tied around her neck."

"That's a big help," Raven said at the front door. "We'll be in touch if anything develops."

"Tell Lou and Mildred I send my best," she said to Raven's back as she walked to the street. Raven just waved.

R aven's chilly, fifteen-minute walk back to the office had cleared her mind and given her time to consider how she would approach Lou about his wife's illness. In the end, she had decided the best approach was no approach at all. She would let him bring it up.

"How is Opal?" he asked from the door to his office.

"About as well as can be expected," she said

"What do you think happened to her dog?"

"Well," Raven began, "the gate to the back yard does not have a latch, so I think it probably just ran off. But I didn't tell her that. I said we would be on the look-out."

"Can I help you?" Hanson said over Raven's shoulder.

She turned and saw Rondell Boyd. Raven had never seen him in their office—didn't even think he knew where it was located. Apparently, Lou had never even met him, so Raven introduced them.

"What are you doing here?" she asked Rondell after Hanson had returned to his office. She tried to hide her surprise, motioning for him to take a seat at the table.

He sat down and looked around. "I need your help with something," he said.

"Are those gangs bothering you again?"

"No, no. Nothing like that," he said. "I know a man—a white man. He's been real nice to me and Essie. He has two dogs that went missing this morning."

Another missing dog case, thought Raven. It was odd how these things ran in spurts. Next week it would probably be a string of horse abuse cases.

"Do you want me to go down and talk to him?"

"I told him I would speak to you," Rondell said. "He's real upset. Says someone stole them."

"Why does he say that? Maybe they just ran off."

"No," Rondell said. "Those dogs didn't just run off. They is working dogs. He uses them to herd sheep down at the stockyards. You go talk to him. You'll see."

Raven glanced at Lou to see if he had heard the mention of the stockyards. He had not, but Raven knew she would need to plan her next move very carefully.

3

*A*bsolutely not," Lou had said yesterday in response to Rondell's request for help. Raven knew that Lou did not want his people entering the stockyards and causing trouble. The animals were destined for slaughter, so their treatment was not up for consideration. All she wanted to do was talk to Ozzie Bunton about his missing dogs. But Lou had been adamant. That is why she had not gone directly to Bunton's place but, instead, sat outside the back door of Rondell Boyd's stable.

"Are you the lady from the welfare association?"

Raven had seen him approaching out of the corner of her eye but decided to let him make the first move. She stood as he approached and offered her hand. "I'm Raven Griffith."

"Ozzie Bunton," he said. "My friends call me Oz."

He was half a head shorter than Raven, with long gray hair that had not seen a brush in some time, and a thick Scottish accent. His eyes would have had a twinkle, had they not been so clouded with sadness.

"I understand your dogs have gone missing."

"Aye, that they have."

"Tell me about them."

"A couple of real sharp lads. Black and white border collies, they are. I call them Thunder and Lightning." His face lightened a bit as he described them. "We work the sheep pens down at the Yard, moving stock into the sorting corrals."

"Is that where they went missing?"

"Oh no," he said. "They went missing from my home."

"And where is that?"

"Back of the Yards," he replied. "Just the other side of Canaryville."

The mention of Canaryville made Raven shudder. It was a tough neighborhood of Irish immigrants who worked in the stockyards on their western boundary and tormented the Negro community along State Street to their East. It was also home to the Malone boys, Brian Sweeney, and a host of violent Irish gangs. The Back of the Yards neighborhood was further west along the southern border of the stockyard and populated largely by Germans, Poles, and other Eastern Europeans. Raven wasn't sure how this Scotsman fitted into all that.

"I'd like to have a look if that's okay."

"Aye," he said. "We can cut through the stockyard."

"No," she replied. "My boss doesn't want me to go in there."

He looked puzzled at that, but said, "We'll take the long way, then."

They walked briskly toward State Street where they turned south, then turned right at Forty-seventh and continued the dozen or so blocks along the southern boundary of Canaryville. They spoke little—Raven out of her unease at being so near the territory of Brian Sweeney and his gang, and Bunton probably due to his natural taciturn character. When they arrived at the southeast corner of the stockyard, they stopped.

The first thing that struck Raven was the presence of the flies. They swarmed in great clouds, crawling on every bit of exposed skin. Raven had to keep her mouth closed. Then there was the smell. She thought she had a strong stomach for animal odors—urine, feces, even dead animals—she had smelled it all. But this was something else. She fought the urge to cover her mouth with a handkerchief. The odor made her eyes water and threatened to shut down her nostrils. And as she surveyed the scene before her from a slight rise in the road, she could understand why. For what appeared to be miles, certainly as far as the eye could see, stretched a massive checkerboard of wooden corrals and in them she could make out cattle and hogs of every description. The animals were being shifted down lanes, up chutes, and into adjoining corrals in some obscure, random choreography that probably made sense to the hundreds of men conducting it.

After she marveled at the spectacle for a moment, she said, "I don't see any sheep."

"Sheep pens are up this way," Bunton pointed up the street and began walking again.

They walked past animal pens on their right and the Back of the Yards neighborhood on their left. Finally, he stopped and led her to a fence where dozens of sheep were being herded into a chute by two border collies. They watched for a moment as the dogs ran back and forth in stealthy movements and in response to whistles from their handler. They kept the sheep bunched-up and moving in the direction of the chute.

"My house is here," he said, turning his back to the pen and pointing toward a neat, wooden bungalow. They walked across the street and stood in front of the home.

"Were the dogs in that fenced section of the yard," she pointed to the side of the house.

"Aye."

"And was the gate left open?"

"Not by me."

"Could your wife have left it open?" she asked. "Or your children—do you have children?"

"My children are old enough to know better," he said. "These dogs are not just our livelihood; they're part of the family." Tears welled up in his eyes and, for a moment, she thought the tough little Scotsman might cry. Finally, he said, "I hope you find whoever took my dogs before I do. I'll murder the bastards."

"I'm afraid there isn't much we can do, Mr. Bunton. We're not the police. We can't go off and try to arrest anyone."

He was silent, so she continued. "Has there been any unusual activity in the area recently—strangers about, or any suspicious vehicles?"

"No, not that I know of."

"What about your neighbors?"

"They would na steal my dogs."

"No," she said quickly, "I didn't mean that. Might they have seen anything unusual?"

"Nobody's said anything."

"Could we ask her?" Raven pointed to a large woman who was bent at the waist pulling weeds from the flower bed along her front porch.

"Lena," Bunton shouted. She stood as they walked to the edge of her yard. "This lady is helping me look for Thunder and Lightning. Have ya seen anything suspicious around here lately?"

Lena eyed Raven with suspicion as she spoke to Bunton. "No," she said and resumed her weed pulling.

Bunton shrugged, and they returned to his yard.

"There was a box truck," Lena said to their backs.

They turned and she continued, "It was painted green and two men were in it. Driving real slow up the street. It was like they were looking for someone—or *some thing*."

These are good," Josephine Washington mumbled through a mouthful of food. "What are they?"

"What are what?" Lou asked.

Raven hadn't heard the door to the office open. Lou hung his coat on the hook behind the door and shuffled over to the table. He looked tired. His thinning, gray hair had not been combed and his shirt looked as though he had slept in it. With his wife's illness, Raven imagined, he probably had.

"Care to join us?" Raven asked brightly.

"What are those?" he said eyeing the half-dozen small, round pastries Raven had placed on the table.

"Those," she said proudly, "are scotch pies. They're filled with minced sheep meat—mutton, I think—and they're good."

She looked at Josephine for confirmation, but the girl could only nod—her already-round face accentuated by her stuffed cheeks. Josephine, or Jo, as she liked to be called, had apparently wandered into the office while Raven was out and had become the Association's newest volunteer.

Madge Bentley, the office manager, trundled out of her office, took one of the pies without asking, and walked back inside.

"Where did you get them?" He picked one up and took a bite, nodding as he chewed thoughtfully.

Raven hesitated, and then replied, "From the wife of Rondell's friend, the sheep herder."

Lou stopped chewing and looked hard at her, so she held up her hands. "I did not go to the Yards. I met him at Rondell's, and we walked to his house."

Lou sat down and continued chewing, so Raven pressed on. She described the dogs and their importance to both the Buntons and the stock yard operation and the circumstances of their disappearance. She watched Lou as she talked and thought she saw him relax as the spicy meat pie disappeared in his hand and he leaned back in his chair. After hearing of his wife's illness from Opal Fassbender, she had a new appreciation for the pressure he must be under. She had no wish to make his work life miserable as well.

"And one of the neighbors," Raven finished her story, "claims she saw a green box truck driving up and down the street. There were two men inside and, according to the neighbor, they appeared to be looking for something." She paused for effect. "That has to be more than a coincidence. That's the same kind of truck Mrs. Fassbender reported."

She watched Lou for a reaction.

"I'm afraid there's more," said Hanson.

She watched him pick at his teeth with his fingernail and make a sucking sound with his lips before he said, "We've had other reports from around the city. Mostly about men rounding up stray dogs, but a few pets, as well."

They sat in silence for a moment as the scope of the problem sank in.

"Why would someone round up dogs?" Josephine asked.

Strays were a problem all over the city. Raven wondered if this might actually be a blessing. On the other hand, she felt they needed to do something for the Buntons and Mrs. Fassbender.

"What should we do?" she asked Hanson.

"I wish I knew," he said. "I've been trying to get the Board to allow me to hire more people, but they say we don't have enough money."

"What about more volunteers?" asked Jo.

"Who's going to manage them?" countered Hanson.

Raven thought that was something she should offer to do, but she liked to work on her own. She had no wish to be saddled with a bunch of do-gooders. Still, they had to do something.

"In the meantime," Hanson said to Raven, "I need you to go over to the zoo this afternoon. We've had a complaint."

"Complaint about what?"

"They didn't say. Just go over there and see how everything looks." He looked at Josephine for the first time and said, "And take her with you."

"What? Why?"

"Because I said so." Hanson stood up to end the discussion. "I want you ladies going out in pairs from now on. It'll be safer."

The Lincoln Park Zoo had a reputation for excellence. It had been a fixture in downtown Chicago for half a century and boasted some impressive facilities, including a sea lion pool, an eagle flight cage, a lion house, and a bird house. Raven knew about zoos. Her father had built and now directed one back home. With all the animal abuse in the city, the zoo was the last place that needed attention, but she wanted out of the office. She nodded at Jo, snatched up her parasol, and walked out into an afternoon that would turn out to be anything but a walk in the park.

4

W hose rig is this?" Raven demanded of the men behind the two wagons outside the Lincoln Park Zoo.

Activity stopped as four teamsters peered back at her. She held the bridle of a tall black draft horse and, as it shook its head, she was thrown off balance. The men laughed as she stumbled and steadied the hat on her head.

"This horse is lame," she continued. "He needs attention."

"That horse," replied one of the men, "is none of your business."

He leaned around the back of the wagon for a closer look at her, and she stared defiantly back. He was a weathered, muscular man who carried a burlap sack of animal feed on his shoulder. The scar running down his jaw and the whip he carried gave him an air of menace. Raven had seen plenty of bullies like him who liked to mistreat their animals. He dropped his load and strutted toward her as his face hardened. Although she couldn't help but recoil a bit, she forced herself not to back up.

Raven and Jo had stopped off at her apartment to get Jo cleaned up before taking the streetcar to Clark and Webster and walking East toward the West Gate of the zoo. Raven did not admit it to her companion, but she wondered how she would know if animals at the zoo were being mistreated and what, if anything, she could do about it. She liked zoos and did not have a problem with the keeping of animals in cages, and the Lincoln Park Zoo was an iconic community gathering place. Most people, she assumed, thought the zoo was just fine as it was. Every time she had been there, the animals appeared comfortable and well cared for. Sea lions swam lazy laps in their pool, big cats lounged majestically on their benches, and zebras appeared to doze standing in the shade. The only complaint she could imagine was that the cages were too small. But this was downtown Chicago. Space was at a premium.

As they approached the zoo entrance, Raven had noticed some men transferring bags of what appeared to be animal feed from wagons into a small shed. The trouble began when one of the horses caught her eye. It was shifting uneasily on its left front hoof. Jo remained near the road while Raven moved in for a closer look.

"You need to take this horse out of service," she said to the man.

"You're the one I seen in the newspaper," the man snarled. He turned to his mates and continued, "This is the woman who defends niggers that come in here and take our jobs."

As his companions moved in for a closer look, the man balled his fist as if to punch her but at the last instant opened his hand and gave her a violent shove, sending her to the ground. She immediately jumped to her feet and readied her parasol to club him. He stepped forward to meet her challenge.

"Hold on, Vinnie," said another man. "There's no need for that."

"Stay out of this, Harry."

Harry stepped between Raven and the man, holding up both hands to stop the action. He then moved quickly to the horse, turned his back to everyone, and pulled up the hoof, lodging it between his knees.

"There's a piece of glass in here," he said, and with a flick of his folding knife he sent the object flying across the driveway. "There," he said. "He's not cut. He'll be fine."

Vinnie stared at Raven for a moment and glanced at Harry before moving back to continue his work as if nothing had happened. Harry did not join them.

"I'm not sure that was such a good idea," he said to Raven. "Those teamsters are some pretty tough customers."

She was still flushed with anger as she looked closely at Harry. He wore the uniform of a zookeeper with his sleeves rolled up and his collar unbuttoned. He was handsome in a rugged sort of way, and he was clearly good with animals.

"You work at the zoo," she said.

"I'm Harold Fischer," he said. "Folks call me Harry. I am curator of birds, but," he glanced at the horses, "I started out in hoofed stock." He paused then asked, "Is it true what he said about your picture in the paper?"

"For the most part," Raven said evasively. "I'm here to look at the zoo, not those guys and their horses."

"The zoo?" asked Harry in surprise.

She nodded.

He smiled, and when Raven looked down and gave a slight smile back, he said, "You can look at whatever you please. I'll show you around—but only if you'll let me buy you a coffee after."

"Thank you, Mr. Fischer," she said, "but that won't be necessary."

"I might like a coffee." They both turned in surprise. Raven had not heard Josephine move up beside them.

"This is my colleague, Josephine Washington," Raven said.

"Call me Jo."

"Pleased to meet you, Jo," Harry said with a polite bow. "And you are?" He turned back to Raven.

"Raven," she said. "Raven Griffith."

"Raven," he repeated. "Like the bird?"

"Yes, like the bird."

Harry had a private word with the teamsters and motioned for Raven and Jo to follow him down a wooded path and into the zoo.

The change in atmosphere from the noisy, dirty street outside was remarkable. Even the air seemed cleaner. Raven had been to the zoo once or twice, but never noticed how pleasant it was. The walkways were wide, paved, and flanked by formal plantings that were now carpeted by fall leaves. Clouds hung low in the afternoon sky.

"I appreciate your doing this, Mr. Fischer," she said.

"Call me Harry, Miss Griffith."

They strolled past the prairie dog village and stopped at the sea lion pool.

"I need to finish my cleaning routine," he said. "You two are welcome to look around and I'll catch up with you in an hour or so."

As they watched him walk away, Jo said, "I like him."

Raven did not reply. She wasn't sure whether she appreciated or resented the way he had stepped in to intervene with the teamsters. She did not like the idea that she needed a man to rescue her.

Harry Fischer was large and powerfully built but moved with a gentle grace. He wore stained khaki pants over well-worn shoes and a tan shirt that indicated by its rumpled appearance that he must be a bachelor. His face was handsome in spite of his pock-marked skin and shaggy mop of sandy-brown hair.

Raven and Jo left the sealion pool and turned north past the Landmark Café and toward the hoofed stock yards beyond.

Jo looked at the ground as they walked. She was a handsome girl, especially now that she had a bit of coloring applied to her recently washed cheeks and wore one of Raven's old blue and white gingham dresses with the hem pinned up.

"That man was going to hit you," Jo continued. "What would you do if he had?"

"I hadn't thought much about it. Why?"

Jo was silent for a few steps before she replied, "I think men like that need to get what's coming to them."

"I would fight back, if that's what you mean."

Their tour took them in a wide loop, through the hoofed stock area, past the elephant and through the bear line with its polar bears, black bears, and a massive grizzly named—according to the sign—George. All the animals appeared to have what they needed, and they did not appear to be abused or neglected. Even the elephant had a large pool to wade in on hot days. When they arrived at the bird house, they sat on a bench inside to escape the brisk wind that had blown in off Lake Michigan.

Raven shared a little of her story with Jo—growing up in a small town and being the daughter of a zookeeper herself. When she was sixteen years old, her father had been hired to open a zoo for her hometown. She had been allowed to clean cages, take care of a confiscated black bear, and bottle-raise some orphan bobcats. She had a lifelong affinity for animals, but she had not been allowed to live out her dreams of working with animals. Her father had sent her away to a boarding school where she could train for a respectable job for a woman—a schoolteacher.

When Raven asked Jo for her story, the girl just told her she was an orphan who had offered to volunteer at the association in exchange for some food. Raven wanted to learn more of her background, but Harry rejoined them to continue their tour. He escorted them to the Lion House—an impressive structure with its barrel-vaulted ceiling, spacious interior public space, and clear-story windows that provided both light and ventilation. It was, Harry informed them, the vision of the zoo's legendary director, Cyrus DeVry.

Jo pointed at a lion in one of the cages as they strolled down the hall and asked, "Who is that?"

"That's Sheba," he replied. "She's alone for now, but our new director is a former circus man and he says he may have a male from a circus that is coming through town."

"New director," she said. "What happened to the old one?"

"Not sure," he replied. "Politics, I suppose. The new man has plenty of ideas. I just hope he's more than just talk. Some of our animal areas are in bad shape."

"What animal areas?" Raven was thinking of a reason to justify her visit.

"Well," he replied, "the bird house, for starters."

"Why?" she asked. "What's the problem with the bird house?"

"The cages are rusting—falling apart, really. I wish they would tear it down and give me a new building."

His passion impressed her, but she could only reply, "Our interest is primarily with the larger animals, Harry. I don't think I could have any influence over the condition of your birds."

He deflated a bit, but said, "Maybe you could just give it some thought."

As they left the Lion House, they learned that he was a city boy—born and raised on the north-side of Chicago—who had a special interest in birds but who cared deeply about the welfare of all the animals in his care. It wasn't unusual, he told them, for him to spend the night at the zoo to nurse a sick animal or feed some newly hatched bird.

A gust of wind caught Raven's hat and blew it across the lawn. Harry retrieved it and they all had a good laugh as he stumbled after it.

"Maybe we need to see about that coffee you promised," Jo suggested, glancing at Raven for confirmation.

"We need to be getting back to the office," Raven said, but seeing the disappointment register on Jo's face, she relented. "I suppose we could spend a few minutes out of the wind."

T his is a nice place," Raven said as they seated themselves at a table inside near a window where the Café Brauer guarded the south entrance to the zoo. "Do you stop here every day?"

"No," he laughed. "This place is a little grand for my means."

"You really don't need to do this, Harry."

"Sure he does," said Jo with a giggle.

Raven pulled out a cigarette and Harry was quick to strike a match. The clouds had parted, and the sun glinted off the lagoon as a pair of swans swam lazy circles. A bright red cardinal sat on the railing outside the window, lending a splash of color to the black iron fence beneath it.

"So," he said as their coffee was served. "What did you expect to find at our zoo today?"

"Nothing," she said. She leaned back in her seat and blew out a puff of smoke. "I can't imagine what the complaint was about—if there was a complaint."

"Why would you say that?"

"Let's just say our boss might have had ulterior motives," she replied. "He doesn't appreciate my taking the initiative and likes to put me in my place."

"I don't want to agree with him," Harry said, "but you taking-on Vinnie and his pals wasn't such a good idea."

"If I hadn't stopped," Raven bristled, "that horse would be walking around with a piece of glass in its hoof until it got infected. It would probably have ended up being put down."

"That's true," said Harry, "but you could also have been hurt in the process."

Raven didn't respond, so he continued. "What did Vinnie mean about your picture being in the paper?"

Raven explained the incident at Rondell Boyd's Livery Stable, how her picture came to be in the newspaper. Harry listened in rapt attention, but when she was finished, he sipped his coffee in silence. Raven eyed him for a moment, sensing his lack of approval for her actions. She felt sure it was because she was a woman. She could not help but pick at the scab.

"Are there any female zookeepers at your zoo?" She asked—already knowing the answer.

Harry laughed as though she had just delivered the punch line of a joke. He stopped himself and looked at her. "Well," he stammered. "Zookeeping is not women's work."

"What does that mean?"

"It means women belong in the home, not shoveling manure for a living."

"What about voting," she continued, getting angrier by the minute. First Lou Hanson yells at her in the office this morning, then a bully pushes her to the ground and threatens to whip her, and now this.

"Do you believe women should have the right to vote?"

"Women should leave the game of politics to men," he said. "It's like playing poker, smoking cigars, or betting on the horses. It's unseemly for a proper woman to be involved in politics—and that includes voting." His voice was raised, and people were turning to look.

The waiter was making his way to their table as Raven stood up and placed her napkin on her plate. She looked at Jo until she, too, stood in confusion.

"Thank you for the coffee, Mr. Fisher," she said. "But I believe I've seen quite enough of your zoo."

His mouth dropped open. He rose from his chair and watched the two women walk away.

Raven's anger subsided with every step as she realized how rude she had been. Jo's disapproval was evident by her downcast eyes and her silence. It had been a long and tiring day.

"He's a nice man," Jo said without looking directly at Raven. "Why were you so mean to him?"

Raven sensed more than just a concern for being polite. She could see how Jo had looked at the rugged zookeeper. He was much too old for the girl, but that's what teenage crushes were all about. And it gnawed at Raven that Jo was probably right. They quick-stepped past a little stone cottage and out to Clark Street where Raven placed Jo on the LaSalle streetcar that would take her back to the office. It was a little early, not much past four o'clock, but Raven wanted respite in her apartment just a few blocks away on State Street. She thought about returning to apologize and involuntarily glanced back to see if Harry had followed. He had not, but she had the feeling someone else had. She sensed she was being watched.

5

The knock at the door startled her. Raven was just out of the bath and still in her housecoat, trying to decide what, if anything, to do about dinner. She was still a little unsettled by the feeling of being watched and thought about not answering, but the knock came again so she padded quietly to the door in her bare feet.

"Who is it?" she asked through the door.

"It's Katherine, dear. I've brought you some dinner."

She opened the door, suddenly grateful for the company. She accepted the warm pot and led her landlord, who held a small Yorkshire terrier under her arm, into the dining room at the back of the apartment.

"Min Lee made a delicious lamb stew, but it was much more than the two of us could eat," Katherine said. She placed the dog on the floor, but it quickly curled up next to the wall.

"How is Pickles?" Raven asked.

"Not well, I'm afraid. I took her to Doctor Adams at the clinic today. He said she has a tumor in her abdomen. There's nothing to be done but make her comfortable."

Katherine busied herself at the counter while Raven kneeled next to the dog and stroked its head.

"I'm so sorry," Raven said. "How long..."

"He didn't say."

Katherine placed a dish on the table and Raven took her seat.

"Do you have any whiskey about?" the old woman asked. "I need a drink."

Raven had just taken a bite, so she pointed to the cabinet with her fork. Katherine found the bottle, poured herself a generous portion, and sat opposite Raven.

Raven figured Katherine Ruebottom must have been about sixty years old. She was a matronly, plump woman whose husband had been one of the richest men in Chicago. When Raven had applied for the apartment six months ago, she learned that Stanley Ruebottom had made his fortune in wholesale meats before being killed in a duel over his mistress. After her inheritance was settled, Katherine threw herself into supporting women's rights, beginning with the right to vote. She rented out the carriage house behind her mansion at a very reasonable rate to young women, probably, Raven figured, in hopes of recruiting them to the cause. Raven didn't mind. She enjoyed the freedom it offered, especially after living in the Eleanor House apartment—a home for single young women with rules that were reminiscent of the girls' school she attended before moving to Chicago. Katherine even allowed her to smoke and drink.

After Raven had eaten and piled the dishes in the sink, they retired to the sitting room with the bottle. The rooms Raven occupied above the carriage shed were simple but comfortable. It was a masculine looking space with dark paneling and richly upholstered furnishings. The space was much too fine for lodgers. Raven wondered if Mr. Ruebottom had once occupied it. A large L-shaped room had a kitchen at one end and the sitting room at the other. An indoor water closet and a spacious bedroom meant she had everything she needed for a comfortable life. So why, she wondered, wasn't she happier?

Raven sat back in the high-backed leather chair, drained her glass of bourbon, and felt herself relax as the whiskey warmed her. She pushed her feet up under her robe, pulled the towel from her head and shook out her hair. It was almost dry.

"Thank you for the dinner," she said as she poured another drink and lit a cigarette. "Min Lee is a good cook."

"She does all right," Katherine said, "especially now that she has learned to cook American food."

Raven had seen the petite oriental woman tending the garden and driving Katherine around town. They had always nodded politely to each other but had never spoken. Raven wondered if she spoke English.

"You're quite the celebrity," Katherine said.

"What?" Raven replied with a coy smile.

"You know—the photo."

"Oh, that."

"I'm still not sure whether that was awfully brave of you," said Katherine, "or awfully foolish."

"Those boys," Raven was beginning to slur her words. "They were going to burn those animals alive just because the owner is a Negro."

"Boys?"

"They were boys wanting to be men," Raven continued. "They looked at me like I wasn't even human—like they were so superior. I wanted to shove that pitchfork down someone's..." She stopped herself and took another drink. "Lou Hanson was so angry with me," Raven continued, as she blew twin streams of smoke from her nostrils, "that he sent me on a wild goose chase to the zoo."

"I don't care for zoos," said Katherine. She stroked Pickles, who was now in her lap. "I don't like seeing those animals pacing around with no place to go."

"Zoos are no different for animals than us riding a horse or keeping a dog on a leash," Raven said. She was on her third drink by now and feeling bolder by the minute.

"I'm not so sure about that," Katherine replied. "What about the sea lions? They should be in the ocean. In the zoo, all they can do is swim around in a glorified swimming pool."

They sat in silence for a moment, listening to the Cicadas buzzing in the cool night air. Raven got up to close the window and stood looking out past the house toward the street.

"I'm thinking about quitting my job," she informed Katherine.

"Why?"

"I'm just tired of it all," she said. "I'm sick of seeing people abuse animals and being powerless to stop it."

"You've just had a bad day, dear," said Katherine. "You'll feel better in the morning."

"Maybe," Raven said in frustration. "But I'm tired of being pushed around by men and being told what I can and cannot do."

They sat in comfortable silence for a moment until both were startled by a knock at the door.

"Were you expecting someone?" Katherine asked.

"No," Raven replied as she rose uncertainly.

"Who is it?" she asked at the door.

"Min Lee," said a soft voice from the other side.

Raven cast a puzzled look toward Katherine and opened the door. Min Lee was a slender woman with attractive features and a humble manner. She smiled warmly at Raven, bowed slightly, and said, "So sorry to disturb you, but a young lady has called for you at the house. I didn't know if you wanted me to show her to your door."

By now Katherine had joined Raven at the door and asked, "What young woman?"

"She says her name is Josephine Washington."

"Oh," said Raven. "Jo is a colleague. You can send her around."

Min Lee gave another bow and descended the stairs.

"I'd best be going," Katherine said. "Thank you for the company, dear."

Raven rubbed the little dog's head and said, "Thank you for the dinner—and the visit." She stood at the door and watched Katherine walk back to the house as Jo walked up the driveway. They exchanged greetings and Jo walked uncertainly up the steps.

"What are you doing here?" Raven asked a little more rudely than she intended.

"Can I come in?"

Raven was annoyed at the intrusion but stepped aside and asked, "Do you want to sit down?"

"No. I won't stay. I just wanted to apologize. You were right to be put-out with that zoo man. I admire how you stand to people." She hesitated before continuing. "I've been pushed around by men all my life. I had a bad experience once, and it has affected me."

"What kind of experience?"

"My father worked for Western Electric." Jo began to pace the room. "My parents were on a ship that sank at the docks."

"The Eastland disaster?" Raven asked.

It was a well-known event that had happened nearly five years ago—but still came up in conversation from time to time. The ship had rolled over while tied to a dock in the Chicago River. More than eight hundred people had died.

"I was an only child." Jo finally sat on the arm of the chair. "And had to go live with my aunt and uncle. When my uncle started coming into my room at night, I ran off."

"How long ago was that?"

"I'm not sure. I've been on the street for a year or so."

"How do you get by?" Raven asked, afraid of what her answer might be.

"Not by selling my body, if that's what you're thinking. There are shelters for young girls, mostly in churches. I stayed in them for the winter, but when the weather warmed, I moved out to the street." Raven did not respond, so Jo continued, "Mr. Hanson took me in to clean around the office and said I can stay there for a while."

Jo lowered her head and sank down into the chair. Raven could see the young woman was deeply affected. The tension had a sobering effect on Raven, but before she could speak another knock came at the door—and this time it was urgent.

Raven hurried to the door as another knock came. Before she could ask, she heard a voice say, "It's Min Lee."

Raven pulled open the door. Min Lee was not so polite this time. There was no bowing, and she stood upright as she looked Raven in the eyes.

"Come quickly," Min Lee said. "It's the dog."

6

Raven had almost dozed off during the streetcar ride the next morning. She was exhausted after spending most of the night comforting Katherine over the death of her dog and, truth be told, she was hung over from the bourbon they had shared.

Yesterday's tour of the zoo had turned up nothing. She thought about confronting Lou to tell him it was a waste of time, but she would not. She wondered if Harry Fisher deserved another chance, but she didn't plan to call on him either.

"Morning," she mumbled to the wagon driver who had stopped to water his horse at the ornate, cast-iron water trough in front of the office.

She pushed through the door at 715 North LaSalle Drive, entered a short hallway, and mounted the stairs to the second floor. The offices of the Animal Welfare Association were perched above the recently vacated Wilson's Tavern and Mr. Woo's bustling Chinese grocery store. The office was dominated by an enormous worktable from which Riley, a big ginger cat, presided.

Lou Hanson's glass-walled office was tucked in the back corner on the left side of the room. On the right side, a storage room spilled its contents of feed sacks, animal crates, and animal capture implements. Next to the storeroom, the closed door of the bookkeeper's office kept prying eyes from Madge's inner sanctum. A peculiar odor—a mixture of cats, dogs, and horses—permeated the space.

Raven placed her bag on the table, sat down, and absently stroked the cat.

"Where is everybody?" she asked.

"Madge hasn't come in yet," Jo said. "And Lou went out in a hurry after a call came in from the police." After a moment of silence, Jo continued, "Aren't you going to ask about the flowers? They're addressed to you."

"Oh," Raven said as she plucked a card off the arrangement of white iris, gardenias, and sprigs of fern at the end of the table.

Sorry if I offended you, the card read, *but even the dumbest of animals deserves a second chance.* It was signed, *Harry.*

She smiled as she tucked the card into her bag and smelled the gardenias.

"Well?" smiled Jo.

"They're from that zoo man."

Jo waited a moment to see if more information was forthcoming. When it became obvious that it was not, she said, "Mr. Hanson said for you to write up your report on the zoo. He seemed annoyed that you were late"

"I'm not late," Raven said as she glanced at the clock and realized that she was, in fact, a few minutes late. She opened her mouth to defend herself when the phone rang. Since she was nearest, she answered it.

"Where's Hanson?" a rude voice demanded.

"Pardon?"

"Where's Hanson?" the man repeated. "I phoned him twenty minutes ago."

"Mr. Hanson left the office a while ago," Raven said. "May I ask who is calling?"

"God damn it!" shouted the man, ignoring her question. "I need someone over here right now or I'm going to shoot this dog."

"Hold on," Raven said. "Don't shoot the dog. Where are you?"

Moments later, after a brief stop at Mr. Woo's grocery, Raven was inside the Lewiston Mule Barn, several blocks north of the office. The place had been riddled with bullets. Sergeant Thomas O'Malley, the overbearing policeman who had called, stood with his back to her, forcing her to peer around him. They were looking at a man sitting on the ground with his back against an animal stall. He had been shot dead.

The smell of blood and manure permeated the space along with something unfamiliar to Raven, the smell of human death. Her stomach lurched as she listened to the sound of Jo throwing up outside on the sidewalk.

A huge Alsatian dog—a German shepherd—paced in front of the dead man, barking occasionally at the small knot of people. The tip of the dog's left ear had been shot off and, although blood caked the side of its head, the bleeding appeared to have stopped.

O'Malley turned to Raven, raised his eyebrows, and said, "Well?"

Raven tore her gaze from the dead man and took a step toward the dog. It stopped pacing and snarled with bared teeth.

She could see O'Malley out of the corner of her eye. He folded his arms and backed up a step with a smirk—apparently enjoying himself.

She took a small package out of her bag and squatted as she unfolded it. The dog stopped and eyed the crinkling paper suspiciously. With slow, deliberate movements, Raven broke off a chunk of cheese, smelled it, and tossed to it a spot midway between her and the dog. The animal stretched its neck for a sniff and inched closer before quickly gobbling up the treat.

When the dog retreated and resumed its pacing, O'Malley drew his revolver. "That dog needs to be put down," he said.

"Wait," said Raven. "One more try."

She nodded at Jo, who had returned and was holding a catchpole with a rope noose fastened to one end. Jo moved cautiously forward as Raven tore off another piece of cheese. She held it out in her open palm and the dog inched forward for another bite but when the noose brushed its head, the dog lunged at Raven's hand and, instead of taking the cheese, took a bite out of Raven. She fell back, O'Malley discharged his pistol, and Jo dropped the noose around the dog's neck.

The dog did not fight the noose. It grew calm and allowed Jo to guide it out of the way. O'Malley holstered his weapon and pulled out a handkerchief. He took Raven's hand to examine it and proceeded to wrap the wound.

"It's just a scratch," he pronounced. "You'll live."

"You're not a very good shot," Raven said, returning the slight.

"I was just trying to scare it," he said sourly, glaring at the smart-mouthed girl. "If I wanted to hit that dog, it would be dead."

She pulled the handkerchief tightly around her hand, ignoring the sting, as she watched O'Malley examine the dead man. The man had blood oozing from several holes in his chest. Judging from the bullet holes and blood smears on the wall above his head, it appeared to Raven that he had fallen where he was shot.

One of the policemen stuck his head out the door of the stall behind the dead man and said to Raven, "You'd better get in here."

Two huge, brown mules lay in the straw. One was dead. The other was trying to raise his head, but his body would not respond, He appeared to be paralyzed—probably due to the bullet holes in his neck. Raven looked up at the officer and gave a slight shake of her head. There was no hope for this animal.

"I'll get Sergeant O'Malley," he said.

Raven moved to the next stall where two gray mules paced nervously. She looked them over carefully. One had a scratch across his hip—probably from a passing bullet—but both animals were otherwise unharmed. The mules were startled by a gunshot as she placed halters on them, but they calmed under her touch and allowed her to lead them into the hall.

"Do you have some place you can take them?" growled O'Malley as he emerged from the other stall holstering his pistol. He looked up and past her, and continued, "Where in the hell have you been?"

Lou Hanson walked in without acknowledging Raven or Jo. "You gave me the wrong address," he replied.

"No, I didn't."

"Yes, you did."

"You must have wrote it wrong," said O'Malley. "Anyway, your girls are getting these animals out of my way so I can investigate this murder."

Hanson glanced at Raven and Jo for the first time and did not appear to be grateful for their efforts. Before he could reply to O'Malley, two more men strolled into the barn. One man was tall and gaunt with sharp features. He was well dressed and walked with the confident air of someone who was accustomed to getting his way. The other man had the look of an adult dressed up in the body of a boy. He paused when he saw Raven but continued to follow. It was Danny Malone and, if he was one of Sweeney's Colts, the other man must be Brian Sweeney. Now Raven really wanted to leave, but she was rooted by a combination of wanting to hear Mr. Hanson's directions and a curiosity at what Sweeney was doing there.

"Is he one of yours?" O'Malley asked Sweeney by way of greeting. He was pointing at the dead man.

"He is," said Sweeney as he examined the body.

"Then what's he doing dead?" asked O'Malley. "I thought you were supposed to provide protection."

"It's those God damned Italians," Sweeney said. "Johnny fucking Torrio is trying to make a name for himself."

He straightened up and looked around the room as if expecting to find the culprits. He glanced at Danny who was still looking at Raven and asked, "Is that her?"

Danny nodded and his boss walked over to face Raven. "She's a looker," he said. His cold eyes bored into hers before he looked at the two mules and the dog. His eyes lingered on the dog for a long moment. He looked at Danny, nodded knowingly, and they both walked out.

An awkward silence filled the room before O'Malley asked Hanson, "Are you going to get those animals out of here?"

"I can take them to Rondell Boyd if you'd like," Raven said to Hanson.

"Fine," he snapped. "Then get back to the office." He stomped out.

Raven pulled three lead ropes from a nail on the wall and clipped one to each mule's halter. She had Jo hold the mules and remove the catch pole from the dog. But when Raven clipped a lead rope to the collar on the dog, she noticed a key dangling from it.

"I wonder what this is for?" she asked Jo as she fingered the key. She stole a glance at the policemen, but they were busy examining the dead man.

"Maybe it's a key to the barn," Jo suggested.

"Hmm," Raven replied. "I guess we'd better get these animals out of here."

They had barely cleared the door to the street when a voice said, "I'll take that dog off your hands."

It was Danny Malone. As he moved forward to grab the leash from Raven, the dog emitted a throaty growl that stopped him in his tracks.

"Is there a problem here?" asked a policeman from the open door.

"I am just collecting Mr. Sweeney's dog," Danny said.

He moved up to face the policeman who was a head taller and a good fifty pounds heavier—and who did not back off.

"That dog is being held as evidence in a murder," said the policeman. "You're not taking it anywhere."

Traffic was light with just a few wagons and trucks on the street and no walkers to interfere with their conversation. Danny looked at the policeman for a moment and glanced at the dog. He locked eyes with Raven before he turned and stalked off.

"Sergeant O'Malley told me to escort you ladies to wherever you're going," the policeman said. "I'm Walter Miller. My friends call me Walt."

Walt was uncommonly handsome—a tall man with close-cropped dark hair and lively brown eyes. Raven felt herself stir as she shook his hand, but immediately cooled when she spied his wedding band. After they had properly introduced themselves, Walt asked, "Any idea what that was all about?"

Jo said, "It was prob..."

"We have no idea." Raven cut her off.

"Let's take the mules to the police station," Walt suggested. "The horse unit has a truck that can transport them to that stable for you."

"Why not leave the mules at the police stable?" Raven asked.

"If that was an option," Walt said, "O'Malley would have offered."

"Can you order a driver to transport them for us?" she asked.

"No," he laughed. "But you probably can. Use O'Malley's name and the murder investigation."

Raven went down on one knee and stroked the dog, careful not to touch his damaged ear as he licked her on the hand. She fingered the key as she glanced up the street. The south end of Lincoln Park was a twenty-minute walk to the north, and she had an idea. She handed her mule lead-rope and the dog leash to Walt and said, "I need to stop by the zoo."

"The zoo?" her companions said in unison.

"I need to see someone."

"Now?" asked Jo.

"Yes now," Raven replied. "I won't be long. I have something I need to do."

7

The Chicago Avenue police station was just a few blocks away from the mule barn. By the time Raven arrived after her trip to the zoo, she discovered that Walt had called the police stable and convinced one of the drivers to bring an old horse-drawn wagon. The motor transport truck had been dispatched to the murder scene to deal with the dead mules and Walt had needed to return there as well. Jo had gone back to the office to make peace with Lou.

Raven rode on the police wagon with the dog on the floor between her legs and the mules tied up in the back. She regretted lying to the driver about O'Malley's approval, but the twenty-minute ride in the vehicle would have taken her an hour to walk—probably longer if she had to drag a couple of lazy mules.

"Pull into the alley," she instructed as they arrived. "We'll unload in the back."

If the driver noticed—or cared—that they were in the black-belt, he did not let on. He did, however, remain on the wagon while Raven and the dog went in search of Rondell. He did not acknowledge Rondell or offer to help them unload, and he drove off as soon as the mules were out of his wagon. Raven watched the wagon disappear and wondered if the driver was afraid or simply indifferent. Either way, she was grateful for the ride and the relative safety of Boyd's Livery Stable.

"So, that's why Sweeney's boys been hangin round across the street," Rondell said, when Raven told him why she was there. "They must a known you'd turn up here."

"Sorry, R. B.," she said, "but I had nowhere else to go."

They stood in silence for a moment, leaning on the fence rail watching the mules.

"What happened to your hand?" he asked.

"The dog nipped me."

A wagon overflowing with a load of hay rumbled down the alley as the mules nosed around in the near-empty feed trough.

"It's this dog they're after," Raven said finally, "not the mules. Those guys will lose interest when they find out I'm not here."

"Why do they care about a dog?"

"He had a key on his collar."

"A key?" Rondell said. "I don't see no key."

They both looked at the dog who sat patiently by Raven's leg.

"He must have dropped it somewhere," she said. She gazed absently around then gave Rondell a sly look out of the corner of her eye indicating that she was not going to tell him the whole story.

Rondell did not look at Raven as he asked, "You want to come inside?"

"No, thanks," Raven replied. "I need to get back uptown. You sure you're okay with this?" She nodded toward the mules.

Rondell rubbed the back of his neck and glanced up and down the alley. Raven followed his gaze. She had been uneasy in the days since her photo had appeared in the newspaper. She could not seem to escape those hushed whispers and sidelong glances that came with a fleeting brush with fame. Now, as she stood in the open with Rondell, she once again sensed that feeling of being watched—that feral instinct, which precedes the need to flee or fight.

"If it'll make you feel better," she said finally. "I'll come inside for a while."

Raven slouched in a kitchen chair, absently stroking the dog's good ear while she sipped her coffee. She was growing fonder of him by the minute. The dog was massively strong and seemed unusually protective of her. He had finally settled down after an initial bout of growling and showing his teeth whenever Rondell or Essie tried to approach. Rondell had gone outside, and Essie finally won him over with a bowl of meat scraps.

Essie turned from the sink, wiped her hands on her apron, and poured herself a cup of coffee.

"Thanks for standing up for us the other day," she said as she sat at the table opposite Raven.

Raven did not look up. "It was the least I could do after what Rondell did for me back home."

"What *did* he do?" Essie asked. "He won't talk about his time in Thomasville."

Raven leaned back in her chair and looked across the table. She lowered her eyes and said, "If he won't talk about it, I don't know if it's my place to say."

"Whatever it was, it still bothers him. He has nightmares."

"So do I," said Raven.

"He says you're a remarkable woman. Says you rescued your brother from a bear."

"That may be a bit of an exaggeration," Raven laughed. "My pa was there, too. My brother got locked in a bear cage at our zoo. He was unconscious. We had to go in and pull him out."

After a pause, Raven warmed to the subject and continued. "When Thomasville started their zoo, my pa was the first director and Rondell was his first real zookeeper. I was about sixteen at the time."

"*Real* zookeeper?" asked Essie.

"The first keeper was the man who came to town with the bear. It was a wrestling bear that killed a man in a match and was confiscated by the sheriff. The man's name was Henry Koch, and he was an evil man. He wasn't right in the head and seemed to take a dislike of me.

One day, he tied me up in our barn and set it on fire. If it hadn't been for Rondell, I would have burned up."

Essie let the pause hang in the air until Raven finally let the secret tumble out.

"Rondell stabbed Koch with a pitchfork, untied me, and pulled me out. My pa buried Koch's remains later and nothing was ever said."

"No wonder you both have nightmares."

"Rondell didn't stay around long after that. He moved back to Alabama and my pa packed me off to boarding school."

"How did you come to be in Chicago?" asked Essie.

"I have a knack for finding trouble." Raven said.

"So I've noticed," said Essie.

Raven looked at her and they both laughed.

"After I graduated from the boarding school, I went to work in their TB sanitorium. They had some horses and mules that were poorly treated, so I wrote to the local humane people. They sent a man out of the Chicago office to investigate."

"I can guess the rest of that story," said Essie. "They didn't take too kindly to you stirring up trouble."

"No, they did not. And to make matters worse, when I got to Chicago to look up the man who left me his calling card, I discovered he had more than just a job in mind."

"Seems like you're settled in pretty well now," said Essie.

Before Raven could reply, the dog raised his head and growled at Rondell's return. Two other Negros followed him into the room. They stood near the door, one with an axe handle and the other with a short length of stout chain. These were men who appeared ready to do battle and had probably seen their share of abuse at the hands of the Irish, the police, and white people in general. Raven suspected why they were there but, before she could speak, Essie moved to the middle of the room with a wooden spoon in her hand.

"What's this all about?"

The two newcomers looked nervously at each other. Essie was a tiny woman, scarcely five feet tall and as big around as a broomstick. But she exuded a power that could take over a room. Raven admired her immensely and took comfort in observing her. Here was a woman who did not need the approval of, or permission from, the men around her.

The room had an earthy smell—a mixture of the meat stew Essie had been stirring on the wood stove, horses, and something else Raven could not quite identify. It was probably the odor of a room full of people who were foreign to her, the Negroes.

"Essie," Raven said. "It's okay. I need to be going, anyway."

"Let us go run them boys off first," Rondell said.

"There's no need to go stirring up that trouble again," Essie said.

"Essie's right," Raven agreed. "I can slip out the back and be gone before they even know I'm here. Besides," she continued, "I'll have the dog with me."

"Where will you go?" asked Rondell.

"I'm going to catch the streetcar at State Street," she said. "I'll be uptown in fifteen minutes."

Rondell looked from Raven to Essie and, finally, to the two men. With a nod of his head, they were gone.

"Thanks for the coffee," Raven said as she rose from her chair and walked toward the door.

Essie grabbed her arm and said, "You watch yourself, child."

"I'll take you to the streetcar stop," Rondell said, looking at Essie for confirmation. Something Raven could not see must have passed because Rondell pulled his hat off the peg by the door and said, "Wait outside. I'm going to lock the front door to the barn and hitch up the wagon. We'll go down the alley."

A few minutes later, she stood at the busy intersection of State and Forty-First, watching Rondell drive home. He had wanted to wait with her but a black man with a white woman would have attracted unwanted attention. She just wanted to blend in with the crowd and get back to the office. The crowd was an unusual mixture of races since they were near the boundary between the black belt and Canaryville.

She glanced nervously around and saw nothing suspicious. People were walking behind her, cars were chugging in the street, and she could see the streetcar heading her way in the distance two or three stops away. State Street was lined with businesses both North and South as far as she could see. The only thing unusual was that she saw very few motor cars since the Negroes could not afford such luxuries. The street was mostly occupied by mule-drawn wagons and horse carts.

"Mommy," a child called behind her.

She turned in time to see a young white boy crying and alone. He appeared to be searching as he rounded the corner out of sight. "Mommy!" he called again. He was lost.

Raven looked up the street. The streetcar was still a couple of blocks away, so she tugged on the dog's leash and rushed after the child. When she rounded the corner, the child was nowhere to be seen. The only place he could be was the alley just ahead, but when she entered the alley at a trot, she pulled up short. A car was parked in her path with its doors open and the child was standing calmly against the wall. Before she knew what was happening, strong arms encircled her, pinning her arms to her sides. Raven's cries were muffled by the coarse burlap sack that was placed over her head. The dog uttered a guttural growl and Raven felt him lunge against the leash, but he was silenced by a gunshot. The last thing she heard before she was thrown to the floor of the car and knocked unconscious was an awful silence.

8

When Raven regained consciousness, she wanted to jump up and see about the dog, but she forced herself to remain still. She listened but only heard water dripping and some type of motor running. She carefully cracked open her eyes but saw only blackness. Wherever she was, it was as dark as a tomb. She gasped and jerked upright, wondering if she had, in fact, been buried alive. As her eyes adjusted, she saw a faint sliver of light before her. It was, she realized, the bottom of a door. She had been placed inside some type of room. Her prison cell was damp and smelled of urine.

Raven had no idea how long she had been there, but it was long enough that she had to relieve herself. She stumbled to her feet and felt her way to a corner of the room where she hiked her skirt and squatted. She then felt along the wall to the opposite end of the room and sat against the wall. She gently rubbed at the source of a deep, throbbing pain—a knot on the crown of her head where she had been struck. She also had a sharp pain in her hand where the dog had bitten her. It reminded her that he had been shot trying to protect her. Tears came to her eyes, and she sobbed quietly. Grief swept over her and threatened to engulf her. She rested against the wall and closed her eyes, preferring not to see the darkness before her. As she let her hands fall to the floor beside her, her right hand came to rest on a half piece of brick. A weapon, she thought. When they came for her, she would be ready—or so she thought.

Raven must have fallen asleep, because when the door opened at last, she was too groggy and blinded by the light to react. She was grabbed by each arm and pulled to her feet before she could use her brick. Someone slapped her hand and forced her to drop it. She struggled and tried to kick at her attackers, but they had her in a firm grasp.

"Let me go," she screamed. "Why did you shoot my dog?"

They pulled her out of her prison and, after her eyes adjusted to the light, she could see she was in a basement. High, narrow windows encircled the room. A furnace dominated the center of the space and a set of wooden steps led up to the main floor.

They laughed and taunted her, and Raven instantly recognized the Malone boys. It didn't take a genius to figure out that she was being held in the basement of their so-called Athletic Club somewhere in the Canaryville neighborhood. She struggled against them as they bound her wrists and chest to a wooden chair.

"Leave me alone."

Danny Malone grabbed one of her breasts as his brother and the others laughed.

"Let's have some fun," he said.

He grabbed her collars and began to rip her blouse open but was stopped by a voice at the top of the stairs.

"Where is she?"

"In the basement, Boss."

"You didn't touch her, did you?" Brian Sweeney asked as he descended the stairs.

"No, Boss," Malone lied. He straightened her blouse, looked at her, and dared her to object.

"Welcome to my clubhouse," Sweeney said. "Sorry it had to be under such circumstances."

When she did not respond, he continued. "It's not my habit to harm women, but I think you have something of mine, and I mean to get it back." He bent forward with a slight smile on his face, smoothed the collar on her blouse and then glanced back at Danny— a signal that he could see what was about to happen when he arrived. She hoped the gangster might confront his goons, but he did not. Instead he bent in closer, screwed his face into a snarl, and said, "Where's my fucking key?"

Sweeney's face was inches from hers. His breath smelled of garlic and peppermint.

She head-butted him, and he slapped her as he backed away and rubbed his nose.

"You didn't have to kill my dog," she snarled. She could not recall a time when she had been this angry. She wanted to kill these evil men who would shoot an innocent dog. In that moment, she didn't care what they might do to her.

"He wasn't your dog," Sweeney growled. "He was *my* dog, and he was wearing *my* key."

Raven's cheek stung as she looked around the room. Its stone walls and small windows made rescue unlikely. She was alone and vulnerable, and she fought the urge to cry.

"The key," Sweeney grabbed her by the neck.

She felt fearful and could not think of a good reason not to tell Sweeney what he wanted to know—except to avenge the dog.

"What key?" She gagged through his chokehold.

"You know what key. Danny saw it on the dog. Now it's gone."

"It must have fallen off."

Sweeney slapped her again, then straightened up and turned around. He walked away, then turned back. He pulled a watch from his vest pocket, checked the time, and said, "I have an appointment. Shall I just leave you with these boys for a few hours?"

He looked at the roughly dressed young men standing against the wall then returned his gaze to Raven with eyebrows raised.

"Or maybe I'll send them over to that nigger's house. Maybe that's where you stashed the key."

"He doesn't know anything," she said with more trembling in her voice than she intended.

"Maybe not, but you sure as hell do."

Water was dripping somewhere, and the furnace roared to life. Raven was silent as she weighed her options. The fear and anger rose in her chest in equal measures—with the likelihood of conflicting responses. Should she give Sweeney what he wants and hope he might let her go. Or should she stall for more time and make him wait—but to what end. Even if she tells him, he might just shoot her like his men did the dog and dump her body in Lake Michigan.

"All right," Sweeney said at last. "You two go to that nigger-house and see what you can find."

"Wait," Raven said. She was stalling for time. "There was no key. Maybe the guys who shot the man took it."

"Bullshit, Boss" Danny said. "I saw it myself."

Sweeney looked from Danny to Raven. Finally, he just nodded at the two boys who turned and walked up the stairs. Raven watched them with some degree of dread, worried what they might do to her friends, but somehow confident that Rondell could handle them. They were a tough-looking pair, but little more than boys.

"You," Sweeney pointed to Danny as he buttoned his coat, "stay here and watch her."

As he turned to mount the stairs, they all heard a loud thump from the floor above followed, before they could react, by a second thump. Sweeney froze and looked toward the top of the stairs, then nodded Danny up the stairs to investigate. Danny grabbed a club that had been leaning against the stair rail and slowly mounted the steps—club at the ready. Raven and Sweeney watched him peer through the open door into the room above. He looked closely at something in the room then turned back to Sweeney with eyes wide but before he could report he was jerked into the room by an unseen hand and became another heavy thump on the floor above.

Sweeney pulled a revolver from a holster under his coat and shouted, "Who's there?"

No reply.

"You're making a big mistake," he shouted. "You don't want to mess with me."

No reply.

He was halfway up the stairs before he looked back at Raven as if struck by a thought. He came back down, slipped the gun under his arm, and took out a folding knife. He cut her bindings, pulled his gun back out and jerked her to her feet.

"If this is about the girl," he said, "we're coming up."

No reply.

Raven thought about Rondell and his friends, armed with axe handles and chains. "He's got a gun," she shouted.

Sweeney punched her and, before she had time to react, he grabbed her by a handful of hair. Blood poured from her nose and her vision was blurred as he pushed her up the stairs ahead of him.

"I do have a gun," he said as they neared the top step, "and I'm not afraid to use it."

He pulled Raven near and listened. She felt his ragged breathing before he pushed her at arm's length into the room while holding the gun to the back of her head. The three boys were sprawled in the middle of the room, but she could see no one else. It had to be Rondell and his friends but how, she wondered, could three large Negroes hide in an empty room?

Sweeney inched her forward but, as they cleared the doorway, she felt herself suddenly yanked backward by Sweeney's grip on her hair. As she spun around, she saw the gun pushed up and heard it discharge into the air. The bullet clanged off something metal and an intense, piercing pain entered the top of her shoulder. As she fell, she caught a glimpse of a person dressed in black holding Sweeney's gun hand in the air. It was Min Lee. Raven saw her deliver a vicious chop with her other hand to the side of Sweeney's neck. Sweeney fell like a sack of feed and Raven's world went black.

9

*I*t's time for me to go back to work," Raven said without taking her eyes off the scene before her. The garden outside the floor-to-ceiling window was carpeted in four inches of fresh snow—the boxwood hedges and grassy lawn forming the foundation of a soft, undulating sculpture. The tall, brick perimeter wall, which provided safety and seclusion, also gave Raven a feeling of being enclosed like an animal at the zoo.

"Nonsense, dear. You're not fully healed yet."

"It's been six weeks. The doctor says I'm fine."

Raven glanced at the woman across the table and returned her gaze to the garden where her dog romped in the snow. His ear had healed into an upright 'V' and a hairless patch of skin on his chest was the only sign of where he had been shot by Sweeney's men. She had grown an enormous attachment to him and felt a twinge of sympathetic pain in her shoulder. Katherine had named him Vincent after the artist who had cut off one of his own ears.

Raven fidgeted with her coffee cup. She longed for a cigarette, but Katherine did not permit smoking in her house. It was she who had sent her cook and bodyguard, Min Lee, to shadow and ultimately rescue Raven—and Vincent. Katherine's personal physician had tried to remove the fragment of the bullet that had ricocheted into the top of her shoulder before finally deciding to leave it there. Josephine had visited her and brought her things, but no one else knew where she was.

"I do appreciate all you have done for me," Raven said. "You have made a new woman out of me." She ran a hand over her hair, which was cut short in a stylish bob. "You've taught me how to walk, how to talk, and even how to eat like a lady. What I've learned from Min Lee is priceless, but I'm just not a suffragette."

"I did think you would be good for our movement," Katherine admitted. "But I've come to appreciate what you do for the animals. I suppose that's important, too."

"I want to see if I can get my old job back," Raven said.

"What makes you think they'll take you back?"

"I don't know. Maybe they won't, but I need to try."

"Did Min Lee put you up to this?" Katherine asked.

They both glanced at Min Lee, who stood at the back door, letting Vincent inside.

"It must be her decision," said Min Lee without turning.

"Humph," grunted Katherine.

They all jumped when Vincent began barking. He had rushed toward the basement door as a mouse disappeared into a hole in the baseboard.

"Vincent!" shouted Raven. "That's enough. The mouse is gone."

The dog kept up the barking as he paced in front of the door.

"Vincent, stop!"

Raven got up from the table, but Min Lee was already moving to quiet the dog.

"He's not barking at the mouse hole," Min Lee said. "He's barking at the basement door."

Raven grabbed Vincent by the collar as Min Lee opened the door to the basement.

"Oh my," exclaimed Katherine as a puff of smoke escaped into the kitchen. "We'd better call the fire brigade."

Min Lee disappeared down the steps.

They all waited in silence, straining to hear a report. Finally, Min Lee emerged and said, "It's all right. The smoke was coming from the electrical box. I pulled the switch, and the smoke stopped." Min Lee got down on one knee and rubbed Vincent's head. She scratched his ears and said, "Good boy."

"Don't build him up too much," laughed Raven. "He'll become self-important."

Min Lee refilled their coffee cups and joined them at the table

"We can't stay in your house forever," Raven continued, looking at the dog. "It's a new year—a new decade," she said brightly. "I'm ready to go back to my apartment."

"I'm afraid that won't be possible," Katherine said, glancing at Min Lee.

"Why not?" Raven asked in surprise.

"I've rented it out."

"What?" Raven looked at both women and both avoided her gaze. "Why?"

"I found someone who needed a place to stay."

"Who?"

"Josephine."

"What about me?" Raven was angry by now. "Where am I to go?"

"You have a place here, now. You and Vincent can keep your room in this house."

That night Raven lay in bed staring at the ceiling, troubled by her feelings. Katherine Ruebottom had clearly taken a shine to her. She had not only saved her life; she had welcomed her into her home and placed all her considerable resources at Raven's disposal. Why was Raven so reluctant to accept?

She got up, put on her housecoat, and rummaged through a drawer. When she found what she was looking for, she grabbed a blanket and padded through the sleeping house, down the stairs, and to the kitchen with Vincent on her heels. She carefully turned the lock and quietly pulled the back door open, letting Vincent into the back yard before closing the door and settling on the back steps with the blanket around her shoulders.

"May I join you?"

Raven let out a gasp and jumped. Min Lee had appeared behind her in the doorway.

"Of course," said Raven, trying to recover her composure.

Min Lee ducked back inside. Raven knew her well enough to expect a pot of tea to appear.

"Sorry if I scared you," said Min Lee when she returned and set a tray on the step between them.

"How do you do that," said Raven.

"Make tea?"

"No," said Raven. "You move without making a sound."

Min Lee just smiled and sat down on the step. She was one of the most remarkable women Raven had ever met. She appeared so average in every way. She was of average height—a little shorter than Raven—average weight, and unremarkable in appearance. She was quiet and would never stand out in any crowd, but she had somehow overpowered four men. The blow she had seen her strike at Brian Sweeney was delivered with deadly force, yet she sat beside her now as calm as could be—her face kind but intense. Raven had enjoyed the self-defense training Min Lee had offered and hoped they might continue working together. Raven was by no means an expert, but she would be much better at defending herself in the future.

"You don't want to stay here, do you?" Min Lee said.

Raven sipped her tea and thought for a moment.

"I don't think I do," she said, "but I'm not sure why."

"Out there," Min Lee nodded her head to the yard and beyond, "you are free. In here you are like prisoner—owned by the house."

"Are you owned by the house?"

"I am where I wish to be," Min Lee answered evasively.

"How did you come to be here?"

"Mr. Stanley bought me."

"Bought you?" Raven looked at her.

"I was born in a railroad camp in the West. When my parents were killed in a tunnel collapse, my uncle took me in. He taught me the martial arts from the old country and many of the ways of my ancestors, but he too met with an untimely death. I made my way east as a servant and cook for a railroad man in St. Louis until Mr. Stanley paid for my release and brought me here. He tried to make his advances on me, but I was too strong for him. He finally gave up and let me cook for the household. Now that he is gone, this is as good a place as any for me to spend my days."

Raven didn't know what to say, so she remained silent and let Min Lee's story soak in.

"You have a sadness about you," Min Lee continued. "I think you have a story, too."

"I was sixteen when a man attacked me," Raven began. "He wasn't right in the head." She looked at the ground and spoke in hushed tones. "He dragged me into our barn, tied me up, and set the barn on fire. He was going to burn me to death." Raven looked at Min Lee with tears trickling down her face. "I still have nightmares. Some nights, I'm afraid to go to sleep."

"What happened to him?"

"A friend of the family happened on us. If it hadn't been for him, I wouldn't be here."

"Is that the man who runs the stable?" asked Min Lee.

"Yes," Raven replied. "That's him—Rondell Boyd." Then she told Min Lee the rest of her story.

"How did you and Mr. Boyd find each other again?"

"We ran into each other at one of the Association's work horse relief events here in Chicago."

They sat in silence for a moment before Min Lee asked, "Aren't you going to take a drink?"

Raven looked at her and Min Lee was looking at the flask of whiskey Raven had brought from her bedroom. They both laughed.

Raven tipped the contents of the flask into her cup as the two women sat on the steps in the dark. Vincent concluded his business and lay down at the foot of the steps with a thump.

"That dog trusts you," said Min Lee.

Raven sipped her whiskey-laced tea and looked at Vincent.

"When the barn burned," continued Min Lee, "What happened to the animals?"

"Rondell and I got them out."

"That was very brave after such a terrifying experience."

"Maybe," Raven said. "I've always had a way with animals."

"Then that is your gift—your calling."

"It's a hopeless calling. Do you know how many animals are being abused in this city right now? I can't save them all."

"You must try."

"But it won't matter."

"It mattered to him," Min Lee directed her cup at Vincent. "Where would he be without you?"

Raven looked at the big dog lying at her feet, oblivious to the conversation, and knew Min Lee was right.

Min Lee stood. She took a final drink of her tea and dumped the dregs off the edge of the porch.

"Confucius was a great teacher of my people who lived over two thousand years ago," she said. "He said, 'Mankind differs from the animals only by a little and most people throw that away'."

"Some people have a calling," she continued. "Some are called to teach children, some to put out fires, and some to serve others. Mine is to serve others. Yours is to help animals. You are one of the special ones who recognize how little we differ from them and refuse to throw it away."

Min Lee mounted the steps and paused at the door. "Maybe it is time to put your past behind you and get to work."

Min Lee silently disappeared into the house, leaving Raven to gaze into the night sky. Her hand shook from the cold as she removed the pack of cigarettes from her pocket lit one. If she went back to work for the Association, she would be stepping right back into a world controlled by men—but she could not imagine a world where that was not a fact. She wondered about the best way to approach Lou Hanson. Should she be contrite and apologetic or bold and forthright?

She smoked and thought about what Min Lee had said. People are not much different from the animals, but that difference is what is important. She thought about how many animals in the surrounding city were suffering and how little she could do about it. Her gaze drifted from the stars overhead to the dog at her feet. He looked up at her, as if reading her thoughts, and for an instant, she read his.

She needed her old job back—for herself and for animals like Vincent. She stubbed out her cigarette, dropped it off the porch, and pushed herself upright.

"Let's get some sleep," she said to the dog. "I need to get back to work in a few hours."

10

"Why should I take you back?" Lou Hanson asked. "You've been gone for six weeks."

He had a Yorkshire terrier sitting on his lap. The little dog had yapped furiously at Vincent when he had entered the office. Vincent appeared not to notice.

Raven leaned forward in her chair and placed her elbows on Lou's desk, prompting another round of barking.

"Max!" Hanson said. "Quiet."

He turned back to Raven and continued, "Word on the street is that Sweeney's still looking for you. That guy from the zoo calls here about once a week. And here you are, all dolled-up with a dog in tow—a dog that the police are asking about. Jesus, Raven."

Raven watched him closely but did not reply.

"You've never been very good at following instructions," he continued.

"I know, Mr. Hanson," she replied. "But I have learned my lessons."

"And what lessons might those be?"

"I'm a better listener, for one thing." When he failed to respond, she continued, "After my accident the doctor insisted that I take the time to heal properly. Strict bedrest is what he prescribed. Doctor Jackson said he spoke to you."

"Yes." Hanson looked out the window and seemed mesmerized by the gray skies and the endless sea of rooftops. It was beginning to snow. "He was a little vague about your accident, though." He looked back to Raven with raised eyebrows and let the questioning statement hang in the air between them.

"It was a gunshot wound."

"So he said. A gunshot wound."

"Would you like to see?" She reached for the top button of her blouse.

"No," he held up his hand. "He told me. A bullet just fell from the sky."

"People fire guns into the air all the time. Those bullets have to fall back to earth. I was just unlucky." Hanson didn't respond, so she continued. "I'll do my old job without complaining."

"That would be refreshing."

"I can help you manage all of these new people." She motioned over her shoulder to the workroom outside his office.

"What about the dog?" He looked at Vincent as he lay by the door to his office.

"I'll straighten it out with the police. He can be part of our program, promoting animal welfare. He can be our ambassador."

Hanson looked over her shoulder at the workroom and appeared to come to a decision.

"Look," he said finally. "I've already hired a replacement for your old job, but I need a small animal officer—someone to take calls, investigate claims, and the like. Do you think you can handle that?"

Her mind raced with excitement, but she remained calm. "Yes, Mr. Hanson. Yes, I can."

"I can't have you confronting people like you did Sweeney's boys last fall. You need to be diplomatic. Is that clear?"

"Yes, Mr. Hanson."

"And quit calling me that. It's just Lou."

"Okay, Lou."

"Some dogs are coming in later this morning," he continued. "We have a new space downstairs that the city gave us after the bar closed down. They even put some wire cages in there. We need to get it ready for animals. We're going to enlarge our animal shelter and open a small animal clinic."

Wilson's Tavern had been a popular pub on the ground floor. The temperance people had been successful in closing it down and, with the prohibition laws about to take effect, it was unlikely to reopen.

"Where is everybody?" Raven asked.

"Madge is running late, and Doctor Adams will be here shortly to check the dogs. Everyone else is working downstairs," he replied. "Josephine is down there with Myron, our new ambulance driver, and Jim and Doris."

Jim and Doris, Raven recalled, were the kennel attendants who lived on the third floor and cared for all the animals that were in residence.

"Who are these people?" Raven asked, nodding to the workroom behind her

"Judge Ross has been assigning people to do what he calls *meaningful work for the community* instead of being locked up."

"They're criminals?" Raven turned back for a closer look.

"Just minor infractions."

Lou let out a puff of air and said, "Get them organized. I'm tired of dealing with them."

"What about the theft of the dogs? Did Mrs. Fassbender get her dog Molly back?"

"No more thefts reported, but Opal never recovered her Molly. I had to find her a replacement."

"And how's your wife?" Raven asked quietly.

He gave her a questioning look and then softened. "Opal must have told you." He paused and looked down at his desk. "Mildred passed away on New Year's Day."

Raven sat quietly for a moment and then stood. "Thank you for taking me back, Lou," she said. "You won't regret this."

"See to it that I don't," he said. "You need to get squared away with the police and with Sweeney. I don't need them coming around here. I have enough problems of my own."

"I'll take care of it."

"And, Raven."

She stopped at the door and turned.

"Tell that guy from the zoo to stop calling here."

She did not respond. She waited for Vincent to follow her out and pulled Lou's door closed. Arrayed before her were three scruffy men of indeterminate age sitting around the worktable looking expectantly at her. Raven glanced nervously over her shoulder to see if Lou was watching her and hoping he might come to her rescue, but he was on the telephone.

Vincent went cautiously toward the table and approached Riley, the cat. The cat watched the dog approach, apparently unconcerned, until Vincent's nose touched his. Raven held her breath. Riley gently swatted Vincent without putting his claws out. The dog jumped back and gave a quiet bark. It appeared that Vincent and Riley were going to get along just fine.

"All right," she turned to the men. "We have work to do."

*T*he new clinic area was a mess. The city had provided wire panels for cages, but whoever had dropped them off must have been in a hurry. Some panels were leaning against the wall and some were stacked in the middle of the room. The floor was littered with bottles, old newspapers, and the filth that somehow accumulates in vacant buildings. Light filtered through cracks in the boarded-up windows.

"Are these guys here to help?" Jo asked as she stopped sweeping and leaned on her broom.

Raven nodded and asked, "What do we need to do?" She removed her coat and draped it over a bar stool.

Jo just nodded toward the pile of wire fence panels that need to be assembled into cages and smiled. "It looks like he took you back."

"Go lay down," Raven commanded Vincent, pointing to a place in the corner.

The rest of the crew had also stopped working and were looking from Raven to the new workers.

"Lou sent these men to help us," she said. "They can work with Myron and Jim putting cages together." She picked up a broom that was leaning against the bar and continued, "I'll help Jo and Doris get this place cleaned up."

Soon, they had eleven cages lining one wall in a section of the room that had a floor drain. They all worked with a sense of urgency since the dogs were expected to arrive at any moment from the City Public Works department. It didn't take them long to have cages assembled and trash piled outside the back door.

Raven instructed the men on how to install the cage doors, while she and Jo sat at a table to watch.

"Are you mad at me," Jo asked.

"About what?"

"Taking your room."

"I was upset at first," Raven admitted.

"I didn't ask for it," Jo inserted. "Katherine insisted. She told me you were moving into the house."

"Not exactly true," said Raven. She watched the men work for a moment before she continued. "I liked the freedom of the apartment out back so I could come and go as I please. But Katherine can be pretty persuasive."

Jo opened her mouth to reply but was interrupted by two men who burst through the door with dogs on rope leads. Vincent was on his feet growling at the new arrivals, but Raven scolded him and placed him in one of the empty cages to keep him out of the way.

Few words were exchanged as Raven took charge. She and Jo took the dogs one by one and pushed them into the new cages. The barking was deafening in the cavernous, hard-walled room. Lou Hanson and Doctor Cecil Adams were soon with them, surveying the new arrivals.

There were four dogs. Three were females—a short-haired, brown mutt, a small, English setter with long, brown and white fur, and a German shepherd that looked like she could be Vincent's sister. The fourth dog had long, curly, black fur that hid its dark eyes and any clue as to its gender. As one of the delivery men coiled up his ropes, the other one came back inside with a small white fox terrier under each arm. Jo placed them in a cage together.

Raven turned to Lou and said, "I may have a home for the terriers."

"We need to find homes for all of them," he said sourly. "The City's only paying us a dollar a month for their upkeep." With that, he followed Myron and the two men who had delivered the dogs out the door.

Jim and Doris went outside to begin cleaning the old kennels, leaving Jo and Raven looking at the new arrivals. Doctor Adams moved up beside Raven.

"Do you need to examine them," she asked him.

"They all look fine to me," he replied.

Raven could see out of the corner of her eye that he was weaving slightly as he looked at the dogs. The alcohol on his breath was as powerful as it was disconcerting. He appeared to be drunk, and it wasn't even mid-day.

"What do you want us to do now, lady?" asked one of the court-appointed workers.

Raven looked around the room. The work inside was done, so she directed them to move outside and help Jim and Doris with the outdoor kennels. Dr. Adams took his leave as Raven and Jo began to lay out the one-gallon cans and fill them with water for the dogs.

"I need to run up to the zoo," Raven said after they were finished.

"Can I come?" Jo asked eagerly.

"You need to stay away from that zookeeper," Raven said.

"That's none of your business."

Raven looked sharply at the girl and then broke into a smile. "Well, well. Aren't you Miss Independent?"

"Sorry, I didn't mean..."

"That's alright," Raven said. "You can come but I need to speak to him privately. You can wait outside the zoo until I call you."

11

"Where have you been?" Harry Fisher exclaimed. "I've been worried sick about you."

He jumped down from the cage he had been scrubbing in the Lion House and wiped his hands on a towel that hung over the visitor's handrail.

"What are you doing over here?" she asked without answering his question. Their voices echoed in the cavernous space.

"I've been promoted," he said. "I'm supposed to get this place cleaned up and ready for the busy season."

"Did you get your male lion, yet?" Raven asked, nodding toward the cage he had been cleaning.

"The circus will be in town in a few weeks," he replied.

She looked around, apparently admiring the building. "I need a favor," she said, finally.

"We're not going anywhere until you tell me where you've been and why you're really here."

She looked at him, feeling a little guilty for having walked out on him the way she did. The flowers he had sent were a sincere enough apology, but that seemed a lifetime ago. Despite his archaic opinions about women, she felt she could trust him. Perhaps it was because of his genuine love and concern for his animals.

"Can we walk and talk?" she said.

"Where to?" he asked, as he hopped over the rail.

"The raven cage."

He grabbed his jacket and cap off a hook behind the door and they trudged through the ankle-deep snow. More snow settled on their hats and shoulders, and Raven pulled her coat tightly around her shoulders. She began their walk by thanking him for the flowers and told him what had happened that had taken her out of his life. They had arrived at the raven cage, and she wanted to get on with retrieving the key, but he had more to say.

"I understand why you got mad at me for what I said in the café," he began, "but I'm not accustomed to having someone walk out of my life without a word."

"Now you know why."

"Yes, but what I don't know is where we stand now."

She looked at the raven cage for a long time without seeing what was before her.

"Look," she said, finally. "I'm sorry I walked out, but it's not like I just forgot you. A lot has happened in my life."

"So, where do we stand?"

"I want us to be friends."

"And you won't walk out on me again?"

"Not if you won't be an ass."

He leaned back against the cage and smiled into the distance. Finally, he turned to her and asked, "Are you all healed up from the bullet wound?"

"It still hurts sometimes. The doctor couldn't find the bullet, so it will probably always bother me."

He seemed at a loss for words, so she continued, "The key is just there," she pointed, "behind that loose brick at the bottom of the cage."

He stepped over the fence, moved the brick, and recovered the key. He presented it to her in the flat of his hand and they both peered at it closely.

"So that's where you hid it," a voice said, causing both to jump.

"What are you doing in here?" asked Raven. "I asked you to wait outside the zoo until I was finished with my business."

"Josephine," said Harry as he closed his fist around the key.

"It's cold and snowing," Jo said to Raven. "And you were taking too long."

Raven suspected there was more to it than that, judging by the way Jo was gazing at Harry.

Harry opened his hand, exposed the key, and asked, "What do you suppose it's for?"

"I don't know," said Raven.

"I do," said Josephine.

They both looked at her.

"It's a key to something in the athletic club across the river on South Michigan."

"How do you know that?" asked Raven.

"I spent time in the railroad yard across the street. That 'C' inside the circle," she pointed to the key in Harry's hand, "is on their sign."

"The Chicago Athletic Association is a men's club," Harry said to Raven. "This is probably to one of their lockers."

They were silent for a moment as they looked at the key.

"Oh no," said Harry as Raven shifted her gaze back to him. "I'm not a member. They won't let me past the front door."

"At least you're the right gender."

"It doesn't matter," he handed her the key. "I would still need to be a member. We need to take this to the police."

Raven snatched the key and said, "I'm not giving this to the police. I got kidnapped and shot over this key. Vincent almost died. I want to see what makes this key so important, then we'll go to the police."

"I'm not getting involved with the police," said Jo. "You two can have whatever it is."

She turned to walk away but Harry said, "Wait." She turned back, and he said, "What if we leave you out of any dealings with the police?"

"Who put you in charge?" Raven said as she squeezed the key in her hand. "I took the key off the dog and I hid it. Now I want to know its secrets." She paused, "And I don't need a man to help me figure it out!"

She turned and stalked toward the South entrance to the zoo, but she had only made it a few yards before she heard shuffling footsteps in the snow behind her.

"Raven, wait," Jo said. "We're sorry. We want to help."

"Come on, Raven," said Harry. "Quit being like that."

"Like what?"

"Like you hate men," he replied. "I'm just trying to help."

Raven looked at the pair and was suddenly glad they had stopped her.

"Sorry," she said, fingering the key. "I really do need your help—both of you. I have no idea how I'm going to get into a men's club."

"I do," said Jo. "But we will need Harry's help."

They both looked at him.

He cast his eyes to the heavens and said, "Okay. What do you want me to do?"

12

Raven and Jo sat in the open door of a boxcar in the rail yard that ran along Michigan Avenue. Their perch protected them from the damp snow that drifted in from the Lake behind them and gave them a clear view of the ornate, multi-story Chicago Athletic Association building—a building that would put most fancy hotels to shame. Raven wondered what rich men did in there and why they needed something so large and magnificent in which to do it. She looked around the train yard and pulled her feet up under her coat.

"When you lived on the streets, how did you sleep outdoors when it was this cold," Raven asked. "I should think you would freeze to death."

"Some do," said Jo. "But I wasn't out much in the winter."

"Didn't the bums bother you? I mean as a young woman."

Raven was looking down the railroad tracks a hundred yards to their left where a dozen or so people were huddled around a roaring fire.

Jo followed her gaze and replied, "I dressed like a man. Not many knew I was a girl." After a pause, she continued, "And they're not bums. They're hobos."

Raven looked at Jo. "There's a difference?"

"Bums," Jo said with some authority, "are just homeless people who live on the street. Hobos ride the rails, mostly looking for work. All those men," she nodded toward the campfire, "work somewhere during the day—at the stock yard or on some building project. When that work dries up, they'll jump a freight car to wherever it takes them."

Raven was quiet for a moment, and then said quietly, "So you didn't..."

Instead of answering, Jo said, "Here comes your boyfriend."

Raven opened her mouth to protest the boyfriend comment but was silenced by the scene unfolding across the street. Jo had figured out how to sneak Harry in through the employee entrance in the alley. Now he was emerging from the front of the building carrying a canvas bag, but instead of bringing it to them, he looked around, stuffed it into a trash bin, and turned to his right. He walked south on Michigan Avenue for a moment, apparently trying to blend in with the crowd, but when another man burst out of the building, looked both ways and hollered at Harry, he broke into a run. Raven's heart raced as she watched Harry turn the corner and disappear up Monroe Street. The man giving chase stopped at the corner where Harry had disappeared. He must have lost him because he turned around and was soon back inside the building.

Raven and Jo hopped to the ground, and Raven took a step forward but was stopped by a hand on her arm.

"I'll get it," said Jo. The girl turned her coat inside out, put her head down, and assumed the furtive shuffle of someone who lives in the shadows. "Nobody will pay attention to me going through the bin."

They had arranged to meet at the Association's office, and that is where they found Harry waiting outside for them.

Raven unlocked the door to the new clinic, and the three of them piled inside and shook off their wet coats.

"I'm glad you found it," Harry said as Raven plopped the heavy bag on the table. "The doorman tried to stop me as I left."

The three of them looked at the bag, unsure of what to do next. It was a heavy, well-worn brown leather satchel.

"I still say we should take it to the police," said Harry.

"I want to know why someone tried to kill me," Raven said, as she unbuckled the straps and dumped the contents on the table—bundles of money and two automatic handguns.

"Jesus!" exclaimed Harry.

"How much money is there?" asked Jo.

Harry fingered the bundles of twenty-dollar bills. "Looks like a thousand dollars in each bundle," he said, "and there must be a hundred bundles here."

He grabbed one of the pistols, pulled back the slide to see that it was unloaded, and aimed it at the wall.

Raven sat down heavily and lit a cigarette.

Jo ran her hands over the money and asked, "What are you going to do with it?"

Raven took a puff of her cigarette and blew the smoke out her nose.

"I'll take it to the police first thing in the morning."

Harry yawned and asked, "Are we done here?"

"Yes," Raven stood up.

Harry turned to go, but Raven pulled him back, grabbed his shoulders, and kissed him on the cheek. He looked surprised and hesitated, unsure of what to do next, but she turned him around.

"Thanks," she said. She gave him a gentle shove toward the door. "I'll see you in a few days."

"So, he is your boyfriend?" asked Jo, when Harry was out the door.

"He's just a friend," said Raven. "He reminds me of my brother."

"Right," said Jo.

Raven looked around the kennel. Most of the dogs, including Vincent, were asleep on their blankets. Only the two little fox terriers had any interest in their activities.

"Can I sleep here tonight?" Jo asked. "The dogs will settle better with someone here."

"Sure."

"Where are you going to put that?" Jo pointed to the money and the guns that were still piled on the table.

"She's going to give it to me."

Vincent sprang to his feet and lunged at the front of the cage barking as Raven and Jo backed in his direction, moving as far away from Brian Sweeney as they could. He must have slipped in the front door just after Harry had exited out the back. Vincent's throaty bark became louder as two of Sweeney's men came in behind him. These were not the boys Raven had dealt with before. These were rough looking characters who looked like they would be spoiling for a fight if they had not been facing two girls and some caged-up dogs.

"Nice of you ladies to retrieve this for me." Sweeney nodded at one of the men, who stepped forward and began to pile the money into the bag. Sweeney picked up a pistol and pulled back the bolt on an empty chamber. "Ain't this a beauty?"

He nodded at the other two men and said, "Lock them in a cage and let's get out of here."

Harry had already shown Raven that the pistol was not loaded and she had not seen any other guns, so when one of Sweeney's thugs placed his hand on her arm she grabbed his wrist with her left hand and punched him in the stomach with her right. When he doubled over, she brought a knee up to connect with his nose and he dropped in a heap.

The man who had grabbed Jo stepped back in shock at what he had just witnesses and, before he could recover, Raven lunged at Sweeney.

Sweeney backed away and pulled his own pistol. "I should just shoot you right now, you little bitch."

"I don't think so, Sweeney."

There were two guns trained on Sweeney, both sub-machine guns. The third man facing Sweeney, the man who spoke, was not armed. He did not need to be because he was, as everyone in Chicago would have known, mob boss Johnny Torrio.

"Give me the gun," Torrio said.

Sweeney handed over his gun and put his hands up—which prompted Raven and Jo to do the same.

"What happened to him?" asked Torrio, nodding at the man on the floor.

Nobody answered.

Torrio took a hard look at Raven before casting his eyes to the table.

"That's my money," Sweeney said defiantly.

"Shut up!" said Torrio. "It's my money now. You're out of business."

"We had a deal, Torrio."

"Gino," Torrio turned to one of his men. "Get this piece of shit out of here."

"What about him, boss?" Gino pointed to the man on the floor.

"Send in a couple of the boys to drag him outside."

As soon as Sweeney and his men were out of the room and the money and guns were bagged, Torrio turned to Raven and Jo, who were now seated at the table.

"Which one of you knocked out Sweeney's man?" Torrio asked as he took a seat across from the women.

Neither of them replied, but Jo stole a glance at Raven and Torrio followed her look.

"Where did you learn to do that?" he asked Raven.

When she didn't reply, he leveled his gun at her but was interrupted by one of his men who returned and gave him a nod. Torrio lowered the gun and got to his feet.

"Sorry for the trouble." He tipped his hat. As he exited the room, he turned to the man who had helped him bag the money and said, "Alphonse, see that these ladies get home safely."

13

I've named everyone," Jo shouted proudly above the barking dogs the next morning.

"It looks like you've cleaned them as well," Raven responded as she hung her coat on a nail by the door. She surveyed the room where the dogs—and Jo—had spent the last few nights. She opened Vincent's cage and kneeled to pet him, letting him lick her on the cheek before pointing to an old blanket in the back corner of the room and saying, "Go lie down." She then moved back, hoping to escape some of the noise, and took a seat on a stool across the room with her back to what once had been the bar. "I want to name one of them."

"Oh," Jo said with a hint of disappointment.

"I want to call the female German shepherd Bea," said Raven. "And the two terriers," she continued, "are going to Katherine this afternoon. Let's let her name them." When Jo cast her eyes down, Raven continued brightly, "So what are we going to call the other three?"

"This one," Jo moved to a kennel and pointed to the brown dog with a white tip on her tail, "is named Tippy.

She moved to the next cage where the English setter stood patiently looking at them. "I'd like to call her Chelsea. It was my mother's name." She hesitated, then continued, "Chelsea is a sweet dog—very loving but probably not terribly bright."

"Are you sure that's how you want to remember your mother?" Raven asked with a grin.

"Well," Jo replied. "If the shoe fits..."

They both burst out laughing.

"And what about that one?" Raven gestured to the black shaggy dog that that was barking and running back and forth. Its eyes were barely visible under its dense fur.

"That one is a female," said Jo. "We can call her Bexley. She is very clever, but silly. She sometimes runs around, jumps up and down, and barks for no apparent reason. She's like a clown in a dog suit."

They laughed, then sat in silence for a moment, watching the dogs. Raven considered their personalities and how much like people they were. She already had warm feelings for each of them.

"Did Mr. Alphonse walk you home last night?" Jo asked.

"No," Raven replied. "He just waited with me until the streetcar came."

"How was he?"

"He seemed nice enough," said Raven. "His name is Capone. Alphonse Capone."

"He works for Johnny Torrio," said Jo. "You know what Torrio does, don't you?"

"He's a gangster—a criminal," said Raven. "Everyone knows that."

"But do you know what kind of criminal?"

"What do you mean?"

"Torrio runs brothels," said Jo. "*Whorehouses.*"

"So?"

"So," Jo straightened up and looked at Raven. "He's known on the street as the Fox. Did you see how he looked at us after he figured out it was you who beat up that man?"

Raven laughed. "You don't think he's looking for me to go to work for him, do you? Do I look like a prostitute?"

Jo did not laugh. "It's not you I'm worried about."

*T*hose two will certainly liven up this house," said Katherine.

"It looks like Vincent agrees," Raven replied.

She took a sip of her tea as she looked out the window into the garden. She could see the breath of the two terriers from the kennel as they scampered around chasing and barking at Vincent. The big shepherd would occasionally turn and drop into a play stance before rushing at the little dogs over the frozen ground. Katherine sat beside her wheezing and occasionally coughing into her handkerchief.

"What are you going to call them?" Raven asked.

"Gracie and Sophie."

"Which is which?"

"I haven't the faintest idea."

"Where is Min Lee?" Raven asked. "I haven't seen her about, lately."

"I understand you don't need her any longer," Katherine replied with a knowing look. "It seems you are taking care of yourself just fine."

Raven's mouth dropped open, but Katherine just smiled and shrugged. "I have my sources."

Raven decided not to press her for details.

"What does the doctor say about that cough?" Raven asked.

"Nothing to worry about, dear."

Raven was worried. She had worked in a TB sanatorium and she knew what a deep, rattling cough might mean. She got up, closed the door to the living room, and let the dogs in—one at a time—carefully wiping their paws before sitting back down.

"You'll need to make sure they understand who's the boss," Raven said.

"Ha," said Min Lee as she pushed through the swinging door from the living room. "I can guess how that will go."

Raven laughed. "I suppose that will be your job."

Min Lee sat at the table and patted her knee. Vincent placed his head in her lap, but the new dogs were wary.

"What are their names?" asked Min Lee.

"Gracie and Sophie," Katherine replied

"Which is which?"

"I haven't the faintest idea," Katherine and Raven said in unison.

They all laughed.

"I need to be getting back to work," Raven said. "I'll leave Vincent here to help Gracie and Sophie settle in."

"Where has Josephine been staying?" asked Min Lee.

"She's been sleeping at the kennel with the new dogs," Raven said. "I'll try to get her to come to dinner with us tonight."

"It's not safe there," said Min Lee. "You need to talk to her about sleeping here."

14

Raven stepped off the streetcar at LaSalle and Huron and picked her way through the wet snow and mud. She hopped across a puddle at the edge of the street and onto the sidewalk but was brought up short by the police cars and the ambulance parked outside the door to the Association office. Her anxiety rose when she saw Jo being carried out the door on a stretcher. She had a bandage wrapped around her head.

Raven rushed forward and asked the attendant, "What happened?" Raven placed a hand on Jo's arm. "Is she all right?"

"She seems fine," said the man. "Just a bump on the head. We're taking her in to be looked at."

"They took the dogs," Jo cried out. "They took the dogs, Raven."

"Who took the dogs?" Raven asked.

"Some of Sweeney's men," Jo said. "The ones you fought with."

"We need to go, lady."

"Wait," said Raven. "How did they know we had dogs?"

"Two of our workers were with them. The men who built the cages."

The attendant began to close the door, but Raven put a hand on it as Jo continued. "Sweeney's man was mad. He pushed me down. I hit my head and blacked out. When I woke up, they were gone with all the dogs."

Raven was stunned. She backed up so the man could close the door, and the ambulance sped off.

What struck her first, as she walked into the kennel, was the awful silence. Lou Hanson was talking in hushed tones to O'Malley, the police sergeant who had been at the scene of the murder. The cage doors all stood open while Officer Walt Miller and another policeman examined the premises, presumably looking for clues.

"Morning, Miss.," Walt said somberly.

Raven nodded at him and walked over to join the discussion with Hanson and the sergeant.

"Did you leave the door open when you left last night?" Lou growled.

"What?" sputtered Raven. "No."

"Hold on, Hanson," said O'Malley. "This isn't her fault. This was the work of pros."

Lou glared at O'Malley, looked around the room, and stomped out. "Get this place cleaned up when they're done," he said to Raven from the doorway.

"What is his problem?" Raven asked O'Malley.

"Don't take it personally," said the sergeant. "Crime scenes tend to upset people. Especially when there's violence involved."

"What happened?"

"We found tire tracks out back where they backed up to the door," O'Malley said. "Not sure how they got in, but they knew what they were doing."

"Did they..." Raven hesitated, "hurt the dogs?"

"I doubt it," said O'Malley. "There was no blood. They usually want the animals alive."

"Usually?"

"We have been seeing a lot of this lately. They sell the dogs."

"Who buys dogs?"

"Companies that do research."

Raven let that sink in. She had heard of the awful things done to animals in the name of science, and she had crossed paths with activists who opposed the practice—anti-vivisectionists, they were called. Her eyes teared-up at the thought of the dogs being used for these purposes. She felt a little guilty for being relieved that her dog, Vincent, was safely at home.

O'Malley glanced at her and said in a soft voice, "I'll have Miller make some inquiries, but I wouldn't hold out much hope."

Raven wiped her eyes and gave a quick nod of appreciation.

*L*et's begin with a description of the animals," Walt said as he placed a cup of coffee in front of Raven and lit the cigarette she held in her shaking fingers.

They were seated at a table in the back of the room. Everyone else had left, and it was eerily quiet.

"Do you like animals, Officer Miller?"

He sat back in his chair and looked at her closely before his gaze shifted into the distance.

"I was at the Belleau Wood," he began. "It would have been," he paused to think, "two years ago this month. I'll never forget the suffering and death I saw there. So many men died. Maybe they were the lucky ones. A lot of men live with horrible scars—inside and out." He spoke in halting sentences and Raven let silence fill the voids. "Anyway, it wasn't just the men who suffered. Those poor horses and mules. You could see the fear in their eyes, and you could hear the pitiful squeals of the injured animals. As soldiers, we knew why we were there. We could put it all down to duty, honor, and all that. But the animals—they had to suffer without knowing why."

She waited a beat to make sure he was finished before she said, "There are plenty of animals suffering in this city right now."

"I know," he looked at her. "but it's the suffering people that I'm sworn to protect."

"Not exclusively, I hope."

"No, not exclusively." He smiled warmly at her for the first time and said, "Tell me about your dogs."

"City workmen brought us six dogs a few days ago," she began.

Walt wrote in his notebook as Raven described the dogs, the workmen who had been there that day, and how the room had been set up when she left. She also suggested how someone might have stolen a key to the building. Finally, she told him about the confrontation between Sweeney and Johnny Torrio a couple of nights ago, leaving out the fact that she subdued one of Sweeney's men.

"So," Walt said looking around the room in surprise, "Sweeney and Torrio were here that night?"

"Yes," she said.

"How did Brian Sweeney and Johnny Torrio come to be at an animal shelter?" he asked incredulously.

"I'd rather not say."

"You'd rather not say," he said. "You'd rather not say. That might be kind of important, don't you think?"

"Not to the disappearance of the dogs."

Walt was silent for a while as he studied Raven.

"You keep some mighty bad company," he said finally.

"Look," she said, "if all you're going to say is 'a girl shouldn't be getting mixed up with those people' then save your breath. I can handle myself."

His look was somewhere between a smile and a grimace when he said, "So if Sweeney was involved in taking these dogs, then maybe you can get Torrio to help you get them back."

She sat up and looked at him.

"I was kidding," he said sternly. "You need to stay away from Johnny Torrio."

"You're probably right," she said evenly.

But staying away from Johnny Torrio was the last thing she intended to do.

15

*H*ow many brothels are there in this city?" asked Raven.

"How should I know?" replied Jo, still angry over the loss of the dogs and the assault on her person.

"How many do you know about?"

"Just the ones downtown. He might be outside of town somewhere."

Raven wrapped her scarf tightly around her face against the cool, damp lakeshore breeze. Jo, however, wore nothing on her head and—except for the bump on her forehead—seemed impervious. She had cleaned up into a lovely young woman with proper clothes and hair that had to be cut before it could be brushed. Although she was nearly a foot shorter—not much more than five feet tall—and several years younger than Raven, she had an air of confidence that was more than a match for Raven's sometimes brash demeanor.

They turned a corner and Jo pointed toward a man standing outside the door just ahead of them. She didn't say a word since this was their fifth stop in the last twenty minutes. She allowed Raven to move ahead.

"I'm looking for Johnny Torrio," Raven said to the doorman.

"Never heard of him."

"He runs this place," she persisted.

"Beat it lady," he said

He turned to two well-dressed gentlemen approaching the door. "Evening Mr. Saxon," he said smoothly.

"Evening, Sammy."

Sammy held the door open, but Mr. Saxon turned to Jo and said, "Well, well. Who have we here?"

"Nobody, Mr. Saxon. They were just passing by."

Saxon grabbed Jo by the arm and said, "Maybe she'd like to come inside with me."

Jo jerked her arm free and backed away as Raven inserted herself between them. She placed a hand on the man's chest and said as nicely as she could, "I'm sorry, sir. We were just leaving. My sister and I got a little lost."

She was close enough in his face that she smelled the cigar smoke and alcohol on his breath. The glazed look in his eyes told her that trouble was about to erupt if they didn't leave quickly. As she tried to move Jo toward the street, Saxon's companion blocked their escape by stretching out two, burly arms and herding them back toward the door.

"We don't allow street girls in the club, Mr. Saxon," Sammy pleaded. He was trying to diffuse the situation and avoid a scene, but Saxon did not like being rebuffed.

Raven pushed back at the bodyguard and nodded at Jo to slip out through the crowd. She looked at the doorman for help, but all he did was shrug his shoulders. He wasn't about to take on a rich customer and risk losing his tip—or his job.

Saxon elbowed his companion out of the way while other customers moved around them to enter the club.

"Look, bitch," he mumbled to Raven as he placed his hands on her shoulders near her throat.

He tightened his grip, moving his hands around her throat so Raven subtly threw up her arms to break his hold. She kneed him in the groin and grabbed him by the lapels as he bent forward. His eyes bulged, and he gagged in pain, but his companion had been standing behind him and did not witness what had happened. Raven deftly turned him toward the other man as she and Jo quickly made their escape onto the crowded sidewalk.

"I've had about enough of this," Raven said as they hurried down the sidewalk. "How many more of these places does Torrio run?"

"I only know of one more. It's a new one, but its down on South Wabash. We can take the streetcar."

"Good," said Raven. "Let's get out of this wind for a while."

Twenty minutes later they were deposited across the street from a four-story brick building at 2222 South Wabash Street. The place was called, cleverly enough, the Four Deuces and—once again—they were faced with a man guarding the door.

Raven set her shoulders and made to cross the street but was held back by a hand on her arm.

"Let's try something different this time," said Jo.

"What did you have in mind?"

Jo took off Raven's hat and scarf and stuffed them into her handbag. She unbuttoned the top three buttons on Raven's blouse, fluffed out her hair, and applied a little lip-rouge. She then did much the same to herself.

"Push your breasts up a little," Jo said as she did so to herself. "Like this."

Raven laughed as she did so. "We look like a couple of proper working girls, don't we?"

"Let's hope so," said Jo. "Let me do the talking."

Five minutes later, they were through the door, having convinced the doorman they were here for their first night on the job. They ran into Al Capone inside the front door and were soon seated in a spacious parlor along with a half dozen other women who were chatting amiably amongst themselves while eyeing the newcomers.

"I didn't expect to see you ladies again," Capone said, "Especially in a place like this and," after an appraising smirk, "looking like you belong here."

"We need Mr. Torrio's help with something," Raven said.

"Can I offer you a drink first?" Capone asked, staring at her chest.

"Sure," said Raven. "Bourbon, if you have it." she sat back, lit a cigarette, and buttoned up her blouse.

"No thanks," said Jo. "But I wouldn't mind one of those." She pointed to the cigar Al held in his fingers.

He held it up and looked from Jo to Raven in surprise. Raven, too, was surprised.

After a moment's hesitation, he broke into a grin and said, "My pleasure."

Raven watched Capone as he got up and walked to the bar. He was not very tall—maybe an inch or so shorter than Raven—but he was solidly built with a broad chest and thick limbs. He reminded Raven of a bear.

When he returned with her drink and he lit Jo's cigar, Raven commented, "You're still serving alcohol."

"Of course," he replied. "I don't expect we'll stop."

He was young—maybe in his early twenties—and had a brash air about him. His round face, thick lips, and close-set eyes further accentuated Raven's impression of a bear. She liked bears, but the thick scar that ran from his left ear to his jawline gave him an air of menace.

"What do you do here?" Raven asked.

"I'm just visiting from New York," Capone replied. "I'm helping Mr. Torrio set up his books for this place."

"You don't look like a bookkeeper," said Jo.

"What do you think a bookkeeper looks like?" His glance at Jo turned darker.

"Well," she said. "I suppose I would expect some mousey little man with thick glasses and a pocket full of pencils."

Capone grinned and said, "I have other talents," but before he could continue, a man approached and whispered in his ear. Al looked at the floor as he listened, but his eyes shot up to Raven and Jo at something the man said.

Al watched the man walk away, then returned his gaze to his guests. "We just received a telephone call from the Aphrodite Club uptown. It seems a couple of dames roughed up one of our best customers outside the doors. Said they were looking for Mr. Torrio."

"That customer was rude," said Jo. "He tried to drag me inside."

"Even the doorman told him no, but he wouldn't listen," said Raven.

"What did you do?"

"I made him listen," Raven said.

Al rolled the cigar in his fingers,

Raven continued, "I need to talk to Mr. Torrio about some dogs that were stolen from our kennel."

"Dogs?" said Al. "We don't have nothing to do with no dogs."

"I know," said Raven. "But Brian Sweeney does."

"Sweeney? What makes you think we know anything about his business?"

"I don't think you do, but you may be able to help us find out where he's taken them."

"And why would we do that?"

"Because," Jo removed the cigar from her mouth and said, "Sweeney's territory is just a few blocks from here. With prohibition going into effect and this stuff," she pointed to Raven's glass of whiskey, "becoming illegal," she hesitated, "You guys will be the only ones providing it. Sweeney may not be in this business yet," she looked around the room, "but I'll bet he's planning something."

Al was quiet as his mind worked. Raven suspected he was not particularly book-smart and probably had not seen the inside of a schoolhouse, but he had to be bright and quick-witted to survive in this business. There seemed to be plenty of money in prostitution, but alcohol had to be the next big thing for anyone who was willing to capitalize on something that was illegal.

"All right," he said finally. "I'll have a word with Mr. Torrio. That's the best I can do."

Raven and Jo rose, and Raven offered Capone her hand. "I appreciate it," she said.

"You keep this quiet," he said as he rose and escorted them to the door. "And stay away from Mr. Torrio's business establishments."

"Now that we know where to find him," said Raven, "we won't need to bother anyone else."

He shook her hand and held it as he looked her in the eye. "You feel free to look me up anytime, sweetheart."

As they emerged into the frigid night air, Jo said, "He likes you."

Raven found the man oddly attractive, even though there was little in his appearance to make him so. She did not reply, so Jo continued, "You'd better not trust him. He's a bad man who works for bad men."

"I'll be careful," Raven said.

16

R aven sipped her coffee and looked out the window of the Huron Street Diner at Lou Hanson. He was half a block down LaSalle down the street directing the loading of a truck. She noticed that he kept glancing angrily in the direction from which Raven should have been approaching. Clouds were building and dust was swirling in the street. She wondered if more snow was coming.

"Shouldn't you be going with them?" asked her companion.

Raven did not answer right away. If Lou were at all intuitive, he would have looked in the opposite direction and seen her staring at him from the diner.

"Probably," she said finally. "But it's just another of his little publicity stunts where he'll have us give out animal food and some *Be Kind to Animals* posters. He calls it his Welcome Wagon. Besides," she continued, "I'm supposed to be the small animal officer, not a welcome wagon hostess."

Raven did not mean to sound negative about the mission of her organization. She was, in fact, proud of the work they did on behalf of Chicago's tens of thousands of work horses—many of which were sick, poorly cared for or just too old to work. She had recently learned that when prohibition closed Chicago's taverns, her Animal Welfare Association would assume responsibility for maintaining the water troughs in front of most of those establishments. Lou had much to do with all of that. She also felt a pang of guilt that, with so many people in the city suffering, she was concerned about animals. But animals were her calling. Someone else would have to worry about the people.

"So," she shifted her gaze through the haze of frying bacon and cigarette smoke toward the handsome man in the tan trench coat across the table. "Why did you call me to meet?"

"Maybe I just like your company."

"Officer Miller," she said with mock formality, "do I need to remind you that you are a policeman—and a married one at that?"

"Shall I remind you that I am off duty today?" He opened his hands and smiled. Was he flirting with her? "Besides, my wife's the reason I'm here."

"Oh?"

He sipped his coffee and looked around the room as he spoke. "She teaches nursing students at Rush Medical College and she's active in several movements—child welfare, women's suffrage, and the like. She is so active, in fact, that I hardly ever see her. That's probably why we have no children. Anyway, some of her friends are anti-vivisectionists. Do you know what that is?"

"Of course, I do."

"Well I didn't until she explained it to me. When I mentioned your dogs to her, she told me her friends are fighting a pharmaceutical company that does research on infections, diabetes, and other human diseases. They use dogs as their test subjects—hundreds of dogs—and they are paying two dollars for every healthy dog that is brought in."

"That doesn't seem like enough money to attract a big-time criminal like Sweeney," said Raven.

"Crooks like Sweeney don't plan something like this. They're opportunists. If it happens in their territory, they want a piece of it."

Raven leaned forward and placed her elbows on the table. "Where is this pharmaceutical company?"

"Thirty miles south and west of town," a new voice replied. "In the middle of nowhere."

Raven sat back, startled by the arrival of what could only be Walter's wife. She took a seat at the table.

"I'm Gladys Miller," she said, extending a gloved hand to Raven. "My friends call me Glad."

Raven had been so lost in conversation that she had not noticed Glad's arrival. She was a handsome brunette with tightly cropped hair, a round face, and large, wide-set eyes. She was dressed in black, from her hat to her shoes, and had a smile that could light up a room. Walter, it appeared, was one lucky man. Raven felt an unwelcome stab of jealousy.

"Roberts Laboratories," Glad began after she ordered a coffee, "operates on a large estate in a forested area on the Des Plaines River. It's out near a place called Signal Hill."

Raven took a drag on her cigarette and stubbed it out in the ashtray. She leaned back in her chair, blew smoke at the ceiling, and asked, "What do they do to the animals?"

Glad looked down at the table as she spoke quietly, "They remove organs and sew the animals back up to study how they are affected. They inject them, spray chemicals on them, feed them poisons..." She stopped.

Raven's eyes became moist at the thought of the dogs from her kennel undergoing such treatment.

"Can't the police do something?" She looked at Walt.

He shrugged and placed his hands palms-up on the table. "Even though they were technically stolen from your kennel, they were still ownerless strays. In fact, looking at it another way, the dogs are being used for the benefit of humanity."

"I've got to do something," Raven said, finally. "I'm going to get them back."

"You can't fight these people," Glad said. "They are too powerful. They pay off politicians and," she stole a glance at her husband, "policemen."

"What about your anti-vivisectionists?" Raven's voice was rising in desperation. "Can't they do something?"

"Believe me, they've tried."

"Raven," Walt said evenly, "I'm afraid those dogs are gone."

Raven looked at him and then looked at his wife. "What if I can come up with a plan? Will you two help me?"

Walt shook his head and put up his hands. "I can't get involved in something like this."

"He'll be glad to help when he's off duty," said Glad.

Raven caught a look between them. She couldn't tell if Walt was exasperated or angry. Glad appeared not to notice—or care.

"We'll just need to be discrete," Glad continued.

Raven stared out the window. A plan was forming in her mind, a plan that involved Walt and a drive into the country. But it might be risky. She would need to be careful how she approached Lou—if she approached him at all.

17

*S*orry I'm late," said Raven as she placed her bag on the table and shed her coat and scarf. "I was seeing what I could find out about the missing dogs."

"That's a police matter," Lou snapped. "I was expecting you to go out with the Welcome Wagon this morning."

"The dogs are most likely at a research center," she continued, ignoring his admonition.

She stood in the doorway to his office, still breathing heavily from the dash across the street and the climb up the stairs to the office.

He looked up from his desk and asked, "How do you know that?"

She looked away, not sure whether she trusted him with her source.

"The police haven't reported any progress," he continued. "Where did you get your information?"

She couldn't tell if he was angry about the dogs or simply irritated at her failure to show up earlier. Theirs was a complicated relationship. This timid little man answered to a board of trustees composed primarily of wealthy women who were used to getting their way. They had most likely selected him to run their organization because few men would have accepted a job in which answering to women was a condition of employment. And employing a woman as superintendent was not something they would ever consider.

"I know someone who follows these things," she replied vaguely.

"What's the name of this place?"

"Roberts Laboratories."

He wrote the name on a slip of paper on his desk.

"They're located out near Signal Hill," she continued. "Let me go out there and speak to them."

"No," he said sharply. "I'll call O'Malley. Let the police handle it."

"But, Lou," she began.

"Let the police handle it." He straightened some papers on his desk as he spoke." I want you out on the Welcome Wagon. You can meet up with Josephine at the South end of the State Street Bridge. Some ladies on our Board are going to be stopping by." He stood up as if to accentuate his authority but was still half as head shorter than Raven. "I want to be able to report that we are on top of things."

So that was it. He was more worried about his image with the ladies on his Board than he was the fate of the animals in his care. She locked eyes with him, then grabbed her coat and stormed out.

If she had to describe the scene before her in one word, it would have been intimidating. She also knew that if Lou found out what she was up to, he would probably fire her on the spot.

The building that housed Roberts Laboratories must have begun its life as the home for someone of great wealth. The towering, brick mansion loomed down a long gravel carriage way that ended in a circular path around a small pond.

Raven got out of the car and walked around to the driver's side. She leaned back on the door and gazed at the building.

"There must be a lot of money in whatever it is they do here," she said.

"I'm sure there is," Walt replied, turning off the motor. "Maybe too much for us to take them on."

When Raven did not reply, he continued. "Alright, you've seen it. Now let's get out of here."

Raven had told Walt that she did not plan to confront anybody. She just wanted to see the place and what better way than with a policeman. That way, if Lou found out she was here, she could claim she was assisting the police in their inquiries. Walt had been reluctant to make the long drive out here but agreed in the end. Raven suspected he was sweet on her and, though she did not like the idea of being involved with a married man, he was awfully useful.

She wondered where they might keep the animals they worked on—surely not inside this mansion. There must be some outbuildings out in back. As she was debating what, if anything, to do next, a man in a white lab coat emerged from the building and made his way to their car. He was tall and gaunt with hollow cheeks, deep-set eyes, and a stooped posture. As he approached, Raven was surprised that he was a good bit taller than she was. His voice was deep and raspy, and he pointedly ignored Raven.

"Can I help you?" he asked Walt.

"We were just passing by," Walt lied, "and wondered what this place is. There are no signs anywhere."

The man did not answer right away. This was a flimsy excuse and Raven knew it as well as the man in the lab coat did.

"My husband and I were looking for a spot in the country for a picnic," she said.

"This place," the man said to Walt with a quick glance at Raven, "is private property. I'll have to ask you to leave."

Walt appeared to take exception to the man's manners because he opened the door to the car and stepped out. He wasn't as tall as the man in the lab coat, but he more than made up for height in bulk.

Raven grew concerned. Walt was wearing civilian clothes, and they were driving an older model, unmarked police car. They were on shaky ground, at best, as far as police business went.

Walt folded his arms across his chest. "And who might you be?" he asked.

"I'm Doctor Archibald Patterson," he said. "This place, as you call it, is the headquarters of Roberts Laboratories. Now, if I need to call security, I will."

"Headquarters?" asked Raven.

The man looked at her for the first time but did not reply.

"Is this where you do research on dogs?" she asked.

He stiffened but remained silent. Raven could feel herself becoming angry.

"You wouldn't have any idea where the dogs are that went missing from the Animal Welfare Association a couple of days ago, would you?"

"You need to leave."

"Let's go, baby," Walt said.

Raven continued to glare at the man.

"Baby?"

She shook her head in disgust, walked around the car, and got in.

Walt looked at Doctor Patterson, then glanced up at the building before he, too, got back in the car and started the motor. As they drove down the lane, Raven turned and saw Patterson standing in the road watching them leave. She glanced over at Walt and said with a smirk, "Baby?"

"I was trying to rescue you," he said. "That place is half a mile from the highway. How could we be looking for a place to picnic? Not to mention you tipping your hand about the dogs."

"Well," she said. "We did learn that this is headquarters. They probably do their research somewhere else. That must be where the dogs are."

When Walt had turned onto the main road to town she said, "Stop the car."

"What?"

"Stop the car." She got out and stuck her head back in to tell him, "Wait here."

"Where are you going?"

"I want to have a look out back to see if their dog kennel is back there." She trotted into the woods in the direction of the big house they had just left.

He pulled the car to the side of the road and followed her.

"Raven," Walt said in a loud whisper. "I'm not letting you go alone," he shouted.

The woods were open and carpeted with leaves and they made good time in their walk back to the house. They skirted to the left, careful to remain concealed in the shadows. When the back yard came into view, Raven was disappointed to see a garage and a few outbuildings, but nothing that looked like a kennel. Her spirits were lifted, however, when she heard the barking of dogs.

They stopped, and she smiled at Walt. "See," she said. "They *are* here."

He listened for a moment and said. "Those aren't your dogs. Those are guard dogs and they're headed this way."

Her smile faded, and they looked around for a place to hide.

"Over here," he said.

They ran to a tree with low hanging limbs. She began to climb but was moving too slowly so he placed both hands on her behind and pushed her up. He then grabbed the branch and hoisted himself up just as the dogs—a pair of Doberman pinschers—bounded to the base of the tree. One of the dogs managed to grab Walt's shoe and pull it from his foot as he climbed up next to Raven.

"Vell, vell," said their handler in a thick German accent. "Vat do ve have here?"

He slipped leads onto the dogs and pulled them away from the tree and allowed Raven and Walt to climb down.

"We got lost," said Raven. "We were looking for a place in the woods for a picnic."

"Picnic?" the dog handler inquired. "Out here?"

"Well," Walt added with a wink. "Maybe a little more than just a picnic—if you catch my meaning."

"Ah," said the man with a knowing grin. "Maybe this is not such a good place for a—*picnic.*" He glanced back at the house, "if you catch *my* meaning."

Walt finished tying his shoe and took Raven by the arm. "We'd better be on our way, then."

The man stood with the dogs and watched Walt and Raven retreat through the woods.

They walked in silence until they returned to the car. Walt started the engine and began the long drive back to Chicago.

"I'm sorry," she said after a little while. "I just wanted to see what was back there."

"What do you want to do about finding the dogs?" he asked.

"Can we meet tonight? Maybe you could bring your wife. Her contacts might be able to find out where their research laboratory is located."

"Where do you want to meet?"

"Let's meet at our clinic at seven o'clock." She looked out the window of the motor car as he drove toward town. "They're not going to get away with this."

18

"Where have you been?" Jo asked, sounding more frustrated than angry. "I'm starving, and I haven't been able to get to a toilet."

"Didn't Lou send anyone with you?" Raven asked.

"Myron drove me down here, but he left the truck and walked back to the office."

State Street and Wacker Drive was a bustling intersection near the Chicago River. Since most of the traffic in this area was street cars and motor vehicles, horses were not common. But they were parked behind one of the many watering troughs that the association maintained.

"Have you given out much?" Raven asked as she inspected the supplies in their small truck.

"Just a sack of oats to an old Negro who was heading down to the Black Belt," Jo replied. "A couple of Mr. Hanson's committee members stopped by, but they didn't stay long."

"Did they say anything about me not being here?"

"I told them you went to the toilet."

Raven smiled. "Let's lock up the truck and find you a toilet. I'd like to get a coffee."

"What about her?" Jo nodded toward a brown dog that lay on the pavement tied to a lamppost. She was large—probably around eighty pounds—with a black face, white muzzle, and a docked tail. "She just wandered by. I gave her some food and water, so she stayed."

Raven looked at the dog and it gazed calmly back at her—no sign of nerves or fear. This dog, Raven thought, was special. She thought of Vincent, who was at Katherine's house. She could read him, too. But he was edgy—constantly on guard, like he was spoiling for a fight. Vincent reminded her of those two guard dogs back at the estate. This dog was calm—at peace with her surroundings—but well-aware of all that was going on around her. Raven also sensed that this dog, like some quiet people, was not to be trifled with.

"We can leave her here to guard the truck," Raven said. "Let's go to Field's." Raven nodded down the street toward the enormous department store that anchored the corner of State and Randolph.

"Field's?" said Jo. "Mr. Hanson will have a fit if we go shopping."

"We're not going shopping," Raven said. "There's a public water closet and a coffee shop in the basement."

"You ladies have anything for a couple of hungry teamsters?" said a voice from above.

Two black draft horses—Percherons by the look of them—had their heads crammed into the water trough. The voice came from one of the drivers on the wagon.

"We have some feed for your horses," Jo replied.

"How about something for me and Charlie?" asked the driver.

"Sorry," Raven said as she glanced up at the speaker.

They recognized each other at the same time. He was the man from the zoo. The man named Vinnie who had shoved her to the ground. He jumped from the wagon and approached her, his expression somewhere between a grin and a snarl. Raven shifted her feet, centered her balance, and balled her fists at her side—looking forward to what was about to happen.

"Your horses are watered. Now, move along." Lou Hanson said sharply. He had his little dog Max under his arm.

Raven almost told him to back off but thought better of it. Instead, she watched in disappointment as Vinnie looked around to see who might be watching. He looked hard at Lou, glanced back at Raven, and climbed aboard the wagon. She was irritated that this bully was inclined to listen to a small, mousy man and not her.

"What was that all about?" Lou asked as the wagon drove off.

Jo looked to Raven who said, "Just a couple of angry teamsters."

"They wanted something for themselves," said Jo. "All we have is horse feed and dog food."

Lou noticed the big dog that was tied up at their feet and asked, "Where did the dog come from?" Max growled as Lou squatted and offered the back of his hand for the dog to sniff. Max grew quiet, however, as the big dog sniffed him all over.

"She just wandered by," Jo replied.

"Have you seen any of the Board members?" he asked without getting up.

Jo glanced at Raven before replying. "A Mrs. Johnson and a Mrs. Lorber. They didn't stay long. Just looked at the truck, watched *us*," this was said with a touch of emphasis and a glance to imply that Raven had been here, "give some feed to an old Negro, and then they walked across the bridge and up State Street."

Lou stood up, looking pleased. He turned to Raven, apparently waiting for her to add to the story. When she did not, he said, "Let's lock up here and go for a coffee."

Jo looked at Raven with her mouth open in surprise.

"Good idea," said Raven. "Let's go to the basement at Field's."

They repositioned the dog, tying her to the front bumper of the truck and walked down the street. Field's had been a fixture in downtown Chicago for decades, but the current building had only been completed a few years earlier. Calling itself the world's largest department store, Marshall Field's was breathtaking in both scope and design, and it never failed to excite Raven when she walked through its doors. Even the basement, with its arched doorways and mosaic tile floors, gave her a sense of being in luxury.

Jo immediately excused herself to the toilet and Lou went for coffee, leaving Raven to wonder at his change of mood. Despite his threadbare appearance, Lou had a spring in his step that she had not seen before. From his uncombed balding head to his scuffed shoes he had the look of a man who was down on his luck, but he returned to the table with three coffees, a large cookie, and a smile.

"Your visit with our Board members today was part of my evaluation," he said as he took a seat. "As long as they were pleased with what they saw, I'll be reappointed for another year at their annual meeting in two weeks."

Raven tensed as he spoke. Her little deception did not seem so little anymore.

"I need your help with something," he continued. He wrapped the cookie in a napkin and carefully broke it into three pieces, placing a piece in front of each cup of coffee. "The Board wants me to begin a dog training program."

"Dog training," exclaimed Jo. She sat down and took a bite of her cookie. "Thanks for the cookie, Mr. Hanson. What kind of dog training?"

"It was Celia Shatz's idea," he said. He took a bite of cookie and a sip of coffee, then continued. "She's always stirring up trouble. She seems to like making my life more difficult. Anyway, this time she may have a good idea. She heard about a program in Europe where shelter dogs are selected and trained as police dogs and guard dogs."

Raven thought about the Dobermans she had encountered a few hours ago.

"I can think of plenty of places here in town that might benefit from dogs patrolling a fenced property after business hours." He paused and looked around. "This place could even use them when they close for the night."

"What does a police dog do?" asked Jo.

"Mostly just walk a beat with an officer," Lou replied. "But first he would need trained."

"What about Vincent?" exclaimed Jo. "He would make a great police dog."

Raven knew she was right, but thought it was a terrible idea—for selfish reasons.

"That's exactly what I was thinking," said Lou. He looked at Raven for her confirmation, but she was still staring at Jo.

Raven could not think of a single argument to oppose the idea except that she loved Vincent and had grown so attached to him she could not imagine letting him go. But there it was. She knew he would be much happier on police patrol than following Raven around to Welcome Wagon events and the like.

"We don't know anything about training police dogs," was all Raven could think to say.

"We could learn," pleaded Jo. "Come on, Raven. It will be good for Vincent and, if it works out, other dogs too."

"Actually," Lou cleared his throat. "The training is quite specialized. He might need to be sent away."

"Sent away?" exclaimed Raven.

"Where to?" asked Jo.

"Celia Shatz is working on that."

"You've already begun the process?" Raven asked with more anger than she intended.

Lou held up his hands. "We're just looking into it. I spoke with Sergeant O'Malley this morning. He said he would run it up the chain of command, but that young officer of his has been pestering him for a police dog since he came on the force."

"Officer Miller?" asked Raven.

"Oh," said Jo with a knowing smile at Raven. "Officer Miller."

Raven did not smile back. She would be having a word with Officer Miller.

19

What do you think he'll do?" Raven asked.

"I don't know," Min Lee replied, "but don't let her dominate him. It will break his spirit."

They stood at the window overlooking the garden watching Vincent—who was in the middle of the yard looking back at them. He obviously knew something was up. Gracie and Sophie had been let in to meet the new dog, but he had not.

"Why do you say that?" Raven glanced at Min Lee.

"Probably because Vincent has been shot," Jo chimed in.

"Twice," agreed Min Lee. She sat down and stroked the new dog that Raven had been calling Lizzie and continued. "This is a strong dog. She comes from the street and will not back down from a fight. Vincent is also physically strong, but he doesn't know it. We will need to teach him. This dog will be good for him, but we'll need to handle them carefully."

Raven stared at her friend for a moment and then glanced at Jo, who looked back at Raven with raised eyebrows. Maybe they wouldn't need to send dogs away for the police dog training. Maybe they had the trainer in their midst.

Following Min Lee's guidance, Jo placed a rope around Lizzie's neck while Raven called Vincent to the back door and clipped a leash to his collar. She brought him into the kitchen where he growled as soon as he saw Lizzie across the room. Raven stroked him and said "all right" in a soothing tone.

"Jo," said Min Lee, "you keep her where she is and let Raven approach with Vincent. Let him feel in control."

Vincent uttered a low, steady growl as they approached.

"Let them touch noses and smell each other all over and then separate them. If we can get that far tonight that will be enough."

Raven and Lizzie walked the three blocks West on Schiller to LaSalle where they waited for the streetcar. Lizzie had done well during the introduction. Vincent, on the other hand, showed little indication that he was about to accept this intruder into the fold. Lizzie, it appeared, would be living at the kennel for a while.

As she stood at LaSalle waiting for traffic to clear, Raven saw the streetcar approaching from the North. She waved her hand to catch the conductor's eye and stepped into traffic with Lizzie in tow. The car stopped, and she ran the last few yards, paid her fare, showed her Association identification badge that allowed her dog to board, and took her seat. Her relief at making the car was short-lived. As she glanced out the window her blood ran cold. Sitting across the street in an open-topped car were Danny and Sean Malone. Danny smiled and gave her a two-fingered salute. It appeared that they wanted her to know they were watching.

She craned her neck as the streetcar pulled away to see if they would follow, but they pulled off in the opposite direction.

Five minutes later she was relieved to see Officer Walt Miller sitting on the steps of the Animal Welfare Association as she emerged from the streetcar.

"Who is this?" Walt asked cheerfully. He offered the back of his hand to Lizzie for a sniff and then proceeded to scratch her behind the ears. "She's a beauty."

"I'm being followed," Raven said.

"What?"

"I'm being followed. The Malone boys were waiting for me at the streetcar stop. They watched me get on and, when I saw them, they laughed and waved at me."

"How could they know where you were going to be?"

"You don't believe me?"

"No," he said. "It's just that..."

"Where's your wife?" Raven interrupted as she unlocked the front door.

"Late," he replied, "as usual."

As they mounted the stairs to the second-floor office, she calmed. Why was she so afraid? She had the skills to handle her stalkers. It was probably just the idea of being watched that bothered her.

"I understand you're interested in having a police dog," she said.

They hung up their coats and took a seat at the table in the middle of the room. Raven was careful to sit facing the door.

"How did you know that?" Walt asked.

"Well," she said, "are you?"

"Yes. The Germans used dogs for all sorts of missions during the war. Now, police departments are starting to use them."

"Would you be interested in this one?" she pointed to Lizzie, who was sniffing her way around the office.

"Why are you asking this?"

"My boss approached Sergeant O'Malley," Raven said. "One of our Board members wants us to start training dogs—police dogs in particular."

"Wow," he said with a grin. "That's great."

The door downstairs opened and closed. Raven tensed as footsteps mounted the stairs but relaxed when a female voice said, "It's just me."

Lizzie emerged from under the table, barked, and rushed toward the stairs.

"Lizzie," shouted Raven. "It's alright."

The dog growled quietly as Gladys entered the room. She gave the intruder a quick sniff and returned to her spot under the table.

"See," Raven said, "she'd make a fine police dog."

"Police dog?" Glad questioned.

"I'd prefer a German Shepherd," Walt said. "They're bred for that sort of thing."

"Like Vincent?"

Walt held up both hands. "I'm not interested in taking Vincent from you."

"Who's Vincent?" Glad asked.

"Right," said Raven.

"Would someone tell me what's going on?"

Raven continued to stare at Walt, and then turned her gaze to Glad who had, Raven noticed, taken a spot two seats away from her husband. How odd, she thought. There had been no sign of greeting or affection. She told Glad about the idea of training police dogs and her concerns about losing Vincent.

Glad waited a beat, and then asked, "So, why are we here? Not to discuss police dogs, I presume."

"I had your husband take me out to Roberts Laboratories this morning," Raven said. "I wanted to have a look around."

"And?"

"Nothing," Walt said. "No dogs. No kennels. Just a mansion that serves as their headquarters."

Glad drummed her fingernails on the table as she thought. "I'll keep asking around," she said, finally. "We're planning a protest at the Roberts office on South LaSalle. Maybe I can turn up some information there."

She addressed Raven as she spoke, paying little attention to her husband. Were they on bad terms, Raven wondered? They were both lovely people, and Raven tried to imagine what they were like as a couple—how they interacted when they were alone. Raven pictured them in bed together and began to blush.

"Well," Raven said suddenly, pushing back from the table and standing. "Thank you both for all your help. I've had an exciting day and need to get home and rest."

She could not know that tomorrow would be equally eventful, beginning first thing in the morning.

20

The Chicago Avenue Police station was bustling with activity as Raven followed Lou Hanson through the front door. The dreary, three-story stone structure sat just a few blocks north of the Association office, but its atmosphere was unsettling to Raven. A policeman led them through the crowded halls and up the stairs. He deposited them in two chairs outside an office with the name of *Captain Everett Yancey* stenciled on the door.

Lou had not said a word on their walk from their office. He was, she could tell, furious and, judging by the shouting from inside the office, so was the Captain. When the door opened, Sergeant O'Malley emerged to usher them in. Raven was relieved to see that Walt was not among them.

"I got a call last night from Mayor Thompson's office," Yancey began, "It seems the mayor received a complaint from Doctor Patterson out at Roberts Laboratories—something about a man and a woman trespassing on their property and asking about some missing dogs. When I questioned my men, Sergeant O'Malley said your organization is missing some dogs. Care to explain what you two were doing out there?"

"Wait a minute," said Hanson, leaning forward in his chair and putting his hands up. "I had nothing to do with that."

Captain Yancey took a long look at Hanson, who appeared ready to become unglued, then directed his gaze toward Raven. Yancey was probably in his fifties with graying hair and ice-blue eyes. He might have been handsome at one time. Now, he just looked hard and cold. When his pointed tongue emerged to lick his lips, Raven thought he looked like a lizard.

"How about you, Missy?" he said. "Do you deny being there, too?"

Raven stared back at him, determined not to show him how much he frightened her. She was saved by a knock on the door.

"Captain," said the woman who had been parked at a desk outside his office. "Someone is here to see you."

"I'm busy."

"I think you'll want to see him."

Yancey pushed himself up. "We're not done here," he said as he left the room and closed the door.

They sat in silence for a moment until O'Malley said, "I'd better not find out that Miller is involved in any of this."

"Who?" asked Hanson.

"Walter Miller," said O'Malley, "is the officer who wants the police dog. He works for me," O'Malley continued with his eyes locked onto Raven. "He would do well to remember that."

Despite his gruff nature, Raven sensed that she could trust Sergeant O'Malley. There was something in the way he carried himself, in the warmth of his eyes, and even the timber of his voice that reminded her of one of the most trustworthy people she knew—her father. Calvin Griffith had lost his wife but managed to raise two children. When the property on which he had lived and raised his children was converted into a public park, he had been asked to continue to live there and run the park. And when the city confiscated a black bear that had killed a man in a bar fight, Calvin Griffith had figured out how to build the area's first zoological park. If her father was given a task, he completed that task—honestly and fairly. That is some of what Raven sensed in Sergeant Thomas O'Malley.

As O'Malley addressed Raven, his eyes widened at something over her shoulder—something outside the glass wall of the office. She turned in her chair and saw Captain Yancey and Brian Sweeney across the outer room, locked in an animated conversation.

Hanson turned to see what they were looking at but quickly turned back as if afraid to see too much.

Sweeney poked an index finger into Yancey's chest and Yancey put his hands up, apparently trying to appease the gangster. It looked, Raven thought, like a stick-up.

"What is that all about?" she asked O'Malley as she continued to look on.

"I'm not sure I want to know."

As she continued to watch, Raven's unease grew. She wondered whether it was because she felt guilty about watching someone's private conversation or, more likely, because the cop and the gangster knew each other, and the gangster appeared to have the upper hand. Her spell was broken, however, when Walt Miller emerged from a doorway adjacent to the office.

He looked around and, when he spied O'Malley through the glass, made his way to the office door. He stuck his head in and said, "You wanted to see me, Sarge?"

"Not now, Miller," O'Malley said. "Come back after lunch."

Walt left without the slightest glance at Raven and, as he moved away, the Captain returned and took his seat. He was flushed and remained silent for a moment. "Since those dogs from the kennel were strays and technically ownerless," he said to O'Malley, "I'm pulling you and your men off any investigation. I want you to find the Lewiston Mule Barn murderer."

"Yes, sir."

"As for you two and your welfare society," Yancey turned to Raven and Lou.

"Association," Raven said. "It's the Animal Welfare Association."

Yancey looked at her for a long moment. She could see something in his eyes but couldn't decide whether it was anger or surprise, so she decided to continue, "Those dogs were in our care. You can't pull us off."

Hanson stood abruptly and said, "We won't pursue the matter any further, Captain." He then turned to Raven and said, "Let's go."

As they stepped into the harsh morning sunlight outside the police station, Hanson turned to Raven and asked, "What are you playing at?"

"We need to find those dogs," she said. "That's our job—at least it should be."

"Don't you see what's going on here?" Hanson pleaded. "Sweeney's got that Captain in his pocket. The police are not only not going to help, they are most likely trying to stop us."

Raven began to walk back toward their office and Hanson followed along. They walked in silence for a while as Raven tried to decide what to do next.

"You're not going to let it go," Hanson said finally, "Are you?"

She did not reply. She was already planning her next move, and Lou was not going to approve.

21

The two-block walk from the police station to their office on LaSalle took less than five minutes, but it seemed like forever to Raven. She thought about making small talk with Lou, perhaps commenting on the snow clouds that were building in the West or their plans to begin police dog training that afternoon by acclimating Vincent to the police station environment, but before she could decide on a subject, they were at the office.

"Get someone out here to clean out this trough," he said gruffly. He nodded toward the horse trough at the curb. "People seem to think it's a water-filled trash receptacle."

"I'll take care of it as soon as I put my things down," Raven said.

As they neared the door, Jo burst out, looked up and down the street, and shouted, "Max!"

When she spotted Lou, she froze.

"Oh," she said. "Mr. Hanson."

"What's the matter?" he asked. "Where's Max?"

"He, uh, well," she stammered. "I can't find him."

"What do you mean *can't find him?*"

They rushed inside and up to the second-floor office. Lou stormed into his office and called, "Max!" He looked under his desk and behind the filing cabinet. He was furious. "When did you last see him?"

"An old man brought in a box of kittens he found in his garage," Jo said.

"Max hates cats," Lou said.

"So, I discovered," Jo replied. She was almost in tears. "The cats wouldn't stop mewing, and Max wouldn't stop barking at the box, so I took the cats downstairs to the clinic. When I came back, the old man was gone—and so was Max."

"Where's Vincent?" Raven asked. She had just noticed that he was missing, too.

Jo looked around. "I don't know," she said, and she began to sob.

"Jesus!" exclaimed Lou. "What a mess."

"Walk us through what happened," Raven said. "What did the old man look like?"

"He was rough looking," Jo began. "He looked like he was homeless."

"Did he want money?"

"No, but he was nervous. He was looking around like he might be looking for something to steal. Max was barking and Vincent was nervous, so I took the box of kittens downstairs. When I came back, they were gone—all of them."

"Did you leave the door open?" asked Lou.

"No. But it was open a bit when I came out of the clinic. I closed it the rest of the way and went upstairs. That's when I discovered everyone was gone." She began to cry again.

Raven looked at Lou and said, "This was deliberate. I think that man was after our dogs."

"Your dog," he said, "wouldn't allow himself to be led away, would he?"

"Good point."

"He was after Max. He wanted the little dog." Lou's annoyance with Jo was turning to anger at the man who took his dog. "And your Vincent let him do it. Some police dog he'll make."

Raven didn't know what to say. Lou was right, but where was Vincent?

"I'm going to the police," Lou said—and with that, he stormed out.

Raven listened to Lou's footsteps thumping down the stairs and, when the front door slammed, she turned to Jo.

"Is Lizzie out back?" she asked.

"No," said Jo. "She's in one of the kennels downstairs in the clinic. We're waiting for Doc Adams to look her over."

"Good," Said Raven." Let's go."

They rushed downstairs and into the clinic. Raven instructed Jo to place the box of kittens on the floor while she clipped a long leash to Lizzie's collar. The big dog licked Raven on the face as she did so. She then led the dog to the box, hoping she would pick up a scent to follow. Lizzie carefully sniffed around the outside of the box and Raven grew hopeful, but when the dog stuck her head inside the box and saw the kittens, she jumped back in surprise and gave a low bark.

"It's alright," Raven encouraged. "Have a good sniff and let's see where this box came from."

Raven led Lizzie around the box in ever-widening circles, then let the dog pull her to the door. They bounded outside and down the steps to the street. Raven figured the man had come and gone from the south since she and Lou had returned from the police station from the north and they had not seen any sign of Max. She was encouraged when Lizzie led her south toward Huron Street. They walked for fifteen minutes, past Huron, past Erie, and Lizzie did not appear to be sniffing the ground. She was just pulling along. Raven suspected they were just out for a walk. When she pulled on the leash and stopped, the dog just turned to look at her.

"You're not tracking anything, are you?" Raven said rhetorically. "Let's go home."

As they backtracked, Raven's mind was racing. What could she do? She had to retrieve Lou's dog both for Lou's sake and—perhaps more importantly—for Jo's. As they approached Grand Avenue, she looked both ways before crossing and did a double take. To her left, a block and a half away, she saw a dog lying on the sidewalk facing a doorway. It was Vincent.

Though she was tempted to retrieve her dog, she decided the best course was to rush back to the office and get help. A few minutes later, she was back at the corner of LaSalle and Grand with Lou and two policemen. She had returned Lizzie to her kennel.

"There he is," she said pointing down the street.

The policemen seemed unsure of what to do, so she said, "Let's go see who he followed."

"No," the older policeman said. "You need to let us handle this. Get your guard dog, then you two go home."

"But." Lou protested.

"Sir, just let us handle this."

They walked down to where Vincent was waiting. Raven kneeled and gave him a big hug as he wagged his tail.

"Good boy," she said. She clipped a lead to his collar and stood up.

Raven looked at the door he was guarding. The roll-up door to *Ernie's Garage & Tire Shop* was closed, which seemed odd for business hours.

"You two can go now," the older policeman said. "Leave it to us."

"What did you say your dog's name is?" asked the younger policeman.

"Max," said Lou.

As they turned North on LaSalle, Raven was surprised—and somewhat relieved—to see two police cars turn onto Grand toward the garage.

"Looks like Max is in good hands," she said. She could not know how wrong she was.

22

"Where is Josephine?" asked Min Lee. "I thought she would want to be here for this."

"So did I," replied Raven. "But something about policemen and police stations puts her off."

"That girl has a troubled past," Min Lee said.

Raven looked up Chicago Avenue toward the police station, wondering why O'Malley had asked them to meet down the street with the dog instead of coming inside the station. A brisk wind was blowing off Lake Michigan and Raven pulled up her scarf to cover part of her face. Yesterdays' clouds had not brought any snow, and they had been chased out-of-town by some freezing cold air.

She knew Min Lee was right about Jo's troubled past and wondered how she could learn about it without prying. She was deep in thought and had not noticed Walt approaching until he was saying hello to Min Lee.

"Looks like you were somewhere else," he said to Raven as he extended his hand.

"I was," she took his hand and enjoyed the firm but gentle pressure of his touch. "But I'm back now."

As Walt bent down to scratch Vincent behind the ears, she asked, "So, what are we doing out here? Why didn't Sergeant O'Malley want to meet at the station?"

Walt stood up and replied, "What we're doing hasn't been approved up the chain of command. He wants to try a few things before he makes his formal proposal."

"A few things like what?" Min Lee asked.

Walt leaned against the wall, took off his hat and scratched his head. He looked back toward the police station as he spoke. "The use of dogs for policing and military work is nothing new. They have been doing it in Europe for years. I saw it for myself and it was impressive. Even New York City has started a program. But this is Chicago. We like to do things our own way—which usually means not following what everyone else is doing."

"Even if it works?" asked Min Lee.

"Even if it works," said Walt.

"So, what are we going to do with Vincent?" asked Raven.

"We'll start slow," said Walt. "Right now, we just need a dog that is big and looks like he could take care of the bad guys. Vincent is certainly that. Just having him walk with an officer on foot patrol in a dangerous neighborhood would be good. Eventually, we would want him to be calm and quiet but to bark when we need him to, and even attack if necessary. We'll use him to search houses and to look for missing children."

"But," Raven persisted, "what are you going to do today?"

Walt put his hat back on and said, "There is one test he will have to pass before we can do anything else."

"And what is that?" Min Lee asked.

"He'll have to be comfortable with this." Walt pulled his pistol from its holster and held it near the dog. Vincent did not react. "I'll need to take him out and see how he responds to gunfire."

"Gunfire?" exclaimed Raven. "How do you think he's going to react? He's already been shot."

"I know," said Walt. "Let's just see how he does. If he's too fearful, we won't continue."

Walt left them standing on the corner and went for a police car. He drove them to an abandoned warehouse west of the river and into a courtyard that was surrounded on three sides by brick walls, offering some merciful relief from the wind. Tables had been set up facing bullet-riddled targets on wooden frames.

"It's an off-the-books shooting range," he explained. "Let's start by leaving him in the car. Let me take a shot or two and see how he does."

Walt walked about twenty yards away and turned his back to the car to shoot down range. Raven was in the front seat of the car watching Vincent, who was in the back seat with Min Lee. He was watching Walt closely, seeming to sense that something was afoot. When Walt fired, Vincent barked viciously. Min Lee had to wrap both of her arms around the dog's neck to prevent him from jumping out the window and attacking the shooter.

"Well," said Raven, "that's clearly not going to work."

"He sure didn't like the gunfire," agreed Walt as he approached the car.

Walt put out a hand to Vincent, who had calmed as soon as Walt put the gun away. The dog licked his hand and wagged his tail as the policeman leaned against the car.

Raven's relief at Vincent's apparent failure was short-lived, however.

"I think that went rather well," said Min Lee.

"How do you figure that?" asked Walt.

"He was barking out of aggression," said Min Lee, "not out of fear. Perhaps he was warning Officer Miller about a threat, but he sees the gun as the threat. I believe I can train that out of him."

Walt rubbed Vincent's head through the car window. "Atta boy," he said.

Raven just sighed.

"There is something else, though." Min Lee was watching Raven as she spoke. "If this dog is going to work with Officer Miller as a partner, he will need to go live with Officer Miller. I believe I can train him to do most of what you want, but you two," she was now addressing Walt, "need to bond with each other." Min Lee looked at the floor of the car as she addressed Raven. "Sorry, Raven."

Raven looked out the car window at the dilapidated buildings that surrounded them. They perfectly matched her sour mood. She and Vincent had been through so much together and he had been like a guardian angel. The thought of him living with someone else felt like a huge loss, but to try to prevent it felt like a selfish act, perhaps even a betrayal of Vincent. He deserved a chance at a life of significance— a chance to make a difference in the world. His tracking of Max and the kittens and his aggressive reaction to the gunfire had to be signs that police work was his calling. Lizzie, on the other hand, seemed to have no talent for any of that. She would make a better companion for Raven.

Raven turned to Min Lee and said, "While you're training Vincent, could you also train Lizzie? Not in police work, but just with some of the same obedience skills."

"Yes," said Min Lee. "It will make both dogs more comfortable."

"How do you know how to train dogs?" Walt asked Min Lee.

"The Chinese have been training dogs for hunting and for guarding property for thousands of years. The uncle who took me in after my parents died taught me many things. He had an old dog named Boots, and he showed me how he had trained Boots with kind words and food rewards."

"Most of the dog training I've seen," said Walt, "involved a rolled-up newspaper and a swift kick."

"You won't want to kick this dog," warned Min Lee as she stroked Vincent.

They all laughed.

"He'll be the first police dog in the department," Walt said. "Like Alice Clement."

"Who is Alice Clement?" asked Min Lee.

"The first female detective in the department—maybe the first in the country," replied Walt. "I'm surprised you haven't heard of her. The newspapers love her. They call her the queen of dramatic arrests with her furs, pearls, and fancy hats. I find her strong-willed, opinionated, and not to be trifled with."

"Sounds like someone else I know," said Min Lee, looking pointedly at Raven.

Raven just smiled. She could not know that she would soon meet the famous detective, but not under the circumstances she had imagined.

23

After saying goodbye to Walt and sending Min Lee home, Raven stayed late at the office to tell Lou about the day's activities. It was well past dark when she left for home, but she decided to walk rather than ride the streetcar. The thirty-minute walk from the office to Katherine's house gave her time to think. She was confused by her emotions—not so much about the dogs, but more about Walt Miller. Lurking in the shadows of her mind was the irrational thought that she wished she was going to live with him. If she unwrapped that thought, she was jealous of a dog.

Raven trudged up State Street, constantly looking over her shoulder and staying aware of her surroundings. She saw nothing suspicious as she approached from the south toward the house which was on the left-hand side of the street about halfway between Bunton and Schiller. She liked to approach the house from the opposite side of the street so she could admire it before she entered. She had never lived in a place this grand, so she paused to take in the view. Much of the facade was obscured by the trees growing near the street, but she could see the three-story red brick structure tucked in amongst the brownstone and limestone residences.

The wide front steps led up to a pair of massive wooden front doors that were set back in the deep, wrought iron framed front porch. To the left of the porch a bay window jutted out toward the street and to the left of that a driveway skirted the house, sandwiched between the neighboring house and Katherine's ivy-covered window-less sidewall. The brick facade of the house was softened by ornate, hand-carved limestone trim around all the windows.

The interior of the house was similarly impressive, but it was only when she inserted her key in the lock and opened the front door that she remembered how decidedly different the atmosphere was from the first time she had stayed there. Gone was the quiet formality of the old widow and her servants. Thanks to Raven, the house had taken on Josephine, two rambunctious fox terriers, and Raven's dog—which would now be Lizzie instead of Vincent. Tonight, Raven was greeted by laughter coming from the kitchen and the clatter of claws on the tile floor as the dogs scrambled to greet her. Instead of tea in the drawing room overlooking the formal garden, on most evenings it was coffee in the kitchen with dogs nosing around under the table looking for dropped food. Raven walked in on Min Lee and Jo sharing some humorous story.

"Have the dogs been outside?" Raven asked.

Min Lee looked at Jo and they shook their heads.

Raven poured a cup of coffee and opened the back yard to let the dogs out. "Where's Katherine?"

"Not feeling well," said Min Lee.

"How was work?" Raven addressed Jo.

"Fine," Jo said. "Mr. Hanson doesn't tell me anything, but I did overhear him on the phone. More dogs went missing over the week-end—from someone important, judging by the tone of the call."

One of the dogs scratched at the back door and Raven got up to let them in. The snow and frozen soil that clung to their paws turned into mud when the animals entered the warmth of the house, so she picked up the old towel from the floor next to the door and carefully wiped their feet before letting them inside.

"You okay?" Min Lee asked her.

"Yes," replied Raven. "Just tired, I guess." She wasn't prepared to share her feelings about Walt, whatever they were.

After she finished with the dogs, Raven moved to the stove and lifted the lid on one of the pots. "Is there anything to eat?"

Before Min Lee could reply, there was a knock at the door that set the dogs barking and running.

"I'll get it," said Raven. "I'm already up."

She was surprised to find Walter Miller standing there in the dark, and he was still in uniform.

"What are you doing here?"

"Nice to see you, too."

"Sorry," she said. "I'm just surprised to see you. How did you know where I live?"

"I'm a policeman," he smiled. "Finding people is what I do." After an awkward pause he continued, "Can I come in?"

"Of course," she said stepping aside.

She glanced up and down State Street out of habit. She thought she saw someone duck back into the shadows, but on closer look, there was nobody there. She must have imagined it.

As she ushered him down the long hallway he said, "Nice house you have here."

"It's not my house. I'm just a lodger." She led him past the parlor, the formal dining room, a couple of rooms whose names escaped her, and into the kitchen where she announced, "It's Officer Miller."

Min Lee rose and gave a small, formal bow. Jo also got up and said, "Can I get you a coffee?"

"No thanks. I can't stay." He stood next to the table with his hat in his hand. "I just wanted to let you know that more dogs have gone missing. You might want to make sure these guys are secure." He nodded toward the dogs that sniffed around his feet.

"Nobody's going to get them out of this garden," laughed Jo. "This place it like a fortress."

"That's what the Second Ward Alderman thought."

"That's our ward," said Min Lee.

"These people are getting more brazen by the day," he said. "It's starting to feel like more than just money for dogs. It seems more personal. Like someone is trying to stir things up."

"Why would someone do that?" Raven asked. "What would be the benefit?"

"I think Sweeney is behind it," Walt said. "I just can't figure out what his game is."

Raven watched the policeman as he stood in the middle of the room. He was tall but did not stoop like some tall men. He moved with grace and confidence, using his hands as he talked and smiling easily. She remembered the feel of his hands on her backside as he pushed her into the tree to escape the guard dogs.

"Why don't you sit and join us?" she said.

"Thanks, but I need to get back to the station."

"Station," Jo said. "At this time of night?"

"When an alderman is involved, we pull out all the stops. It was O'Malley himself who told me to come see you. If you find out anything, he wants to know."

"I'll talk to Lou in the morning," said Raven as she walked him to the door. "I'll stop by the station later in the day."

"Thanks," he said as they stood alone in the darkened hallway.

"Where's Vincent?" she asked.

"He's at home. O'Malley doesn't want him around the station just yet."

He shook her hand formally but held it carefully in both of his for a moment longer, she thought, than strictly necessary. He looked directly into her eyes and said, "I look forward to seeing you tomorrow."

24

G one!" Raven exclaimed. "What do you mean they're gone?"

"I had to pick up Katherine from the hair salon," said Min Lee. "I was only away for twenty minutes."

Heads began to turn at the curious sight of the hysterical woman berating a calm, composed Chinese lady. Raven had been passing out *Be Kind to Animals* flyers at the Michigan Avenue Bridge when Min Lee had approached.

"I want to see." Raven grabbed up the rest of her flyers and ran to the car with Min Lee following. The drive to Katherine's house only took five minutes, but it seemed longer, and no words were spoken.

"You were meant to be watching them," said Raven as they arrived at the house. "What were they doing in the yard without you here?"

"They're often in the yard with no one here," said Min Lee. "It's a walled garden. I considered it safe."

"Did you leave the gate open?"

"See for yourself." Min Lee pulled the car down the driveway beside the house to where a gaping hole in the wall was evident.

Raven was shocked at the violence of it. Someone had rammed the gate with a large vehicle, smashing a portion of the wall. Katherine appeared from inside the yard. She was in tears. They hugged for a moment until Raven regained her composure and allowed her anger to subside.

"Sorry," she said to Min Lee.

She walked through the hole in the fence and paused when she heard a couple of cars arrive. After the doors slammed, policemen appeared in the yard. Walt, with Vincent on a leash, stopped briefly at the wall before walking over to Raven. He appeared unsure of what to say or do until she threw herself into his arms.

He held her for a moment, then took her by the shoulders and pushed her to arm's length, glancing at the other policemen who were eyeing him carefully. They stood side by side looking around the yard.

"Is this typical?" she asked him, trying to regain her composure by petting the dog.

"That's not." He nodded at the gaping hole in the fence. "They wanted these particular dogs very badly."

The thieves, he was suggesting, were not just after some dogs, they were after her dogs. She was relieved that Lizzie had been at the office.

She watched him walk around the yard looking at the ground. Finally, he stopped and nudged something with the toe of his boot as he pulled Vincent away from it. He nodded for Raven to join him. Min Lee, who had been standing with Raven, came along as well.

"This," he said, pointing at the ground, "is typical."

"What is it?" Raven asked. "It looks like a piece of meat."

"It's probably laced with some kind of barbiturate," Min Lee responded, looking at Walt for confirmation. When he nodded, she continued, "They must throw the meat over the fence and wait for the dogs to eat it and fall unconscious, then break in and load the animals into their vehicle."

"The whole operation is over in ten or fifteen minutes," Walt said.

Raven pushed her fingers through her hair as she tried to take it all in. She felt bad for the two terriers. They would be waking up about now in a strange place. They had trusted her, and she had let them down.

She bent down to hug Vincent and asked, "Are you any closer to finding out who's behind this?"

"We have our suspicions," Walt said. "But nothing we can prove."

She looked up at him for a moment. She knew what those suspicions were and suspected that his hands were tied. She stood up.

"What does your wife have to say about all this?"

"Why don't you ask her? She'll be at that anti-vivisection protest this afternoon at the downtown office of Roberts Laboratories."

"I thought she liked to keep a low profile," Raven said bitterly.

"She does," he replied. "She won't be carrying signs or in a position to be photographed. She'll be off to the side, lending support. You might want to be there as well."

"I have something else to do first." She turned to Min Lee and asked, "Will you drive me somewhere?"

Min Lee and Raven turned for the car.

"Hold up there," Walt said. "Don't do anything stupid."

She had an odd feeling as Min Lee pulled the car to the curb in front of Sweeney's. She had been here before—and so had Min Lee.

"Wait here," she told Min Lee as she exited the car.

"Not a chance," said Min Lee. "They are my dogs, too."

Sweeney's place was in the heart of Canaryville—a large two-story frame house at the corner of Wallace and Forty-Third. It was marked by a green sign next to the front door with black script lettering that read *Southside Athletic Association*. Two men Raven did not recognize sat on the porch. If they were guards, they were not very good at their job. Raven and Min Lee breezed past them as they rose from their seats. Min Lee seemed to know where she was going, and she took the lead.

Sweeney's office was off the main corridor—a spartan room, devoid of any decoration, with an unused fireplace on one wall and a desk facing the broad window that overlooked the front yard. Min

Lee had parked in front of the house next door, so they had walked to his front door unobserved.

His hand went to a drawer in the desk as the two women surprised him. He relaxed a bit and smiled when he saw it was Raven, but his eyes darkened, and his hand moved to his desk again when he recognized Min Lee.

"What's he doing here?"

"He's a she," said Raven. "And she's with me."

Sweeney's mouth dropped open in surprise, but Raven did not hesitate.

"Where are my dogs?"

The two men from the porch appeared in the doorway behind the women, but they backed into the shadows when Sweeney dismissed them with a wave of his hand. Raven took the opportunity to glance through pocket doors behind his desk toward the back of house. It was the first time she had seen the room in which Min Lee had subdued Sweeney and his men and rescued her.

"Hard to find good help," he quipped. He leaned back in his chair and lit a cigar, obviously enjoying himself. He shook out the match, tossed it in an ashtray, and blew a smoke ring at the ceiling.

Raven grew angrier by the minute until, when she made a move toward Sweeney, Min Lee grabbed her by the arm.

"Even if I knew about your dogs, why would I tell you anything? First your friend here comes into my place and assaults me and my men, and then you steal my money. You two need to get out of here while you still can."

"My friend assaulted you because you shot my dog and kidnapped me." Raven shook off Min Lee's hand and took a step forward. "And Torrio took your money because you let him get the drop on you. That was pretty sloppy." Raven glanced back at the men by the door to see if they got the jab, but they were oblivious.

Sweeney's eyes hardened, and he leaned forward. "You need to get the fuck out of my office."

He was looking at Raven, but she did not flinch. He had her dogs, and they both knew that she could not simply walk out and forget about them.

"Are you two part of Torrio's little harem?" he continued. "I'll bet he likes you two—the black-haired Amazon and the quiet China doll."

Raven felt Min Lee tense. Sweeney reached into his drawer and pulled out a revolver, slowly placing it on the desk in front of him and raising his eyebrows. "I've seen what you two can do, but you're not so tough now are you, *ladies?*"

Raven knew what her friend was capable of, but fighting Sweeney and his men would not get the dogs back—and it might get them killed. They turned and left without another word.

"You can drop me off downtown," she directed Min Lee. "I'm going to see if I can find Walt's wife."

25

Raven awoke the next morning with a pounding headache and an upset stomach, made worse by her sudden shift to a sitting position. She crossed her legs and sat back against the brick wall. Her eyes slowly focused on the iron bars, and she tried to remember how she had come to be in jail. Four other women slept on the concrete floor and a fifth was standing with hands gripping the bars and head pressed into the gap. She must have heard Raven stir because she spoke without turning.

"That was quite a dust-up yesterday." When Raven did not reply, she continued. "Don't worry, our lawyers will have us out of here in time for a late breakfast."

Raven had no idea who this woman was, nor did she recognize any of the others. She had gone to the anti-vivisection protest hoping to find Gladys and, as she pushed her way through the crowd, the police moved in to break it up. She thought she may have punched a tall, skinny policeman who had grabbed her arm. The last thing she remembered was attempting to duck his partner's night stick just before it connected with the top of her head.

"I wasn't really part of the protest," Raven said to the woman at the bars.

"Well, you are now."

"I just went to see Gladys Miller," Raven continued. "Do you know her?"

"Oh yes," said the woman. "She's Val's friend. She was there alright. But I don't know if she got picked up."

Raven thought about asking the woman her name but was too tired to engage in idle conversation so she just sat, slightly nauseated at the smell of urine and stale vomit. She was angry at the police for hauling her to jail when she hadn't done anything wrong, angry at these women who seemed to take it all in stride, and angry at herself for thinking she could walk into a melee without consequences. Her thoughts were interrupted by the sound of footsteps in the hallway outside the cells. It was the unmistakable clomp of a woman's heeled shoes—a short woman by judging by the quickness of the steps. She stopped somewhere down the hall, walked a little and stopped again, and finally appeared at the front of the cell.

"Who is Raven Griffith?" she asked.

Raven recalled Walt's description of Alice Clement, the famous woman detective as she struggled to her feet.

"O'Malley saw your name on the list of women who were picked up," Alice said curtly. "He's busy and asked me to retrieve you."

"What about us?" asked the woman at the bars who had retreated to the center of the cell, causing the other women to stir.

"What about you?" Alice retorted. "This is nothing to do with you."

Raven gathered her coat and scarf and shuffled to the door as the jailer appeared with a large ring of keys. Raven and Alice walked up the stairs in silence and the jailer returned to his desk in the hallway.

Alice stopped the lobby and pointed to a line of chairs. "You can wait here," she said curtly. "Someone will be with you shortly."

As she turned to walk away, Raven said to her back, "I wasn't part of the demonstration. I was just there looking for someone."

Alice stopped and turned. "You punched a policeman," she said. "You're lucky the constable dropped his complaint against you."

Raven didn't know what to say. She wanted the female detective's approval, but she wasn't sure why. Alice Clement was the kind of independent, successful woman that Raven strived to be. But, for the moment, it appeared that the admiration was not returned. Alice turned and walked away.

Raven leaned back in her chair. She wrapped her arms around her coat to fight the chill in the hallway and looked down at her scuffed shoes. Never one to care much about her appearance, she was suddenly taken with shame—shame at her unkempt appearance and shame at being imprisoned. Then the anger began to return, the anger that had taken her to the protest in the first place.

"You're quite a sight."

Raven bolted upright. Her left hand went to her face, an unconscious effort to hide herself. Walt Miller had plopped down in the chair beside her.

"How did you know I was here?"

"O'Malley told me you got picked up. Said you knocked out one of our constables."

"Oh, God," she said through closed eyes.

"It's alright. The guy doesn't want to make an issue of you assaulting a police officer. He's ashamed that a woman got the better of him." By now Walt was grinning broadly.

Raven looked at him for the first time and said, "You think this is funny?"

"Well," he replied, "actually, I do." He paused, "But I also wanted to let you know I have not heard anything about your missing dogs."

"I thought you had been pulled off the case."

"I have, but I'm still keeping my eyes and ears open, just in case."

Raven glanced down the hall toward the desk sergeant who appeared to preside over the comings and goings in the police station. A man in a camel overcoat with matching fedora was handing a piece of paper to the sergeant. The sergeant looked at the paper and pointed to Raven, sending the man in her direction.

"Raven Griffith?" he inquired as he approached.

She stood and shook his outstretched hand in mute reply.

"I was sent to secure your release," he said. "But it appears that all charges have been dropped. You're free to go."

She looked at the man for a moment, trying to process what he was saying, and then turned to Walt who was now standing.

"Thanks," she said to Walt.

He winked at her shy smile.

"Who sent you?" Raven asked the man as they walked down the hall.

"I'm not at liberty to say."

"Was it Katherine—Katherine Ruebottom?"

He did not reply.

As they strolled into the morning sunshine, he shook her hand once again and handed her a note. "I was instructed to give you this." With a tip of his hat he said, "I'll bid you a good day, Miss."

She unfolded the note and read it, then glanced up to see the man disappear into the crowded sidewalk. She pulled her coat around her shoulders, unsure of whether the note left her worried or relieved. She felt dirty—both physically and mentally—from being arrested and hauled to jail like a criminal. She needed to get home, clean herself up, and get some sleep. Tomorrow, it appeared, she had someone to thank.

26

The Four Deuces looked to be deserted on this bright weekday morning. Raven pushed her way through the unguarded front door and walked into the lobby, her footsteps echoing inside the cavernous space. The gamblers had long since gone home to their families and the ladies who worked through the night would, no doubt, be sleeping upstairs. The place gave Raven the creeps and she would not be there but for the note Al Capone had sent and the car that had picked her up. The note said he had news about her dogs.

"How was your stay in the slammer?"

"I suppose you find that amusing," she said to a smirking Capone who had appeared in the doorway to her left.

"Hey," he said with hands outstretched. "It's no big deal."

"Well, it is to me."

"Come in and have a seat," he said, turning back into the room and lighting a cigar. "I've got some news about your mutts."

He led her into the same spacious parlor she and Jo had been in just last week—only now it was deserted. It made her a little uncomfortable being alone with this young gangster, but there was something about his charm and his brash persona that Raven found intoxicating. He had probably killed people and had surely slept with anyone he wanted. Why, she wondered, was he being so nice to her? What would he expect in return for his help?

"The dogs are being held at a place outside of town," he began without preamble, "at some kind of research facility."

"Roberts Laboratories?"

"Yea, that's the place."

"I've already been out there. It's their headquarters. It's just a big office building."

"The place we saw is no office building," he lit the cigarette she had just removed from her purse. "It's an old farmhouse with a couple of barns on the back side of the property. They hold animals there."

"Did you see my dogs?"

"No. We didn't go inside."

"Then how do you know the dogs are there?"

"Because," he said. "We were tailing a couple of Sweeney's goons yesterday when they snatched some dogs."

"Tailing who?" asked Johnny Torrio from the doorway.

Al looked surprised and rose quickly. "Hey boss."

Raven had seen Torrio when he got the best of Sweeney at the kennel, but she was too shaken to notice much. He was not an impressive man by appearance alone. He was of average height, average build, and thoroughly Italian in his appearance. But he had an aura of menace about him that made men—even men like Capone—nervous. Torrio stepped into the room, offered Raven a firm handshake, and took a seat at the table. There was something shifty and dangerous about him. Raven could see why he was known as *the Fox*.

Capone continued, "I was just helping Miss Griffith with some stolen dogs."

"Stolen dogs?" asked Torrio.

"Sweeney's men took them from the dog pound," said Capone with a hand gesture toward Raven. "That's where she works."

Torrio snapped his fingers and pointed at Raven. "I thought I'd seen you somewhere. I can see why you're helping her," Torrio said to

Capone with an appraising look, "but we're not going to war with Sweeney over a bunch of dogs."

"There's more, Boss." When Torrio tore his gaze from Raven, Capone continued. "I think Sweeney is supplying dogs in exchange for space in one of the barns. I think he's got a distillery going in there."

Torrio leaned back in his chair and lit a cigar, so Capone continued. "While we were watching them unload the dogs, a truck load of grain pulled up—must have been fifty bags on there. Why else would they need all that grain?"

Torrio eyed Capone through the haze of smoke, then glanced back at Raven. He was deep in thought. Raven knew that, with Prohibition as the law of the land, people were figuring out ways to get around the law. Raven wasn't surprised that these gangsters were getting ready to set up their illegal liquor businesses. She was, however, surprised by Torrio's response.

"Big Jim says we're not getting into the liquor business," he said. "You know that."

'Big Jim' Colosimo, Raven knew, was the well-known owner of Colosimo's Café and the less well-known owner of the dozens of brothels that Torrio ran. He was, in effect, the man who employed Torrio.

"But boss," Capone pleaded. "If we don't put Sweeney out of business, he'll have a monopoly. He'll be raking in a fortune and turning that money back into making war on us."

Torrio got up and began to pace. Capone kept quiet while his boss thought. Raven found the dynamics between these two gangsters fascinating. It was like a dance that was choreographed by the devil himself.

"Alright," Torrio said finally. He stopped and looked at Capone. "Take a couple of cars out there in the morning. If there is a still, bust it up." He puffed his cigar, took it out of his mouth, and pointed it at Capone. "But if there's no still, none of our guys had better get hurt—especially going after some dogs. You understand?"

Torrio left the room without expecting an answer and Capone visibly relaxed.

They sat in silence for a moment, and then Raven said, "I'm going with you."

"Like hell you are!"

"If it wasn't for me and my dogs, you wouldn't even be going out there."

"So what? I'm still not taking a dame out there."

"Look," she said. "If I don't get my dogs out of there now, what chance will I have in the future—especially if you shoot the place up?"

"We're not going to shoot the place up. We're just going to bust up the still—if there is one."

"What do you mean if there is one? You saw them unloading grain?"

"Yes," he said. "But it may have been for the cattle."

"Cattle? But I thought you said..."

"I know what I said. But Johnny wasn't about to let me go out there with his men without a good reason. I just made the reason sound a little better than it is."

"I need to be there, Al. Without me you won't know which dogs to grab."

She was right, and he knew it. That is why he told her to be in front of the Four Deuces at six-thirty sharp the next morning.

27

*I*t was still dark when Raven stepped off the Wabash streetcar at the curb of the Four Deuces the next morning. The air was crisp and cold with a full moon setting in the Western sky. She was wearing men's trousers, a heavy jacket, and her hair pulled up under a tweed cap. The city was still asleep with little in the way of traffic—either vehicles or pedestrians. She had stopped by the office last night to get some leashes for her dogs. She had told no one what she was up to and had slept poorly. Her mind was on the dogs and the fact that she might be too late to save them—if they were even there.

There was something in the way Capone had emphasized that if she were late, they would leave without her that made her show up forty-five minutes early. As she suspected, a few minutes before six she saw headlights and soon, two large black cars were parked at the front door. Six thirty departure, indeed. But if Capone was surprised to see her, he hid it well.

The drive out to Signal Hill took nearly two hours. When she had made the drive with Walt Miller a few days ago it had been a pleasant outing, with a stop for coffee in Cicero. This drive seemed to take forever, made longer by the dusting of snow that covered the roadways. She was in the back seat, wedged between young Sal, who seemed intent on trying to charm her with his constant banter, and a large, hairy man named Remi who smelled of cigar smoke and day-old fish.

She was relieved when they pulled up a gravel track about a half a mile beyond the lane that she and Walt had taken to headquarters. The car stopped next to a cow pasture and everyone piled out. As the men from the car behind them walked up, Capone turned in the front seat and said to Raven, "You stay here." He pointed to his driver and continued, "Benny will stay with you. We'll call you when the coast is clear."

Capone, surrounded by six men with an assortment of machine guns, shotguns, and rifles, walked calmly down the dirt road, their shoes crunching on the frozen gravel, and disappeared around a bend. They could have been soldiers going off to war.

Benny got out of the car and leaned against the hood, so Raven joined him. Her stomach rumbled loudly, and she clutched it in embarrassment.

"You want some coffee?" Benny asked. Those were the first words he had spoken to her all morning.

"You've got coffee?" she asked.

"It's in a thermos under the seat."

He straightened up and arched his back to stretch. Benny moved slowly. His face was long with deep creases and sharp angles. His expression was unreadable. He could have been a kindly grandfather, or he could have been a cold-blooded killer. Perhaps he was both. He carefully removed the lid from the thermos and poured her half a cup of steaming black coffee.

"Don't got any cream or sugar," he said as he placed the thermos on the hood of the car.

"Black is fine."

She lit a cigarette and sipped the coffee, grateful for the warmth it provided. Five or six cows with white heads and reddish-brown bodies had moved to the fence next to the car and appeared to be curious about the new arrivals. She was about to walk over and pet them when a staccato burst of a machine gun up ahead stopped her. Benny jerked a large, black revolver from under his coat and rushed forward. "You stay here," he said without turning. As soon as he was out of sight, she grew anxious. Staying safe at the cars seemed far worse than not knowing what was going on. If those machine guns were spraying bullets, the dogs might be in danger. She placed her coffee cup on the front of the car, stepped on her cigarette, and walked cautiously toward the bend in the road, trying to peer around the corner as she went.

She ducked behind a tree as the scene opened before her. A two-story farmhouse loomed to her left. It was well kept and looked to be lived in, judging by the two cars that were parked in front of it—two cars that sheltered Capone and his men as they shot at the barn to her right. The barn had the look of a building that had been here for many years, but the roof was new, and the walls sported a fresh coat of red paint. Behind the barn, in the hayfield beyond, Raven could just make out another, newer building. It did not look like it had been here for long. It was a long low structure with a new shiny metal roof and white walls. It looked out of place on this old farm, and Raven wanted a closer look.

She crossed the street to her right and entered some woods, carefully working her way to the back side of the barn that Capone was shooting at. The gunfire stopped, forcing her to move more quietly, watching each step until she emerged behind the barn. She was momentarily confounded as to what to do because there was no cover around the building. It had no windows, but she would be totally exposed as she approached it. She bolted forward and pressed her back to a side of the building, easing around back. Her heart leaped when she heard the barking. Running along the backside of the building was a long wire mesh kennel with rows of cages inside. It was full of dogs.

She rushed forward and realized as she formulated a plan to free them that she had neglected to bring the leashes. Bea, the German Shepherd, was there along with Tippy and Chelsea. But she did not see Opal's dog Molly, the black shaggy dog that Jo had named Bexley, nor did she see Gracie and Sophie. There were eight other kennels, and one of them held two border collies—probably Ozzie Bunton's dogs, Thunder and Lightning.

The kennels did not appear to be locked, but the entire bank of cages was surrounded by a separate fence that was secured by a locked gate. Raven needed help to get inside. Maybe she could convince Benny to shoot the lock off with his pistol.

"What are you doing here?"

She jumped and wheeled around to face a young boy who had emerged from a back door to the building carrying a broom and bucket.

"I'm just looking around," said Raven. "I live up the road."

"I live up the road," said the boy, "and I've never seen you around here."

With her lie called out, Raven's mind worked furiously. This country boy was obviously here to clean the kennels. She had not seen any cars in front of this building, so he was probably alone. The door stood open behind him.

"Look," she decided the truth might work best. "I work for the Animal Welfare Association in Chicago and some of these dogs were stolen." She pointed to the dogs behind her.

His blank look made her wonder if he was simple and didn't understand her, until he looked over her shoulder at the dogs and asked, "Are you here to take them back home?"

"Yes," she said. "Will you help me?"

"No," he replied. "I'll lose my job." He turned to go back inside.

"Wait," she said. He stopped, and she continued. "I'm missing some dogs—a female golden retriever, a big, black shaggy dog, and a couple of small fox terriers."

"They're inside the laboratory," he said. "At least the big dogs are. We don't have any little terriers that I know of."

She watched him for a moment as he processed what was going on.

"Come on," he said, finally. "The lab workers will be here any minute." With that, he dropped his tools and ran back in with Raven right behind him.

Inside was a small reception area with three doors behind the desk. The one to the left was labeled *Lab,* the one in the center was labeled *Administration,* and the one to the right that the boy opened was the *Kennel.* He flipped a switch and the lights in the long hallway came on. He pointed to a door as he passed it and said, "Your black dog is in there. She is on today's schedule. The golden is down the hall."

She opened the door, causing Bexley to jump back and bark at the intrusion. Once she recognized Raven, the dog jumped on her and knocked her back into the hallway. She growled at the boy as he ran down the hall toward them with Molly in tow. The boy also had several rope leashes slung over his shoulder.

"Whoa," Raven said to Bexley as she held on to the scruff of her neck. "It's okay, girl."

They quickly placed rope leashes on each dog and ran outside to the kennels.

"What's your name?" Raven asked the boy as he helped her gather the rest of her dogs.

"Isaac," he replied. "Isaac Newton. My friends call me Zack."

"Isaac Newton?" Raven repeated.

"Don't say it."

"I sure appreciate this," she said as she tried to gather the leashes of the seven dogs she had just rescued.

"That's okay," he said. "I love animals. I don't know what they do here, but I'm pretty sure it's not good for the dogs." He took a long look at the building, and then continued, "I think I'm done working here. I might as well help you."

Raven heard a car arriving on the other side of the building as they sprinted toward the woods with the dogs in tow.

The shooting had stopped, which made their trek through the woods and back to where Capone had parked the cars more difficult to conceal. The dogs ran with enthusiasm, appearing to think it was all a game, and a few of them barked at the cows that had wandered back to the middle of the field. Raven's relief at having not been left behind turned to concern when she realized that Capone and his men were not with the cars.

"Where are your drivers?" asked Zack.

"Good question," Raven replied. Raven smoked a cigarette and paced in front of the cars while Zack held the leashes of the dogs. "How come that car we heard at the lab didn't see these cars?"

"That would have been Doctor Driscoll," Zack replied. "He comes from the other direction. There's a road from the big house."

Finally, she threw down her cigarette. "I'm going to see about my driver," she said. "Will you mind the dogs for a few minutes?"

She walked quickly down the road without waiting for a reply. As she rounded the bend in the road, the house and barn came into view and she was relieved to see Benny calmly standing guard outside the door to the barn. He reached for his gun when she came into view, but relaxed when he recognized her.

"Hello, Benny."

"You should be at the car."

"I found my dogs."

A flicker of surprise passed across his largely expressionless face, but he said nothing. The sounds of crashing metal, splintering wood, and breaking glass told her that Capone had found a distillery and was making sure that no spirits would be coming from it.

"Where are the rest of the men?" she asked, as if there could be any question.

"Inside, dealing with a situation."

She moved to open the door, but he put his hand out. "You can't go in there."

She had no desire to press the issue, so she backed up a few steps. The door opened and Capone emerged. His clothes were disheveled, and he was winded and flushed as though he had been working hard.

"What are you doing here," Capone growled. "I told you to stay with the cars."

"I found the dogs."

Capone looked at her as if unsure of what to do with her. Finally, he turned to Benny. "I'm not putting a bunch of dogs in one of our cars," he said. "Go get one of those cars." He pointed to the cars near the house that must have belonged to Sweeney's men. "Take her and her dogs back to town."

Four pistol shots rang out from inside the building. She jumped at the sound, but Capone and Benny hardly flinched.

"Get going," Capone repeated to Benny.

"Sure, Boss."

Benny grabbed her by the arm, but before he could turn her, the door opened. Her seat mates from the morning ride, Sal and Remi, stepped out followed by the men from the other car. As they emerged, what she saw over their shoulders inside the building gave her a chill.

Four men were sitting against a pile of smashed barrels and bent metal pipes that Raven guessed would have been part of the distillery. Each man had a single bullet hole in his forehead. Capone had ordered the execution of four of Sweeney's men, and the one nearest the door had his face turned in her direction. It was Danny Malone's brother Sean.

28

The midday sun had risen directly overhead by the time they pulled up to the Animal Welfare Association office on LaSalle. Raven stood on the sidewalk with seven dogs at her feet and watched Benny drive away. He had been courteous enough to help her get the dogs out of the car, but he had not said goodbye or looked at her as he left. She wondered if he was angry or, more likely, he was just that way.

The door to the clinic which still had the tavern name in gold letters on the window above it, was locked, so Raven knocked.

When the door finally opened, Jo exclaimed in surprise, "Where have you been?" When she saw the dogs, she was even happier. "And where did you get them?"

Together they wrestled the dogs inside and Jo busied herself hugging and petting each dog. She carefully placed her dogs in their kennels, found space for Molly and the sheepdogs, and provided all of them with food and water. She wiped her hands with a towel and plopped down at the table opposite Raven. Jo's excitement at seeing the dogs was barely contained.

"Where did you get the dogs?"

"It's a long story," Raven said curtly. As Jo sat looking down at the table between them, Raven softened. She explained about how Capone had happened on their location by accident and agreed to let her ride along on their parallel missions. She told Jo about Zack and the rescue of the dogs and about Capone's men breaking up Sweeney's distillery. She left out the account of Capone's murderous conclusion to the whole affair, partly out of deference to the young girl but mostly because she simply did not want to talk about it.

They were sitting in silence when the door to the back room opened and Lou walked in. He looked surprised to see Raven, but his eyes really narrowed when he saw the dogs.

"The police told us to back off," he said.

"No, they didn't," she replied. "Besides, they can't tell us what to do."

"Like hell they can't." He was practically shouting now. "If you knew where the dogs were, you should have told the police and let them handle it."

"They weren't going to handle it, and you know it." She was angry now—angry at Sweeney for stealing her dogs, angry at Capone for spoiling her triumph by murdering four men, and angry at Lou for being so cowardly. "Somebody has to stand up to Sweeney and his crooked policeman."

"Sweeney?" exclaimed Lou. "How was he involved?"

"He stole the dogs in the first place," she said. "He sold them to a lab. That's where we found them."

"We?"

Raven clammed up. She had already said too much.

"If Sweeney was involved," Lou waved his hands, "He'll be coming after us now."

Raven had no answer for that. She didn't dare tell him how bad that situation really was.

"I've had enough of your shenanigans," he said.

"But Lou," she pleaded, "I got the dogs back. Isn't that what matters?"

He stomped to the door and turned, "You can leave Opal's dog," he pointed to Molly in her cage. "But get those border collies out of here. You're fired!" He stormed out and slammed the door.

God, what a mess," Raven said.
Essie Boyd sat opposite her at the kitchen table. Rondell had gone to take the dogs Thunder and Lightning to Ozzie Bunton after Raven had filled them in about how they had been recovered.

"What will you do now?" asked Essie. "Move back home?"

"I don't know," said Raven. "But I'm not moving back home."

"You do good work here," Essie said. "Find some other way to continue that work."

Raven wasn't sure how to respond, but she was saved by a quiet knock at the back door.

"I wonder who that could be?" said Essie as she got up.

They were both surprised to see Josephine standing outside asking if Raven was there.

"Why yes, child," Essie said. "She's sitting right here. Come in."

Raven stood up and moved around the table. "What's wrong? How did you find me?"

Jo entered the kitchen and looked tentatively around. "I figured you'd come here with the border collies," she said. "This is where your picture was taken—the one in the newspaper. And this is where you met the man about his missing dogs in the first place."

"Sit down, dear," Essie said. "Would you like some coffee?"

"No, thank you."

"Why are you here?" asked Raven.

Jo sat across from Raven. Essie joined them after pouring herself a cup of coffee.

"I don't think Mr. Hanson meant to fire you," Jo said to Raven.

"He sounded pretty definite to me."

"He was upset," Jo said, "and maybe a little drunk."

"Drunk?" said Raven. "I've never known Lou to drink on the job."

"After you left," Jo explained, "I went to his office. He had a bottle on his desk."

They were interrupted by the door opening and light flooding the room.

"Old Ozzie Bunton sure was happy to see them dogs," exclaimed Rondell. "And they was happy to see him, too. He said to tell you..." He stopped talking when he realized that there was one more person in the room than he had expected.

"This is my friend Jo," Raven said by way of introduction.

"You must be Mr. Boyd," said Jo. She extended her hand and, after a slight hesitation that Raven knew to be a concern over touching an unknown white woman, he shook it.

"Call me Ron," said Rondell, "or if you want to follow her lead," he nodded at Raven, "I'm just R. B."

Jo turned to Raven and said, "Max is missing."

"Again?"

"Yes, but this time he has no idea who took him."

"Who is Max," asked Essie.

"Max is my ex-boss's little dog," Raven replied.

"Little dog," said Rondell. "What kind of little dog?"

"A Yorkshire terrier," said Raven.

Rondell and Essie exchange a knowing glance, prompting Raven to ask, "What?"

"Did your boss go to the police?" Rondell asked Jo.

"He said the police weren't interested."

"I'll bet they weren't," said Essie. She got up and moved to the sink and Rondell began to look uncomfortable.

"What's going on?" asked Raven. She looked at Rondell awaiting a reply and then shifted her attention to Essie, who was looking at Rondell.

"You need to tell her," said Essie.

"Tell me what?"

"I don't think we should get involved," he said.

"Tell me what, R. B.?" Raven insisted.

After a brief hesitation, he pushed himself up from the table. "Come with me," he said.

Raven and Jo followed him out the door and down the alley. About half a block toward State Street, he turned into the back yard of a barn-like building that faced Fortieth Street and pushed through the back door. The place was deserted and had no windows. In the dim light from the open door, Raven could just make out a box-like structure in the middle of the room. It was ten or twelve-feet square with waist-high wooden walls. The room smelled of urine and dog feces.

"What is this place?" asked Jo.

"It's a dog fighting pit," said Rondell.

"Dog fighting?" said Raven. "What does this have to do with Lou's dog?"

"He might have been stolen by people who train dogs for fighting."

Jo burst out laughing. "Max couldn't fight anything." She stopped when she saw Raven and Rondell looking at each other.

"They don't use the little dogs for fighting, do they?" said Raven.

"No," Rondell replied. "They use them for bait. They let their fighting dogs kill them to get their blood up."

"That's awful," gasped Jo.

"Maybe we could hide down here," said Raven, "and see if Max turns up on fight night."

"Your dog won't be down here," said Rondell.

"How can you be so sure?" asked Jo.

"This is a Negro operation down here. These folks wouldn't risk stealing dogs from the white end of town. Your dog will be in a white operation."

"How come I've never heard of this?" asked Raven. "Why don't the police shut it down?"

"The answer to both questions is the same," said Rondell. "It's not talked about up there because the police are involved. Policemen and firemen run most of the fights."

29

I need to see Officer Miller," Raven said to the desk sergeant.

"Which one?"

For a moment, Raven thought the sergeant was just being difficult. He stood behind the counter in the hallway of the police station writing something so important that he did not bother looking up at her. But she quickly realized that it was such a common name, there probably was more than one Officer Miller. She considered slapping the desk to get the sergeant's attention but simply said, "Officer Walter Miller."

"He's out on a case with Sergeant O'Malley," he said, still without looking up at her.

"I'll wait."

"They may be awhile."

She ignored him and took a seat in the hallway—the same hallway in which she had awaited her release from jail a few days ago.

Essie had insisted she report her concerns about dog fighting and about Lou's missing dog. Raven trusted Essie's instincts but did not believe the police were likely to act upon them. The only one she wanted to talk to—the only policeman she trusted—was Walt Miller. She would sit and wait for him to return.

She had a sick, empty feeling inside. She had successfully rescued her dogs, only to see four men shot dead—and for what? For making whiskey. Sean Malone had been the voice of reason all those months ago when his brother had wanted to burn down Rondell Boyd's stable. Now, his brother would be looking to avenge his Sean's death. Where would he direct his wrath? On top of all that, she had no job—no way to support herself. She could probably find work at Marshall Field's selling cosmetics or ladies' apparel, but her heart was with the animals.

"What are you doing back in here?"

Raven looked up to find Alice Clement staring down at her. The look on Raven's face must have caused Alice's harsh tone to soften as she continued with a nod down the hall, "Care to talk about it?"

Alice led her to a room off the main hall. The sign on the door said Records. It was a musty smelling room with high windows, stacks of boxes on tall shelves, and a row of tables down the middle of the room.

"I don't have an office," Alice said apologetically, "and the ladies' toilet is little more than a closet. So, this is where I come when I want to have a think."

"But," Raven said as she took a seat at the table opposite Alice, "You're a detective."

"Ha," Alice snorted. "That may be, but these men don't want me here and they will do whatever they can to make my life uncomfortable. That's the way it's going to be for you too, Hon. Men don't like independent women."

"I'm beginning to see what you mean," Raven said bitterly and asked, "What about Officer Miller and Sergeant O'Malley?"

"Miller's not a problem," said Alice. "He admires you for how you stood up to that mob in the black-belt last fall. I looked up your picture in the newspaper files. As for O'Malley," she went on, "I haven't figured him out yet. He's as tough as an old boot and definitely one of the boys. But he'll stick up for what's right when the occasion calls for it."

"You looked me up in the newspaper?" said Raven. "I didn't know people could do that."

Alice shrugged modestly, so Raven continued. "Do you know anything about the police being involved in dog fighting?"

"No, but there is a lot that goes on around here that I don't know about," Alice said. "I'm not a member of the boys club, if you know what I mean." After a moment, Alice said, "So, I understand you were involved in a shoot-out yesterday."

Raven's head jerked up. "How did you know about that?"

"I hear things and put two-and-two together," Alice said eyeing Raven across the table. "Sweeney was in here first thing this morning talking to Captain Yancey. He was furious. I don't know everything that was said, but I did hear that there was a shootout between Torrio and some of Sweeney's men over an illegal distillery operation somewhere out west of town. Several of Sweeney's men are dead. And," Alice continued after a pause, "I know there was a woman there looking for some dogs at the laboratory. Ring any bells, yet?"

Raven placed her elbows on the table and buried her head in her hands. "Oh, God," was all she said.

"Is that what's got you so upset?"

"I suppose," Raven said through her fingers. "At least, that's part of it. I got fired from the Animal Welfare Association for my efforts."

"So, you *were* at the shootout."

"I was there, but I didn't do any shooting." She went on to tell Alice about the stolen dogs and her efforts to track them down—efforts that led her to Johnny Torrio's man Alphonse Capone, who is visiting from New York.

"That's impressive," Alice said. "Most girls your age would never disobey a boss and then team up with a gangster like Torrio."

"I just do what I need to do."

"Hmm." Alice appeared to be in thought. "Ever thought about working for the police department?"

Raven chuckled softly and got up to leave.

"Sweeney is planning something to avenge his men," Alice said ominously. "I imagine his wrath will be directed at the other gangsters, but you never know. He might blame you for just being there, or he might just want to make an example of you as a message to anyone who consorts with his enemies."

R aven stood on the steps of the police station and looked carefully up and down Chicago Avenue, using her hand to shield her eyes from the late morning sun. Walt had still not returned from his assignment with O'Malley and she had grown tired of waiting. Alice said she would let him know to get in touch with her. Now it was time to do something about employment. She was about to dismount the steps when she caught sight of a familiar figure. She shielded her eyes again and looked closer at his approach.

"Hello, Lou," Raven said as he mounted the steps.

He pulled up short and squinted up at her. "What are you doing here?" he asked.

"I was just about to ask you the same thing."

She wanted to be angry with him for firing her but, in truth, she was not. She figured she got what she deserved. Lou had been generous in taking her back after her disappearance over the winter and he had tolerated her insubordination like an understanding father. He was, now that she thought of it, the closest thing she had to a father-figure in this town and she missed his company. She suspected that since his wife died last winter that he was a lonely man who seemed to live for his job.

He moved up a step above her so he could look her in the eye and they both shifted out of the line of traffic streaming in and out of the station. He turned his attention back to the street and, without glancing at her, said, "Max was stolen yesterday—right out of my back yard."

"Oh?"

She decided not to let on that she already knew, so they stood there in silence for a moment. The spell was broken, however, when a police car pulled up to the curb and Walter Miller emerged along with Sergeant O'Malley.

"Sergeant," said Lou, moving away from Raven. "Can I have a word?"

O'Malley looked to be in no mood to talk, but Lou was not easily deterred. Before he followed the sergeant into the building, Lou turned to Raven and said quietly, "I may have been a bit hasty yesterday," he did not look her in the eye, "You're welcome to come back to work if you want to." He looked up at her briefly for a response. She nodded, and he went inside.

"Where have you been?" she asked Walt, who had joined her in surveying the street.

"Let's have an early lunch and I'll tell you."

The Billy Club was a bar across the street from the station that catered to police officers. Since it was only eleven o'clock, the lunch crowd had not begun to arrive, so Raven and Walt had the place mostly to themselves. They took a table near the back of the room and both ordered coffee and the Irish stew special. Her spirits were high, and she was not sure whether it was because she had her job back, or—to make things really confusing—because she was in Walt's presence.

"There was a shooting at the Four Deuces," Walt began after their coffee was poured. "One of Torrio's men was killed."

"Who was it?" Raven asked, trying to conceal her concern.

"One of his drivers. The guy was just sitting in his car. Never stood a chance."

Raven thought about Benny. Though he hadn't done much to endear himself to her, she still hoped it wasn't him.

"I understand you are on a first-name basis with Torrio and his men," Walt said.

She sipped her coffee and looked away, so he continued. "These are violent men, Raven."

She held up her hand to silence him. "Don't say it."

He gave her a hard look and continued, anyway. "Don't get dragged into something you'll regret."

"I'm afraid it's too late," she said. "I'm already in it."

Their food arrived so they ate for a few moments in silence while Raven surveyed the room. A horseshoe-shaped bar dominated the space with square tables scattered along the surrounding walls. A half-dozen men sat at the bar, none in uniform, but all looking like policemen. She was, of course, the only woman in the place and elicited several furtive looks.

"What do you know about the police department's dog fighting ring?" she asked.

"What?"

"You heard me. The police are involved in dog fighting. What do you know about it?"

He was quiet for so long she thought he was not going to reply. Finally, he said, "I know there is something going on, but there is some kind of code of silence. I haven't been around long enough for them to trust me."

"Is O'Malley involved?"

"I don't know, but I doubt it. O'Malley is a pretty straight arrow. Captain Yancey, on the other hand..." He let that thought hang in the air before he continued. "You need to leave this alone."

"If they've taken my dogs, I have no intention of leaving this alone," she said loud enough to elicit some looks.

Walt put his finger to his lips and ducked his head. "Keep it down. Maybe you need to lie low for a while."

"How am I supposed to do that?"

"I don't know. Don't you have somewhere you can go? Go home to your family."

"I'm not running away," she said. "I need to face this."

"Do you have a gun?"

"No," she said. "But I can take care of myself."

He leaned forward across the table and said in a low but forceful voice, "I'm getting you a small gun that you can carry in your purse, and I'm going to see that you know how to use it."

She scraped the rest of her stew out of the bowl and chewed thoughtfully. She had learned self-defense from Min Lee and knew how to apply deadly force. Violence seemed to come easily for her so perhaps having a gun of her own would not be such a bad idea.

"Does your wife carry a gun?" she asked.

"My wife," he replied, "doesn't consort with gangsters." He hesitated and appeared unsure about what to say. "These guys are bad news, Raven. They won't hesitate to murder anyone who gets in their way."

Raven thought about how effortlessly Al Capone had ordered the murder of four of Brian Sweeney's men. They were gunned down as easily as someone might take the trash to the curb—dead, gone, and forgotten. The worst part was that she felt complicit. If not for her seeking help to recover the dogs, those men would still be alive.

She looked into her empty bowl. "You must think me an awful woman."

"Oh no," he said. "Quite the contrary. That's why I want you to arm yourself. I don't want anything to happen to you while you're out there making our city safe for its animal citizens."

She didn't know what to say. She looked up and caught him smiling at her. As much as she would have liked to reach across and hold his hand, she did not want to get involved with a married man. Still, she had to admit that being admired by this handsome policeman was a bit of a thrill. She hoped his admiration would continue when he found out where she was going after lunch.

30

*H*ow did you find me?" Capone asked angrily. "Did Sal tell you?"

"No," said Raven. "After I heard Sweeney shot up the Four Deuces, I went over there. Sal and Remi wouldn't tell me anything. The only other place I knew about was here, and it's only a block away."

Capone stood in the doorway to Colosimo's Café and looked out at the street. He was uneasy, and Raven wondered if he was going to let her in. Finally, he seemed to come to a decision because he backed away so she could enter and closed the door behind her. He ushered her into a small private dining room and ordered the man who had first greeted her at the door to get her whatever she wanted to drink. She asked for coffee, lit a cigarette, and waited alone. The long room had a table down the middle with walls of dark paneling below red-patterned wallpaper above the wainscoting. The only other furnishing was a well-stocked liquor cabinet. This room must have held many a meeting between the gangsters and their lieutenants.

Capone came back about five minutes later, poured himself a whiskey from a decanter and joined her at the long table. He appeared a little more relaxed than when he had greeted her earlier.

"Who got killed?" she asked.

"Johnny's driver," said Capone. "A guy named Moe."

Raven wasn't sure why, but she was relieved that it wa

"What are you going to do?"

"That's not for me to decide. I'm just a guest here. Johnny, and some of the lieutenants are planning something."

Raven knew better than to ask what, so she said, "Someone's been watching me."

"It's not us."

"I know that. It's Danny Malone, and it's only going to get worse when he finds out what happened to his brother."

"That redheaded midget is a punk," Capone spat. "I hope he tries to come after me. I'll put a bullet in his head."

Capone's instant conversion from charming host to vicious thug was startling, even to Raven. It was as if someone had flipped a switch. She wondered briefly what it would be like to live with such a man and was grateful that she could walk away from him. Jo had been right to warn her about Capone.

They sat for a moment, then Capone got up and began to pace. "Look," he said finally. "I've got to get back in there." He nodded over his shoulder to where, Raven supposed, the planning for retaliation against Sweeney was taking place. "Maybe Malone will get caught in the middle of something he's not bargaining for. Maybe..." He glanced out the window, "Shit!"

He dove across the table and knocked Raven to the floor as the windows shattered behind him. The staccato report of a Thompson submachine gun being fired from outside reverberated and bullets smashed through the windows, shattering pictures hanging on the wall, coffee cups on the table, and a vase full of flowers by the door. Raven covered her head as Capone crawled into the hallway and returned, still crawling, but with a machine gun of his own. He turned a table on its side and peered over the top. Raven was still flat on the floor trying to watch Capone without lifting her head. Suddenly, the shooting stopped, and she heard the roar of a car engine followed by the squeal of tires. She assumed their attackers had sped off. She was relieved as silence engulfed them and was still shaking when Capone helped her to her feet and sat her in a chair in the corner.

Four men rushed into the room. One she recognized as Johnny Torrio. Two remained by the door with guns drawn. The fourth man must have been Colosimo, the owner of Colosimo's Café. He was running around, screaming and cursing at the damage to the room. She could see why he was called "Big Jim." He wasn't tall, but he was large in other ways, including girth and personality. He had a big nose, a bushy mustache, and caterpillar-like eyebrows—and he was furious.

He kicked at the debris on the floor and stomped over to look out the shattered window.

"Son of a bitch," he said to no one in particular.

When the big man turned to leave the room, he spotted Raven and seemed to calm down immediately.

"Who the fuck is this?" he asked.

"She's a friend of Al's," Torrio replied, looking questioningly at Capone. "But I'm not sure what she's doing here."

"She's..." Al began, but was cut off.

"She's fucking gorgeous," said Colosimo. "Is she coming to work for us?"

Raven looked at Capone in panic but was rescued by Torrio. "No, Boss. It's nothing like that."

Colosimo leered at her for a moment, then stomped out of the room with the other two men behind him.

"What is she doing here?" Torrio asked Capone.

"Sweeney's got someone watching her house. They may be gunning for her, too."

Torrio stared at Raven long enough to make her uncomfortable and then turned to Capone. "Get some of the boys to clean this place up and board up the windows," he said. "Do we have someone who can fix all of this?"

"I know a guy," Capone said. "I'll get him on it first thing in the morning."

Torrio grunted his approval and left. Capone picked up the over-turned table and began to straighten up the room.

"You okay?" he asked Raven—the first person to do so.

She did not reply right away. Her ears were still ringing from the noise of bullets whizzing through the air and shattering everything that got in their way. The lethal force was astonishing. She had to hold her hands together to keep them from shaking. Her eyes were watering, but she wasn't sure if it was from crying or from the acrid smoke that filled the air.

"I'm fine," she said, eyeing Capone. "You look as though you're used to this—like it happens all the time."

"Not all the time," he gave a shrug of his shoulders. "But it happens."

"I'd better go," she said. She pushed herself up from the chair and stood on wobbly legs.

"You'd better sit." Capone pushed a chair up to the table, laid a hand on her shoulder, and had her sit down. He crossed the room and returned with a glass of whiskey that he had retrieved from an unbroken bottle in the cabinet. He lit the cigarette that she held in her shaking fingers and moved to look out the shattered window.

"The boss is going to take care of Sweeney," he said without turning.

"Why did you have those men killed?" she asked. "The men in the barn."

"It was just business. It had to be done—to send a message that we mean business."

She took a sip of whiskey and felt its burn snaking down her throat as she thought about what he said. *Just business.* What kind of business murders people without remorse? Maybe the same kind of business that steals little dogs and allows another dog to kill it for sport.

She watched Capone's back and wondered if he could kill a dog as easily as he kills people. She knew she should feel a loathing for him, but she did not. In fact, she felt drawn to him by some strange attraction. Not the physical attraction she felt for Walt. It was more like being drawn to the spectacle of a burning building where the bigger the fire the stronger the pull. Capone was a big fire, and she was drawn to the flames.

31

Raven stepped off the streetcar at Schiller Street and glanced nervously back down State, half-expecting to see someone following. Al had sent Benny to see that she got on the streetcar safely, but she was still shaken by the shooting even after the half-hour ride to the North end of town. She should have gone back to the office to see Lou but decided she had had enough for one day. As she made her way across the street to Katherine's house, her mind was a jumble of shattered glass, staccato gunfire, and a brooding Al Capone. What was she to make of her fascination with him or his casual approach to murdering his rivals? She should be appalled by his casual admission that his boss was planning to *take care of Sweeney*, but she was not.

She mounted the steps to the house, took one last look around, and let herself inside. The hall was dark and the house quiet—too quiet—causing a moment of panic. Then she heard the clatter of Lizzie's claws on the floor and realized she could smell something baking in the kitchen. Relief flooded over her as the big dog rounded the corner and she kneeled to receive a whining, face-licking welcome. This was the reason she had come straight home.

"You're home early, dear," said Katherine as Raven entered the kitchen.

"Rough day," she said.

She helped herself to a cup of coffee and a warm cookie from the counter next to the stove and joined Katherine at the table.

"What happened?" asked Min Lee from the sink.

Lizzie pushed her muzzle into Raven's lap, demanding to be petted. Raven bent over, gave her a hug, and said, "Go lie down."

The big dog gave her one last look, then plopped down noisily at her feet under the table.

"I ran into Lou at the police station and he gave me my job back," Raven said.

"That sounds like a good day," said Min Lee.

"That was the good part. But Lou was there to see if they will help him find his dog Max. Since his wife died that little dog means everything to him."

"And you don't think he's going to get Max back," said Katherine.

Raven had already prepared Katherine for the worst when it came to her dogs, but Katherine was not as attached to Gracie and Sophie as Lou was to Max.

"I don't know." Raven took a bite of her cookie. "These are delicious," she said. "What are they?"

"Peanut butter cookies," replied Min Lee.

"You haven't told us the bad news from your day," said Katherine.

She told them of her visit with Al Capone at Colosimo's Café and the hail of bullets that punctuated their meeting. She told them of her fitful ride home on the streetcar and her feeling of being watched.

"I'm okay now," she declared. "I just need to be home for a while."

She took a bite of her cookie and a sip of coffee and then asked Min Lee, "How is Vincent's training coming along?"

A loud knock at the front door caused Lizzie to erupt from under the table and scamper barking to the front door.

"You can see for yourself," said Min Lee. She wiped her hands on a towel and glanced at the clock as she took off her apron. "That will be Officer Miller and Vincent now."

Raven felt her pulse quicken slightly as Walt Miller entered the room. He smiled when he saw her. Min Lee let the two dogs into the back yard for a little romp and joined everyone at the table.

"What do you want to work on today?" she asked Walt.

Katherine poured Walt a cup of coffee and placed the plate of cookies in the middle of the table.

Walt took a bite of cookie, tipped it toward Min Lee to show his pleasure, and said, "He's been good with the commands *sit, stay* and *bark, quiet.* I had him out to the gun range, and he is getting better with the sound of gunfire. I need him to be able to chase down a fleeing suspect, search a building, and find a lost person."

Min Lee thought for a moment and then said, "You'll need to get some of your colleagues to help you with the fleeing suspect and the building search. You could do both of those out at that gun range. What do you want him to do with your suspect?"

"I just want him to hold the man until I can get there and cuff him."

"Then you'll need to train him to do that," Min Lee said. "Otherwise he will go for the throat and try to kill the person."

"What do you suggest?" Walt asked.

"You could train him to grab a leg, but that leaves the suspect's hands free to hit the dog," Min Lee said. "I would suggest you train him to grab one of the arms and knock the man to the ground. He can hold him there until you arrive."

"And how do we train him to do that?"

"Dress one of your policemen in a padded suit," said Raven. "Have him attack you and run away."

"That would work," agreed Min Lee, "but you will need to begin with teaching him to grab the arm. Maybe your target could wear some type of mask and have him taunt the dog with a padded arm until the dog bites him."

"I've got just the guy for that duty," said Walt with a laugh.

"You'd better make sure his arm is well padded," warned Min Lee. "Vincent's bite can break a man's arm if he gets excited."

"Okay," said Walt. "So, let's work on finding a lost person."

"I need to get dinner started," said Min Lee. "Why don't you and Raven go up to Lincoln Park and let him follow someone. Find a stranger who is walking around. See if he will follow their trail."

Walt looked at his pocket watch and said, "Four o'clock. I've got about an hour before I need to be back at the station." He looked at Raven. "Is that okay with you?"

"Sure," she said, hoping she didn't show how eager she was.

As they emerged from the house and descended the steps, preparing to turn left toward Lincoln Park, Raven glanced to her right and froze. Parked at the corner was an open-topped car with the familiar figure of Danny Malone at the wheel. He was watching them.

She tugged on Walt's sleeve, causing him to look in that direction.

"Danny Malone," he muttered as he turned. "What is he doing here?"

"Someone's been following me," she said. "I just knew it was him. He probably blames me for his brother's death."

Walt broke into a trot in Malone's direction with Vincent at his side, but the car started up and sped off as they approached the corner.

32

Raven approached her house for the second time that afternoon but from the opposite direction and with a policeman and his dog at her side. She was still apprehensive about Danny Malone and looked in all directions for his car. It was nowhere to be seen. The trip to the park had not been particularly successful. Vincent did not seem too interested in following his nose. But she had enjoyed an hour with Walt and Vincent in the park. She almost felt like they were a couple on an afternoon outing.

"You're welcome to join us for dinner," she said as she mounted the steps to the front door.

"Thanks, but I need to get back. I'm already late."

They locked eyes for a moment before he turned and walked down the street.

She watched him, took one last look around, and went inside.

Once again, she was greeted by Lizzie clattering down the hallway to greet her. And once again the house was filled with good smells, but now, it was meat and vegetables instead of baked cookies. And something else was different. The voices of Katherine, Min Lee, and Jo were joined by another—a man's voice.

Raven's eyes grew wide and her mouth fell open when she walked into the kitchen and found Lou Hanson sitting at the table. All she could manage to say was, "Lou?"

She could feel everyone's eyes on her—everyone but Lou, who looked meekly at his plate.

"I brought Mr. Hanson home," said Jo. "Katherine invited him to dinner."

"We're fellow dog-owners who have lost our dogs," said Katherine brightly.

Lou smiled into his plate.

When Min Lee pushed back from the table, Raven realized that dinner had already been served.

"Sit down," said Min Lee. "I'll fix you a plate."

Min Lee raised her eyebrows at Raven and nodded sternly toward Raven's empty place at the table.

Raven was not upset or angry to find Lou in her home, just surprised—perhaps even shocked. She sat down, Min Lee brought her a plate, and conversation resumed.

"You were about to tell us how you came by Max," said Katherine.

Lou finished chewing and swallowed. He turned to Min Lee and said, "This is delicious, by the way."

"Thank you," Min Lee said with a slight bow in his direction.

"Max was owned by a teamster named Hank Huckabee. People called him *Hammerin Hank* because he was a bar-room boxer at night. Fought at a place called Finnegan's at the south end of the Loop."

He pushed his empty plate away and paused.

"There's more if you'd like another plate," said Katherine.

"No thanks," Lou said. He leaned back in his chair. "As a widower, I'm not used to big dinners."

He rubbed his stomach and continued. "Hank took Max everywhere. The dog was like his mascot—the big, burly boxer with the little fluffy dog under his arm. Hank was killed when his horses ran away with him and overturned his wagon." He looked at Raven for the first time and asked, "Remember that team you took to your friend in the Black Belt?"

"That was Max's owner?"

"Yes."

"But that was ages ago."

"I offered to take Max then, but Hank's wife refused. Said she wanted something to remember him by. Unfortunately, she discovered that Max hates women."

"That explains a lot," Raven said and shared a laugh with Jo.

"She offered Max to me a few months ago," Lou continued, "right after my wife died. He was a welcome companion."

Raven had never seen Lou like this—animated, conversational, almost human.

They sat in silence for a moment, their dinner finished, until Lou looked at the clock and said, "I'd best be going. Thank you for a delightful dinner."

"Dinner's not finished," said Katherine, "until we've had coffee in the Drawing Room."

Katherine rose from the table. Lou followed her lead but looked tentatively in Raven's direction.

"You two go ahead," Raven said. "Jo and I will help Min Lee clean up."

Lou smiled and nodded at her and followed Katherine out of the room.

"Sorry if that was awkward for you," said Jo when they had left.

"It's alright," said Raven. "It was nice to see him like that."

"He seems like a nice man," said Min Lee.

"Yes, he does," said Raven. She lowered her voice and continued, "But we don't often see that side of him at the office."

She and Jo shared a chuckle as they ferried dishes to the sink.

"How did Vincent do at the park," asked Min Lee.

"What were you doing at the park?" asked Jo.

"Walt and I..."

"Oh, I see," interrupted Jo. "You and Walt were at the park and took Vincent along as a chaperone."

Jo laughed and Min Lee joined her.

Raven blushed and said, "He's a married man. We were trying to train Vincent to track a missing person, but he was more interested in tracking squirrels and rabbits."

"Lincoln Park may not have been the best place to try that," said Min Lee. "We've taken him there too many times for play. Tell Walter to try a neutral location—someplace Vincent's not familiar with."

"We're going to take him to that gun range," Raven said. "There are lots of empty buildings there."

There was a pause in the conversation and Min Lee changed the subject. "There was a man watching the house today—a red-headed man in an open-topped car."

"Danny Malone," said Raven. "He was there when we left for the park. Walt ran him off."

"He came back," said Jo. "He was down at the corner when Lou and I came home."

"Did he see you?" asked Raven. "Did he see you come in here?"

"I'm sure he did," said Jo.

Raven looked at Jo with fresh concern. Danny Malone now had a new target.

33

Raven sat in Lou's office with the threat of Danny Malone fresh in her mind, but eager to get back to work. Lou had wanted to talk to her about starting something he called the Chicago Equine Shelter.

"So," said Lou as he hung up the phone after an inconsequential conversation with a woman about her missing parrot. "Where were we?"

"A shelter for horses and mules," Raven reminded him.

"Did you ever stop to think about what it's like to run an organization like this?" he asked, changing the subject. "Trying to please the Board of Directors, hoping we have enough money to run the operation, and dealing with people like this lady and her lost parrot." He nodded at the telephone.

Raven was taken aback. She had never even considered all of that and did not know what to say.

"I know I'm not easy to work for," he continued, "but you've handled this job better than most."

Raven stared absently at the office through the glass wall pondering her response. When the door to the outer office slowly opened, she tensed and leaned forward, but relaxed when a young boy about eight or nine years of age entered the room.

Lou got up and approached the boy.

"Can I help you?" he asked.

The boy handed him an envelope.

Lou glanced at it and handed it to Raven. "It's for you." he said with a puzzled look.

She stood as she accepted it and slit it open with a letter opener from Lou's desk. The note was handwritten and said:

its you I want not the girl. come to the stearns quarry on halsted tonight at midnight. come alone. no police or the girl gets it.   *sweeney*

"Sweeney's got Jo," Raven said aloud. Her hand shook as she handed the crudely written note to Lou.

"What's this about?" asked Lou after he read the note. "Why does he want you?"

"He and his men have been after me since I stopped them from burning Rondell's stable."

He looked up from the note to search her face. "That's it?"

"Some men were killed when Capone busted up their still and we rescued the dogs. Sweeney probably blames me for that, too."

"Jesus," Lou said. "There's nothing out at Stearns Quarry. You can't go out there alone."

"Where is Stearns Quarry?" she asked. "I've never heard of it."

"It's a limestone quarry down on South Halsted and twenty seventh—in Bridgeport." He stood up and began to pace.

"What choice do I have? I can't just not go and let them kill Jo."

"We need to tell the police."

"No," said Raven. "You know as well as I do that Captain Yancey is on Sweeney's payroll."

"Why are you still here?" Lou snarled at the boy.

"He's probably waiting for my answer," said Raven.

The boy nodded.

"Tell him I'll be there," Raven told the boy.

The boy ducked out the door and Lou sat down heavily. They listened to the ticking of a clock.

"I can't let you do this," he said finally. "I can't just sit here and let you walk into something like that."

"Lou," she said as gently as she could. "We have to let this play out. Once Jo is free, I'll talk my way out of it. I don't believe Sweeney is going to kill me in cold blood." She stood to leave. "He's a bad man, but even he's not that bad. He probably just wants to show his power."

She walked out and Lou did not try to stop her.

The Billy Club bar was bustling on a Saturday at lunchtime. Raven and Walt were fortunate to find a place to sit. As he looked carefully at the note from Sweeney, she surveyed the room. It was more of a civilian crowd on the weekend, but still hosted plenty of police officers and plain-clothes detectives.

Walt sat the note on the table and pushed it back to Raven. He sipped his beer and surveyed the room as he thought. "You're not seriously thinking about going, are you?"

Her silence was his answer.

"I can't believe Hanson is letting you do this."

"He doesn't have a choice," she said. "And neither do you."

"I don't like not telling somebody," he said finally, "but I'm not sure who I can talk to. I'm fairly sure I can trust O'Malley and there are others who despise Yancey and what he stands for."

"No," she said. "It's bad enough that I need to go out there alone. I don't want to wonder if I've been betrayed."

He leaned back and smiled. "I guess I should be flattered that you trust me."

She placed her arms on the table and looked him in the eye. "It looks like I'm trusting you with my life."

He pulled something from his pocket and slid it across the table toward her. He carefully raised his hand so she could see a small, nickel-plated revolver with pearl grips.

"At least, take this with you," he said in a low voice. "It's a Smith and Wesson .38-special. It's small, but it packs a wallop."

She hesitated but covered it in her hand and slid it to her lap and into her handbag.

He got up and said, "Let's go out to the warehouse so I can show you how to use it."

When they arrived at the shooting range, Walt told Vincent to stay in the car. As they walked to the target area, she took the little gun out of her purse and allowed him to show her how to open the cylinder and feed bullets into the chambers. After she had tried loading it herself, he showed her how to hold the gun in both hands. When he stepped behind her, wrapped his arms around her, and enclosed her hands in his in order to help her aim at her target, it took all of her willpower not to turn and wrap him in an embrace. She could not stop herself from pushing back into his embrace. It felt good to feel safe and protected, especially considering what she was about to do.

34

"You alone?" asked Danny Malone.

Raven could see his breath in the frigid night air.

"Where's Sweeney?" She responded with a question of her own.

"Not here. He sent me."

Something was wrong. Raven had come alone, as instructed, against the advice of everyone she had told—and even one she had not told. Min Lee had wanted to drive her, but Raven insisted that she could drive herself. She told Min Lee that she wanted to practice what Min Lee had been teaching her about driving Katherine's big car. It had taken her over half an hour of jumpy starts and stops to make the ten-or-so mile drive and she was relieved to pull the car through the broken gate and past the entrance to the quarry.

She was worried because she had missed the twelve o'clock dead-line and was now even more uneasy to be looking at Danny Malone under a streetlight with a gun to Jo's head. They were a hundred yards from Halsted Street and behind Danny was a darkened road that presumably led down to the bottom of the quarry. Sweeney had chosen an isolated spot. Lou was right. She was totally alone.

Raven felt the weight of her handbag and casually tucked it under her left arm. She began to inch her right hand to its opening as she said, "I want to talk to Sweeney."

"He's not coming. This is my deal."

"You wrote that note?"

The shock must have registered on Raven's face because Malone just laughed.

"Sweeney's not going to like you using his name," she said. Her right hand was almost up to her purse. She was desperately trying to remember what Walt had taught her just a few hours earlier—grasp the gun with two hands, finger on the trigger, pull back the hammer.

"Drop your handbag and step away from it."

Raven hesitated—thought about going for the gun—but placed her bag gently on the ground and raised her hands. Malone's actions were nervous and abrupt and Raven was frightened for Jo. This operation appeared to have been poorly thought out. Malone's car was behind him and he did not have any support. She hoped she could get close enough to him to act, but she needed to keep him talking.

"What's this all about, Danny?"

"You know what it's about. It's about my brother being dead. It's about you being there and helping those fucking Italians."

She held her hands up, palms forward and took a step, hoping to get near enough to make a move on him. "All I wanted was to get my dogs back. I had nothing to do with shooting your brother."

"Shut up." He began to cry. "He's dead, and you were there. That's all I need to know. I'll deal with Torrio later." He grabbed Jo by the hair and raised the gun to her head.

"Wait," shouted a voice from behind Raven. Lou Hanson walked out of the darkness and stood beside Raven. She and Malone must have been too distracted to hear him arrive.

"Wait," Lou said again. "Don't hurt the girl. You can take me instead. I've got influence in the community. I'm the superintendent of the welfare association."

Raven knew he was wasting his time. Danny Malone cared nothing for any of that.

"Lou," she turned to him and tried to turn him around. "You need to leave."

"What's he doing here?" Danny pointed his pistol in their direction. "I told you to come alone." He was screaming.

"This is my boss—our boss," she said, pointing at Jo and trying to appease Malone. "He's just trying to help."

Malone appeared confused and was becoming more agitated. She had planned to exchange herself for Jo and wait for an opportunity to disable her captors and escape. But she had expected Brian Sweeney and a few of his goons, not an unstable Danny Malone who was acting on his own with a poorly thought-out plan.

"Let her go," pleaded Raven, "and Mr. Hanson will leave with her. Then it will be just you and me."

She was relieved when he appeared to be thinking this over, but Lou would not take the hint.

"Come on, son. This has gone on long enough."

To Raven's horror, Lou began to walk forward with a hand stretched out like he was going to take Danny's gun.

"Lou," she tried to grab his arm, but he pulled away. "Lou, please."

"Just give me the gun, son."

"Stay back!" Danny shouted. "Don't come any closer."

Lou took one more step before Danny pulled the trigger. They were only separated by a few yards and the bullet hit Lou squarely in the chest. He clutched at the front of his blood-stained shirt, dropped to his knees, and fell face down. Raven knew he was dead when he hit the ground. Her stomach lurched, and she had to swallow hard to keep from throwing up.

Danny appeared in shock as he looked at Lou, then looked at his gun as if he were surprised it had gone off. When he loosened his grip on Jo, she broke away and ran toward Raven. She was about halfway to Raven when Danny raised his gun again and took aim at Jo's back.

"No," Raven screamed as she put her hands up and lurched forward.

Things seemed to unfold in slow motion. She expected to see Danny shoot Jo in the back, but the shot never came. Instead, a small hole appeared in his forehead, like a third eye. Then the back of his head exploded in a shower of blood and brains as the report of a rifleshot echoed through the quarry. Danny Malone dropped to the pavement.

Jo jumped into Raven's arms and they hugged and cried until hands touched them on their shoulders. It was Walt, and he had a rifle slung over his arm.

They rushed to Lou and turned him over, but he was, in fact, dead.

"What should we do?" asked Jo.

Raven looked at Walt for an answer, but he appeared unsure, himself. "I wish I could have saved him," he nodded at Lou. "But I couldn't get a shot."

Raven and Jo continued to look at him, so he continued, "I was a sniper in the war."

They moved to a nearby rock ledge where Jo and Raven sat. Walt propped up his rifle and placed a foot on the ledge with his elbows on his knee.

"What are we going to do now?" asked Jo.

Raven looked at Walt and said, "I don't imagine we want to involve the police, after what you just did."

"He saved our lives," said Jo.

"Yes," said Raven. "But two men are dead, and he was on the scene. He'll have a hard time explaining why he was here on his own."

"Oh," said Jo.

"Let's just go," said Raven.

"I can't do that," Walt replied. "She's right. Two men are dead, and I'm more or less responsible."

"Walt," Raven said, grabbing his hand. "This will ruin your career and may even mark you for retaliation. This could get you killed."

"I'm not afraid of those bastards."

"Leave your rifle here next to Lou and let's just go," said Jo. She stood up to accentuate her point. They looked confused, so she continued. "What will the police find when they get here? They'll find two dead men who somehow shot each other." She answered her own question. "The biggest mystery will be why they were out here in the first place."

Raven looked at Walt and shrugged. "She's right."

"I don't know," he said. He scratched his head and looked around. There was nobody around. "Will you two be able to get home alright?"

"We'll be fine," said Jo. Raven nodded her head slowly in agreement.

"Then get going," he said. "I'll clean up here." When they hesitated, he continued. "I need to make sure there's no trace of us here."

The car lurched forward as Raven clumsily drove away with Jo in the passenger seat. Her thoughts were a jumble. She was glad that Danny Malone was dead—especially after he almost pulled the trigger on Jo—but worried about the impact his killing may have on Walt. She was sad for Lou's death but a little ashamed at her worries over what it may mean for her own future. She would be even more upset if she could foresee the impact this incident was going to have on Josephine and the secrets that were about to be exposed.

35

*L*ou would be disappointed to learn that, even in death, he was not front-page news. The Sunday edition of the *Herald and Examiner* had the story of his death on page four as a robbery gone bad. The report also speculated on why Lou had been at Stearns Quarry so late in the evening, suggesting that he must have been up to no good. That, Raven assumed, was why she and Jo had been summoned to the police department's South Precinct where they had been seated in an interview room.

"Thank you for coming in this morning. I am detective Stanley Woburn, and this is detective William Wallace." The interview began. "We were wondering if you can shed any light on why your boss may have been meeting with a known gangster last night."

"I have no idea," Raven said. She looked at Jo, who only shrugged.

Jo had been reluctant to accompany Raven to the station, and she was now looking nervously around the room. Raven was worried that she might be ready to tell them what had actually happened.

"Are you alright, Miss.?" Detective Wallace asked Jo.

"Yes," Jo replied abruptly. "Of course."

Detective Wallace was the younger of the two men. He was heavy set, not quite fat but in a few years, Raven guessed, he would be. He seemed nice, and after he showed his concern for Jo, Raven decided she liked him. Woburn was a different story. He was also a big man, but he was a good bit older and harder looking. He did not seem nice at all. He looked at Jo with a frowning, puzzled look that made Raven uncomfortable. Jo eyes were cast down at the table and she did not see his look, but he did draw her attention when he abruptly got up and left the room.

After he closed the door, Jo stood up looked at Raven and said, "We need to go."

Raven stood and looked at Detective Wallace.

"We have a few more questions," he said. He stood and placed his palms out in a signal to stop. "Let me go see where he went, so we can finish our interview."

Jo brushed past him, but as she reached for the door, it sprang open and the bulk of Detective Woburn blocked her exit.

"I thought you looked familiar," he said. He held up a poster that said WANTED across the top. There was no mistaking Jo's photograph.

"Josephine Washington," said Detective Woburn. "You're under arrest for the murder of William Truman."

Jo staggered back and fell into a chair.

Raven was shocked, but all she could think to say was, "There must be some mistake here."

She looked to Jo for some protest—some denial—but none came. She then looked at Detective Woburn and wanted to wipe the smug, satisfied look off his face. He finally looked at her and explained.

"This young lady murdered her uncle eighteen months ago." He looked at Jo as if he expected confirmation, but she just sat, staring at the floor.

"Don't say anything," Raven told Jo. "Do you hear me? Don't admit anything. I'm going to find you a lawyer."

Raven sat alone in what she still thought of as Lou's office. The memory of the testy exchanges they had had, erased by how he had lost his life trying to save hers. At first, she could not bring herself to sit in his chair, so she had turned one of the other chairs so she could see out the glass wall and into the outer office. That is where, an hour earlier, she had sat like a prisoner awaiting a verdict. Her judge and jury were gathered around the worktable outside the office. After a heated discussion, much of which centered on the concept of having a woman run their organization, the all-female board of trustees of the association did not reach a decision but left Raven temporarily in charge.

Now, Raven leaned back in Lou's old chair—still feeling a little uncomfortable in it. Walt Miller was across the desk where she had once sat. After the meeting broke up, Raven called Walt then began to dig through Lou's files, trying to understand just what he did. When Walt walked in about an hour later, she welcomed the break. She was comfortable in his presence but uncomfortable with what she had to tell him.

"What did you need to see me about?" he asked.

"Jo is in jail," said Raven.

"What?" He sat upright.

"We were called down to the South Precinct," Raven explained. "A couple of detectives wanted to ask us why Lou might have been down at the quarry. One of the detectives recognized Jo from a wanted poster."

"Wanted poster," said Walt. "Wanted for what?"

"Murder."

"That's crazy. That little girl never murdered anyone."

"They said she murdered her uncle a year or so ago." They sat in silence for a moment until Raven continued, "I need to find her a lawyer."

"The women on your board are well connected," said Walt. "Aren't any of them married to attorneys?"

"Yes," Raven replied. "Mrs. Silverstein's husband Marvin is a prominent attorney. But I don't want to ask a board member to get involved. Especially for a murder case. I may ask Katherine, but I hate having people think Jo is a murderer."

"They're going to read about in the newspaper soon enough."

"God," Raven said, turning back to him. "I hadn't thought of that."

"Sweeney came to see Captain Yancey this morning," Walt said. "After Sweeney left, Yancey told O'Malley to start looking into the shooting at Stearns Quarry. Yancey thinks there might be a connection to the murder at the Lewiston Mule Barn last fall."

"The shooting where we found Vincent?"

"That's right. So, O'Malley is sending me out to the quarry to have a look around," he said. He leaned forward and placed his arms on her desk. "I wonder if I'll find anything."

"Good Lord," she said. "What are you going to do?"

"I'll go out there and poke around. There's nothing out there to find. I made sure of that."

She leaned back in her chair and looked out the window, vaguely aware that she has seen Lou do that a hundred times. "I'm sorry I put you in this position."

"It had to be done," he said with a wave of his hand. He paused and then continued. "How are you holding up?"

"My whole life is upside down," her voice quivered. "Lou's gone, Jo is in jail, but Sweeney is still out there lurking like a monster under my bed. If not for my friends..." her voice trailed off.

They sat in awkward silence for a moment until he got up and moved to the door. She also rose and moved around the desk.

"Let me know if there is anything I can do to help Jo," he said

"I don't know what to do. I don't even know where to begin."

He smiled and placed his hand on her shoulder—a hand she desperately wanted to reach up and grab.

"You probably need begin by going to see Jo," he said as he removed his hand and reached for the door. "That South Precinct is a rough place."

She was glad no one was in the office. She did not know whether to be thrilled by her interaction with the policeman or terrified for her friend in jail. The only thing she had any control over was her own actions, so she would begin in the morning with a visit to the jail.

36

S he's a murderer," said the big detective over his shoulder as he led her down the stairs. "You'd do well to steer clear of her."

"You don't know that," Raven replied.

"The evidence is there—witnesses, motive, and opportunity."

"Sounds like you've already convicted her. What do we need a trial for?"

"I'm just telling you what I know, lady."

Raven had been relieved when Detective Wallace had been the one to respond to her request to visit Jo in the South Precinct lock-up. He had been much nicer than the older detective when they had taken Jo into custody the day before yesterday. Now, she found his smugness irritating.

He had led her from the lobby of the police station at LaSalle and Harrison down two flights of stairs to the basement, through a locked gate with a sign over it that said *Women*, and down a short hallway.

"Washington," he said as they stood in front of the lone cell in the hall. "You have a visitor."

The cell was large with a wooden bench that ran around its perimeter. It smelled of sweat and stale air. Jo sat up when they appeared but did not approach the bars.

"I want to go in," said Raven.

"That ain't happening."

"Why not?" Raven asked. "You can have me searched if you want."

"It's not that," he said. He nodded toward the other corner of the cell and continued, "I just don't think you want to mess with Mabel and her pals."

Mabel stood half a head taller than Raven and must have weighed nearly three hundred pounds. She was flanked by two smaller women who were so average in every way that they almost disappeared in her shadow. It was like three people were rolled into a single body. As they moved forward Raven could sense Jo cowering.

"Open the door," Raven insisted.

"Look," he said. "I can't be responsible for what might happen."

"Nothing's going to happen." Raven looked at Mabel, who was near enough to hear. "Is it Mabel?"

Mabel smiled a toothless grin and put up both hands. "No, officer. She'll be fine. We won't mess with her and her little friend, will we girls?" Mabel looked at her companions, who both smiled warmly and shook their heads.

The detective looked unsure of what to do so he called to the guard at the end of the hall.

"Ollie. You want to come and open the door?"

Ollie shuffled down the hall with his keys, looked at Raven, and then said to the detective, "You sure about this?"

"Just open the door," Raven said.

After the door swung shut behind her, the two officers watched for a moment. When nothing happened, they retreated down the hall. Raven went immediately to Jo's spot on the bench and sat beside her.

"How'd you get that?" she asked Jo, pointing to the bruise on her cheek.

Jo looked at Mabel without replying, causing a cold anger to well up inside Raven.

"Raven, don't," said Jo.

"Don't what?" Mabel smirked from the middle of the cell.

Raven stood up. She knew she should control her anger. Mabel might be a prisoner and a criminal, but the police would take a dim view of having someone injured in their custody unless, of course, they were the ones doing the injuring.

"You're a big girl," said Mabel. There was that toothless grin again. She reached out, grabbed one of Raven's breasts, and gave it a squeeze. Raven did not react, just as Min Lee had taught her—show no fear, feel no pain. She was satisfied to see the surprise register in Mabel's eyes.

Mabel backed up a step and said, "Maybe I'll let my girls have some fun with you."

"It's you I want to have fun with," said Raven.

Mabel was accustomed to confrontations and her doubt barely registered, but it was there. Raven could sense that Mabel was on her heels.

"Did you do that to her?" Raven nodded over her shoulder at Jo.

"What if I did?"

Raven moved in close. She could smell Mabel's foul breath and see the meanness in her dark eyes. Her companions moved in on either side of Raven.

"She's my friend," Raven said. "I'll hold you responsible if anything happens to her."

Strong hands grasped each of Raven's arms as Mabel's glare turned into a smirk. She opened her mouth to reply but was cut short. Raven's right fist jabbed across her body and caught the woman to her left on the chin. The same arm whipped back and chopped across the throat of the other woman. They both dropped without a sound as Raven's left hand closed into a fist and punched Mabel on the side of her neck. The big woman was stunned, but conscious. Raven placed both hands on her chest and pushed her back against the wall and into a sitting position on the bench. The two women behind her struggled to their feet but backed away with hands up in surrender when Raven looked at them.

"Who the hell *are* you?" Mabel asked. She rubbed her neck where Raven had hit her.

"I don't want any trouble with you," said Raven, "or," she glanced over her shoulder, "with your girls. But I'll be your worst nightmare if anything happens to my friend."

Mabel grimaced in pain as she nodded her head. "She'll be fine. I'll see to it."

Raven held out her right hand and when Mabel took it to shake hands, Raven pulled her to her feet and said, "Thanks."

"A little short tempered this morning?" said Jo as Raven returned to her seat.

"I may have overreacted," said Raven, "but this day is not going so well."

"What's wrong?"

"I didn't want to trouble you with this, but Katherine is in the hospital. She had chest pains at breakfast, so Min Lee called an ambulance."

"How is she?" Jo sat up.

"Something to do with her heart, they said. She's resting and she'll probably go home tomorrow."

They sat in silence for a moment and Raven absently watched Mabel and her companions tend to their wounds. She felt bad for abusing these women but felt sure it was the only way to ensure Jo's safety while she was locked up with them. She heard muffled voices at the end of the hallway and the guard's keys jingled as he opened the gate. Footsteps edged their way.

Detective Wallace emerged at the front of the cell.

"You've got another visitor," he said to Jo.

Raven expected to see Walt or Min Lee emerge from the shadows, so her mouth dropped open in surprise when zookeeper Harry Fischer appeared. What was he doing here? She glanced at Jo, who was openly smiling and did not appear to be surprised at all.

37

T hanks for not making a scene back there," Harry said.

"That wasn't the time for questions," said Raven, "but what is going on? Isn't she a little young for you?"

Harry sat across Raven's desk, turning his hat over in his hands. When she last saw him with Jo as she left them in the jail cell, he was holding both of her hands in his and they looked like they wanted to embrace.

"She's old enough to decide what's right for her," he said defensively. "And I've done nothing to take advantage of her. We just like being together."

"When did you start seeing her?"

"A couple of weeks ago. Right after we recovered that stash of guns and money."

Raven's mind was racing. How was this possible? She and Jo lived under the same roof and worked at the same place.

"How did you meet up?" she asked him.

"We've had lunch a few times at that café across the street from where you work," he said. "And we strolled the zoo one night, after hours."

"In the dark?"

"Sure," he replied. "That's a special time in the zoo."

For the first time, Raven felt a pang of jealousy. Her father was a zoo director, so she knew that special feeling of having the animals all to one's self. The zoo at night was a magical place full of exotic smells, animal calls, and the presence of life all around you. It was that feeling that had first drawn her to the work she was doing now and, even though she had no romantic interest in Harry, she was ashamed of the resentment she felt toward Josephine and her involvement with the zoo.

"Look," he continued. "I know what you're thinking, but our age difference isn't as great as you might think—maybe eight or ten years. We're just friends at this point but I won't say that I'm not interested in being more than her friend. When we first met, I had eyes for you. But you're clearly not interested in me. So why stand in the way of happiness for your friend—or for me."

"I'm sorry," she said. "I don't mean to judge. You just caught me off guard. Do you want to go for a coffee?"

The lunch crowd was shuffling out of the Huron Street Diner and they quickly found a table by a window. A waitress cleared the dishes and brought them a pot of coffee with two cups. Raven lit a cigarette and leaned back in the booth.

"What do you know about the charges against her?" she asked Harry. "She won't tell me anything."

"She won't talk to me about it, either." he said. "She doesn't deny doing it, though." After a pause, he continued. "I just can't imagine the circumstance where a girl like her could stab a man—her own uncle."

Raven took a drag on her cigarette and let the smoke drift out of her mouth while she gazed out the window. "I can," she said.

Harry looked at her and she turned her gaze back to him. "Think about it. What could a man do to a woman that might make her want to defend herself with whatever means she had at hand?"

"Oh," he said. "I see what you mean. Then, it should be self-defense, not murder."

"That's why I'm going to find her a good lawyer."

Harry glanced at the clock and said, "I need to be going." He stood but was interrupted by Raven's rapping on the glass to get someone's attention outside.

Raven introduced Rondell Boyd to Harry and the men eyed each other with suspicion. Raven wondered if Harry's feelings toward Negros were as primitive as his views on the place of women. After Harry left the café, Raven motioned Rondell to join her at the table.

"I can't sit here," he said. "We'll have to go back there." He pointed to a sign that read *colored* over the hallway to a back room. She hesitated, so he continued. "Why don't we just go to your office? I just have some news for you."

"No," she said. "We're here so we might as well stay here."

She followed Rondell down a hallway, past the kitchen, and into a smoke-filled room with a door that lead to the alley. The men seated at the tables were clearly surprised to see a white woman joining them, as was the Negro waiter who took their order.

"What's your news?" she asked as she watched the waiter walk away.

Rondell looked around as though someone might be listening and lowered his voice. "They had a fight-night over at the dog pit on Saturday night," he began. "I asked a couple of the boys to keep their ears open and find out what they could about the dog pits in the North end of town, where the white folks go."

"And?"

"Well, they didn't find out much. But they did meet the man who makes the leather muzzles for the dogs, a Negro by the name of Dorky Slaughter. He runs a saddle shop over on State and Thirty-Ninth."

The waiter brought two cups of coffee and a plate of biscuits. Their conversation paused while they each buttered a biscuit and sipped their coffee.

"I had a couple of harnesses in for repair, so I went over to pick 'em up."

"What did he tell you?"

"Nothing."

"Nothing?" she asked. "Then why are we having this conversation?"

"A man came in while I was waiting—a white man. He was there to pick up some muzzles. Dorky told him the muzzles weren't ready, and the man got angry. Said he needed them for Wednesday night."

"That's two days from now," Raven said. "Did the man say where it was taking place?"

Rondell did not reply. He carefully spread some jam on a biscuit.

"R.B.?" she said. "Where is the fight?"

"Look," he said. "You and I have known each other a long time. If I tell you what I know, you need to promise me you won't go and do something stupid. You can't go busting in there. Those guys are bad news. They'll hurt people just as quick as they'll hurt dogs."

Raven pushed back in her chair and smiled. "How do you define *something stupid*?"

He leaned into her and said, "Don't try that on me. I promised your pa I'd keep an eye on you and I'm not going to lead you straight into trouble."

Raven sat bolt upright. "What does my pa know about any of this?"

"I wrote to Calvin a while back. Told him what I was doing and thanked him for giving me a chance at his zoo back in Thomasville. I may have mentioned that you were here and a little of what you were doing."

Raven was too stunned to speak. She thought of Calvin often but had never written to him. She had been angry when he refused to let her work in the zoo and grew even angrier when he sent her away to a school for girls. But he had fueled her passion for working with animals and encouraged her in every way except allowing her to make animals her career.

"You had no right to do that," she said.

"Calvin's your pa. He deserves to know where his girl is and what she's doing."

When she did not respond, he continued, "Just write to him. He'd be proud of you." He looked at her for a long moment before continuing. "Promise me you won't go charging in there, and I'll tell you what you want to know."

"I have a friend who is a policeman," she said finally. "I won't do anything without him being involved."

He looked at her closely, and then said, "The man who ordered the muzzles wanted them delivered to the Lewiston Mule Barn. That's where they hold the dog fights."

38

Katherine had summoned her attorney. She was, Raven assumed, getting her affairs in order—not a good sign. Aaron Goldsmith had been standing on the porch ready to knock when Raven arrived home from the office thirty minutes ago. Now, Raven could hear the murmur of voices coming from Katherine's bedroom above where she sat at the kitchen table.

"How does she seem?" Raven asked Min Lee.

"Weak," replied Min Lee. "but otherwise okay."

Min Lee filled Raven's coffee cup and sat across from her.

"Thanks for calling me when the doctor released her," said Raven. She rubbed Lizzie with her foot.

"She thinks of you as a daughter." Min Lee paused, sipped her coffee, and continued. "I've told her I don't want any of this." She looked around the room.

"What? Why not?"

Min Lee got up and moved to the window. She gazed into the backyard as she spoke. "I don't want possessions, especially things as grand as all this. It would just be a burden to me."

"But," said Raven, not sure of how to respond. "You're a part of *all this*." She waved her hand around the room for emphasis.

"You mean I'm one of the possessions."

"No. that's not what I mean, and you know it!"

"That's how I feel sometimes. Just another piece of furniture." Min Lee returned to the table, sat down, and sipped her coffee.

Raven wondered, for the first time, how much it must cost to keep up with the expenses of running a household like this—the house, the car, the people. Katherine paid the gardeners and the service people. She probably paid Min Lee. She gave shelter and food to Raven and Jo. Raven created an expense ledger in her mind, like the one she had seen at the office—food, utilities, gasoline, salaries. And there were the incidental expenses—the little things that no one ever thought of, but that added up, such as salt to keep the ice off the front steps, medicine, cleaning supplies. The cash outlay must be considerable. In a moment of panic, Raven worried that if Katherine did not have enough money in reserve, the house might need to be sold.

"I'll be taking my leave."

Raven was startled by Mr. Goldsmith's appearance at the kitchen door. She stood up and Min Lee joined her. Lizzie growled but was silenced by Raven's hand on her head.

"Did you get your business taken care of?" asked Raven, hoping for some clue about what was discussed.

"I did."

"Is there anything you need from us?" Raven was still fishing, but Goldsmith was not biting.

"Thank you, but I believe I have all I need." He tipped his hat and turned to leave. Min Lee escorted him to the door where he turned and said, "She does want to see both of you at your convenience."

Katherine's bedroom was dominated by the four-poster bed where she was propped up sipping a cup of tea that Min Lee had just served her.

Raven sat next to the bed and Min Lee stood at the window looking over the garden—still acting moody and unresponsive.

"How are you feeling?" Raven asked Katherine.

"I'm tired, but otherwise okay."

"What did the doctor say when he released you?"

"He said there's nothing more they can do for me. I have a bad heart. I may have more episodes like the one I had this morning. I just need to stay off my feet as much as possible and get plenty of rest." She picked up a bottle of pills and handed it to Raven. "He gave me these little pills to put under my tongue whenever I feel pain in my chest."

"Nitroglycerine," Raven read from the label.

Min Lee turned from the window. "Nitroglycerine? That's an explosive."

"It's alright," said Katherine, waving her hand. "It's perfectly safe."

The three women sat in silence for a moment, each lost in their thoughts.

"Did you get your business with Mr. Goldsmith concluded?" Raven asked.

"I did."

Raven was saved from prying further by Lizzie's low growl followed by the chime of the doorbell.

"Who could that be?" said Min Lee as she headed for the door.

"I want to rest," said Katherine as everyone left the room. "I'm not up to seeing visitors."

*H*ow is she?" asked Walt.

Raven filled him in on Katherine's condition as Min Lee busied herself at the stove and the dogs played in the back yard.

"It sounds pretty serious," he said.

"I suppose it is," said Raven. "But she's taking it well. She's in good spirits and just needs to rest."

"Will you join us for dinner?" asked Min Lee.

"No," he said. "I just wanted to pay my respects."

He rose from the table, took a final sip of his coffee, and moved toward the door. Raven called in the dogs and followed him out.

"How's Vincent doing?" she asked as they stood on the front porch.

"He seems to have an instinct for police work," Walt said. He rubbed the dog on the head as Lizzie looked on from inside the door to the house. "He's good with people, but he can sense a bad guy from a mile off. The only problem I have is with Captain Yancey."

"Why is he a problem?"

"I'm not sure," said Walt. "He just doesn't want the dog around the station."

"Maybe he doesn't like dogs, in general," said Raven. "Some people are like that."

"Maybe," said Walt. "But he's as crooked as a dog's hind-leg, and I just don't trust him."

"Maybe he's worried about being sniffed-out by a good police dog." They shared a laugh.

"I'm sure that's it." Walt kneeled and pulled Vincent toward him. "He's afraid you can sniff out crooked cops."

Raven felt an odd sensation creep into the middle of her chest as she watched Walt hug the dog. It felt like jealousy, but its origin eluded her. Was she jealous of the man who had the love of a dog that had once been hers, or was she jealous of the dog who had the affection of a man she could not have?

"Give Katherine my regards," he said.

He was near enough that she could have grabbed him for a kiss, but she just watched him as he left and hoped he did not find out what she would be up to tomorrow.

39

Raven had Washington Square Park all to herself. People had been coming and going all morning, but it was too chilly for them to linger. Raven, however, was on a mission. She sat sideways on a bench and peered over her shoulder down the length of West Delaware Place toward LaSalle. It had been over an hour since she had watched three officers carry an armload of boxes inside the Lewiston Mule Barn.

Lizzie was stretched out on the lawn at her feet, allowing the sun to warm her brown fur. Raven put the hood down on her jacked, hoping the sun would do the same for her. She glanced back down the street but saw nothing new. Doubt began to creep into her plans for the day—observe, snoop around, and rescue some dogs.

Raven both felt and heard the movement on the bench behind her as someone sat down. The park was filled with empty benches. Why would anyone want to sit on hers?

"Nice dog you have there."

She froze. It was a man's voice. She did not turn or reply, but the man did have Lizzie's attention.

Raven turned her head slightly and could make out his form. His long hair, scruffy beard, and multiple filthy sweaters marked him as a panhandler—a point confirmed when he asked, "Could you spare a nickel for some food?"

"I don't have any money," she lied.

The man leaned back, placed his hands behind his head, and looked absently up at the cloudless sky.

"You need to leave me alone," she said.

"It's a free country," he said. "I can sit where I like."

"You see those police cars." she nodded down the street. "If I holler, they'll come running."

The man glanced over his shoulder and laughed. "They don't care about you. They're getting ready for the dog fight tomorrow night."

Raven swiveled in her seat and faced the man for the first time. "What do you know about that?"

He folded his arms and stared into the distance.

After a brief standoff, Raven pulled a few coins from her coat pocket and handed one to the man, but before he could take it, she snatched it back. "Tell me about the dog fights."

The man eyed her fist as he said, "Wednesday night is fight night. Customers will come through the front door, but the fight is staged in a back room of the barn. The dogs are held and trained inside an abandoned warehouse across the alley."

"What else?"

"That's all I know." He held out his hand, and she gave him the money.

As he shuffled off, she asked, "How can I get into the warehouse?"

"You can't," he replied without turning. "It'll be guarded until the fight, and then it will be crawling with cops. Best to steer clear of that place for the next few days."

She watched him move away then returned her attention to the barn only to discover that the police cars had left.

"Darn," she muttered. She thought about taking Lizzie for a walk around the block and, perhaps, down the alley. If the panhandler was right, she knew where Max and Katherine's dogs were being held—if they were still alive. But he might also be telling the truth about the guards.

She picked up Lizzie's lead, and the dog stood as she stood. They walked to the west gate of the park at Clark Street and looked down Delaware, unsure of how to proceed.

As she stood, lost in thought, she became aware of a dog rounding the corner from LaSalle in the distance and heading her way. It was Vincent. He was in pursuit of two men wearing masks and carrying bags and guns.

Lizzie must have seen him, as well, because she began barking and straining at her leash.

Walt came into view a few paces behind the dog. He had his gun drawn and was yelling something but was too far away for Raven to understand.

Raven edged herself behind the brick pillar of the gate and pulled Lizzie back as she watched the scene unfold.

One of the fleeing men turned and fired a pistol in Walt's direction but missed. His stopping gave Vincent time to catch up and grab the man's arm to bring him to the ground.

The second man must have seen this as an opportunity because he also stopped, raised a shotgun, and fired in Walt's direction.

As Walt fell to the ground, Raven came out of her trance with a gasp. She let go of Lizzie's leash and placed both hands over her mouth in horror. She wanted to run to Walt but was rooted to the spot in fear that he was seriously injured.

Lizzie bounded across Clark Street, causing a delivery truck to slam on its brakes and skid sideways into the curb. The driver emerged cursing and shaking his fist at the dog. Raven took this opportunity to run after her.

As Lizzie bounded up Delaware, the gunman reloaded his shotgun and walked ominously toward Walt, who appeared alive but was bleeding from his leg and unable to get up. Two more policemen emerged from around the corner. One stopped to give aid to Walt as the other drew his gun. The gunman and the policeman fired at the same time. The policeman missed, but the man with the shotgun did not. The policeman fell in a heap.

All of this gave Lizzie time to close the gap. The gunman must have heard the dog approaching from behind because he turned and raised his gun at her, but he was too late. Lizzie hit him in the chest with both of her paws and sent him sprawling onto his back. His head hit the pavement with a thud, and he went still. Lizzie stood over the lifeless man until Raven arrived to pull her off. A policeman ran up with his gun drawn, but the man did not move.

Another policeman was hollering at Vincent to back off, but the dog would not listen. He was, Raven suspected, waiting for his master to call him off, but Walt was lying in the road half a block away.

She trotted toward Walt, who was conscious but in pain. She made eye contact and pointed toward the dog. "Tell him *off*," Walt said. "He'll listen to you."

A moment later she was back by his side with both dogs in tow. The place was swarming with policemen so any further surveillance would be a waste of time.

"Are you okay?" she asked.

He was clutching his groin with a bloody hand.

"It's just a scratch," he said. "But it sure hurts like hell." He looked at her and asked, "What are you doing out here, anyway?"

She averted her eyes.

He looked down the street at the mule barn then back at her as his eyes widened in realization, but before he could say anything, an ambulance arrived, and everyone but Raven stepped back.

"Let's have a look there, officer," said one of the attendants. He began to pull down Walt's trousers.

"Whoa," said Walt. "What do you think you're doing?"

"I need to get a look at the wound."

"Not out here you don't."

"He must not be hurt too bad," Raven grinned at the attendant.

"This is not funny," Walt said. "I came within inches of losing my manhood."

"Officer Miller," she said with a hand over her mouth to cover her relief. "That's more than I needed to hear."

"Just hold on to my dog," he said. "I'll pick him up tomorrow."

40

Raven sat at her desk and gazed out the window allowing her mind to drift back over the morning—watching the mule barn, her surprise at seeing Vincent intrude upon the scene, and her feeling about Walt's being shot.

She turned at the sound of the door to the outer office opening and her blood ran cold. Brian Sweeney strolled in with one of his men. The man remained by the door as Sweeney approached.

"Whoa," he said as he entered her office and saw the gun she held. It was in her lap so his man by the outer door could not see it, but it was pointing directly at Sweeney. He put up both hands and said, "I come in peace."

"I should just shoot you now."

"That wouldn't go over very well with the police," he paused and nodded over his shoulder toward the man by the door, "or with Finbarr."

"What do you want?"

"Mind if I sit down?" he asked as he sat. "So, this is what the boss's office looks like." When she failed to respond he sighed as one would sigh at a difficult child and continued. "I hear you're still having trouble with dogs."

"That's a police matter," she said. She leaned forward in her chair and brought the gun into view. "Unless you're responsible for dog fighting, too."

When Finbarr saw the gun, he pulled his and rushed forward, but stopped when Sweeney raised a hand. His smile melted into something evil—the face of a man with no soul. He leaned forward, taunting her. "Go ahead. Pull the trigger. But you'd better make the first shot count because Finbarr won't miss with his."

She looked at Finbarr and knew Sweeney had the upper hand. She placed her gun on the table and leaned back in her chair.

"Why are you here?"

"I'm here to help you."

"Ha," she said. "Somehow I doubt that."

"I do know about the dog fighting," he said, "But not the way you think." He looked around the office for a moment, then continued. "You probably think I have the police on my payroll," he said, "but you'd be wrong."

"How so?"

"Because it's the other way around."

It took a moment for that to sink in. "You mean?"

"That's right. Captain Yancey is the one calling the shots in this town."

"Everything?"

"Everything but Torrio," said Sweeney. "Nobody's going to control those fucking Italians—pardon my French."

"What about your boy, Danny Malone?" she asked.

"Ah, yes," he said. "Ole Danny boy. He went and got himself killed, you know? Out at the Quarry with your boss. Only I don't think your boss had anything to do with that—and neither do the cops."

Raven was silent, so he continued. "I'm glad Danny got clipped. He was Yancey's guy, not mine. He's been double-crossing me for months. It was Danny who killed the guy in the mule barn that got this whole mess started. He tried to steal my money and guns until you happened along and outsmarted him. That was beautiful."

"I still don't understand why you're telling me all this," said Raven.

"There's an old Irish proverb that says *the enemy of my enemy is my friend*," he said.

"I don't think that's Irish."

"Whatever. Anyway, I figure that you're Yancey's biggest problem right now so whatever I can do to help you, will help me."

"So, you're double-crossing Yancey?"

He just shrugged.

She opened her drawer to get a cigarette and Finbarr came back to attention. She brought out her hand slowly and held up the package. She lit one and slid the package across the desk. Sweeney lit his and tossed the package back across the desk.

"I'm not going to do anything to help you," he said He pushed himself up from the chair and continued, "But I'm not going to stand in your way, either."

He looked hard into her eyes and she held his gaze until he nodded at Finbarr, who led the way out of the office.

D oes it hurt?" Raven asked.

"Of course, it hurts," Walt replied. "What kind of question is that?"

Raven sat on a straight-backed wooden chair next to his hospital bed and looked around the room. Walt occupied one of six beds along the wall of a long room. Another six beds were across the central aisle. The patients were all men. Some were sleeping, a few had visitors, and one man was sitting up in bed reading the newspaper. An antiseptic smell permeated the hushed space, lending a somber air.

"Back in the street you said it was just a scratch."

"Back in the street it didn't hurt as much as it does now. They've been poking and prodding and scraping and cleaning. Now they've got it wrapped so tight I won't be able to walk."

"Oh, don't be such a baby," said a voice over her shoulder.

Raven turned to see a grinning Gladys standing in the doorway. She felt suddenly exposed and embarrassed, as though she had been caught doing something wrong.

Glad walked into the room and kissed her husband on the forehead. She didn't appear unduly concerned that he had been shot. She lifted the covers, exposing his bare legs and the bandage just below the bulge of his underwear. Raven felt herself stir before she averted her eyes.

"Jesus!" he exclaimed, as he jerked the covers down.

"I see you haven't lost anything vital," she said.

"I'd better be going," Raven said. She got up to relinquish her seat to Glad, who showed no sign of taking it.

"Wait a minute," Walt said to Raven. "I need to know why you were snooping around the Lewiston Mule Barn."

"I wasn't snooping around there. I was just walking Lizzie in the park."

"You expect me to believe that?"

"You can believe what you like," Raven said. "Now, I'll leave you two to visit. I need to get back to work."

"I'll be in to pick up my dog on Thursday."

"Thursday?"

"Yes," he said. "I'll be stuck in here for a couple of days."

Raven tried not to show her relief. Interference from Officer Miller was one thing she would not need to worry about tomorrow.

41

You can't come in here, buddy." The man put his hand on Raven's shoulder and pushed her back onto the sidewalk.

She made no effort to resist—did not even offer a reply. She just looked carefully down the dark alley, absorbing as much as she could before she moved on. She recognized the man as one of the policemen who had been carrying boxes into the mule barn the day before. He had also turned up at the shooting just a few feet from where they stood. But she was confident he would not recognize her.

Min Lee had helped her with her outfit, gathering some of Mr. Ruebottom's old clothes and taking a stitch here and there to help with the fit. They had worked quietly in order to prevent Katherine from discovering what they were up to. Raven wore a pair of trousers and a shirt covered by an old, threadbare, navy blue pea coat. She hoped her feet were not too visible since the best they could do was a pair of Katherine's old garden boots. The most important feature of her disguise was the hat. It was a dark green, long-billed military cap that hid much of her face and allowed her hair to be tucked up inside its soft top.

Raven walked casually back the way she had come to the end of the street, crossed at LaSalle, and angled inconspicuously back into a position that allowed her to observe the operation. People were beginning to file into the front door of mule barn where two men—

presumably off-duty policemen—took money and guarded the entrance.

"What did you see?" asked Min Lee from the shadows of a doorway.

"The alley is piled with crates and boxes," Raven reported. "But men are walking from the mule barn to the warehouse." She nodded toward the building directly across the street from they stood. "That has to be where they are holding the dogs."

"I don't like this," said Min Lee.

"I'm going to see if I can sneak in and have a look around," Raven said. "You stay here and see that nobody comes in after me." When Min Lee did not reply Raven looked at her. "Just give me five minutes. If I don't come out, you can come in and rescue me—again."

Raven retraced her steps to the end of the street and circled back toward the mule barn, trying the doors to the warehouse as she passed. The second one she came to was not locked, but she was in clear view of the guards at the alley. She settled back into the shadows of the opening, glanced over at Min Lee, and waited. Soon, an empty flat-bed truck pulled into the alley and she used the distraction to slip inside.

The room was long and narrow with a counter running most of its length. It looked like an old reception area where customers would be greeted and give their order. The back—both then and now—was where all the action occurred.

She edged up to the opening and peeked around the corner into the dimly lit room. The smell of urine and feces was overwhelming, but the atmosphere was uncommonly quiet for a room filled with dogs. The big dogs—presumably the ones used for fighting—were chained to pillars that allowed them to move around but not reach each other. They were quiet because they were all wearing muzzles. They were a sad-looking bunch with their stitched-up faces and chewed-off ears. A few of them were lying down, but most paced nervously. They knew, she could see, that this was fight-night. She also knew there was little she could do for them.

She carefully scanned the room until she found what she was looking for. Tucked in the back, left-hand corner of the massive space was an open door through which she could see wire crates that held the smaller dogs. Her mind raced. How could she get them out of here without being seen? For that matter, how could she even get herself back there without being seen? She thought about starting a fire as a diversion, but that was too dangerous, both to the dogs and to the city. People still talked about the Great Fire of 1871. She had to act quickly, or Min Lee would be coming to the rescue.

A small bark cut across the silence, and she stopped worrying and started moving. She strolled confidently into the warehouse, picked up a box, and edged her way toward the back room. One of the fighting dogs blocked her path and, as she tried to decide whether to step over him or alter her path, a voice shouted, "Hey!"

She froze.

"Get over here and help us load this truck!"

She peered out from under the brim of her hat. The flat-bed truck she had seen entering the alley had backed up to a loading dock and a couple of boys were filling it with burlap sacks and boxes of what appeared to be dog waste. The man who was supervising them was looking at Raven with his hands on his hips. She had little choice but to obey him.

She dropped her box and walked to where the boys were picking up their loads, but the man said, "Come here."

She balled her fists and prepared to defend herself as she approached him.

"Who are you?" he asked.

Before she could respond, a voice behind her said, "What's taking so long? I want this truck out of here."

"I know, Captain," said the man before her. "I'm just trying to get our help lined up."

Raven's plan to rescue the dogs was falling apart. Getting out of here alive was her new objective. She glanced over her shoulder at Captain Yancey and saw that he was accompanied by two men—men who looked like they could take care of anyone who stood in their way. It was time to leave.

Raven's left hand shot out. The heel of her hand connected with the supervisor's chin, rocking his head back. She bolted for the exit behind him but was tackled from behind. Handcuffs were quickly and expertly applied and as the men stood her up and turned her around. Yancey ripped off her cap and the men let out a collective gasp as her hair cascaded out.

"A girl," one of them laughed. "Charlie got knocked down by a girl."

Charlie was getting up off the ground, rubbing his chin. He did not appear to be amused.

"I know you," said Yancey. "You're the girl from the welfare association."

Raven did not respond.

Yancey looked around the room at the dogs. He glanced at the back room where the small dogs were kept.

"Shit," he said. "We can't let her leave here."

He turned back to Charlie and said, "Get some of that chloroform that we use on the dogs."

When she woke up, she was bouncing down the road in the back of a truck. She was still handcuffed, and her feet were tied. She was face down with a heavy weight on her back. Judging by the smell, she was buried under the bags of dog manure. The last thing she remembered hearing was Captain Yancey's instructions to tie her to some of the bags and dump her in the river.

She rolled onto her side and pushed up with her legs, working herself free of the pile. She sat up and edged to the side of the truck and threw up. It may have been the effect of the chloroform, but the intense smell of being covered in dog feces did not help.

Her head ached, her stomach hurt, and a feeling of hopelessness fell over her. She had failed miserably—let down all those animals—and now, it appeared, she would pay with her life. People that cared about her would never know what had happened. And bad men like Sweeney and Yancey would carry on hurting people and animals.

When her stomach settled, she edged her hands down past her butt and slowly and painfully pulled them past her legs and to her front. She examined the bindings on her legs and soon had them free. The truck was speeding along at a pretty good clip, making it too dangerous to try to jump off onto the roadway, but when it slowed to make a turn, she made a split-second decision. She shuffled quickly to the back, gauged the distance of the cars behind them, and slid off the truck—rolling along the road to absorb the impact and hoping she would not be run over.

42

Raven stood in the cavernous space and looked around. The door she had entered the previous evening was still unlocked, but the view before her was vastly different. The only thing left from last night was the smell. Everything else was gone. Even the room at the back where the small dogs had been kept was wiped clean. Raven wondered if this was a normal cleanup or if her escape had spooked them.

Her footsteps echoed as she walked through the empty room and out to the alley. The mule barn was locked, but she had no doubt that it was empty, as well.

She had thought Yancey and his men would be sleeping late after last night and hoped she might be able to rescue those poor little dogs. She walked slowly out of the alley turned toward LaSalle and then turned north for the six-block walk home.

The experience of last night should have been fresh in her mind, but it was more like a distant nightmare. When Raven did not come out of the warehouse, Min Lee had gone inside in time to see Raven being loaded onto the truck. She was following when Raven slid off. They had retrieved one of Walt's handcuff keys from Gladys and spent much of the night getting Raven cleaned up. She rubbed at the abrasions the handcuffs had left on her wrists to remind herself that it was all too real. Her behind was bruised and her elbows raw from where she had hit the road, but she was otherwise okay.

She walked up LaSalle, turned right on Schiller, and left on State, where she was stopped in her tracks by the ambulance and police car angled in the street in front of her house. She rushed up the steps and had to step aside to allow the ambulance attendants to exit the door. Their stretcher was bearing a body covered by a sheet. Min Lee followed them out on the porch where she and Raven embraced.

"What happened," Raven asked as they turned to watch Katherine Ruebottom's body take its final ride in an ambulance.

"She must have died in her sleep," said Min Lee. "She was gone when I went in to wake her up."

"Why are the police here?"

"*Routine,* the coroner says. They need to make sure there is nothing suspicious."

They turned as a short, balding man emerged from the front door.

"Had Mrs. Ruebottom been ill?" the coroner asked.

"Yes," said Min Lee. "She had a bad heart. Doctor Washington is—was—her doctor if you would like to speak to him."

"I will speak to him," said the coroner. "Then I can sign the death certificate and release the body for burial." He shook their hands, offered his condolences, and was gone.

They watched his car drive away and retreated inside. Raven sat at the window that looked over the garden where Vincent and Lizzie sniffed around, oblivious to the tragedy that had just befallen their home. Min Lee brought Raven a cup of coffee, but before she could sit down, there was a knock at the front door.

"I'll get it," said Raven, jumping up. "I expect I know who that is."

Walt was propped up on a single crutch and moved awkwardly down the hallway to the kitchen. He sat stiffly at the table between Min Lee and Raven.

"You look like you are in pain," said Raven.

"It's not so bad," he said. "They've got me bandaged up pretty tight, so it hurts when I move."

He sipped the coffee that Min Lee brought him and continued as he peered into the back yard. "So, how has Vincent been?"

"I should let him in," said Min Lee. "He'll be glad to see you."

She got up and opened the back door. The two dogs sprang into the kitchen and both greeted Walt, but Vincent was more enthusiastic, wagging his tail, whining, and—when he discovered the location of the wound under Walt's pants—sniffing intently at Walt's crotch.

"Whoa, boy," said Walt, pushing the dog's head away. "Let's not get too personal, there."

When the women did not laugh at his embarrassment he asked, "What's going on here? Why the long faces?"

When Min Lee told him, he said, "Oh my God. I'm so sorry. I'll just collect my dog and be on my way."

"That's not necessary," said Raven. She looked at Min Lee, who nodded in agreement. "It was not unexpected. We're just trying to figure out what to do."

After a thoughtful pause, Walt looked at Raven and said, "You look like you may be limping a little, as well. What have you been up to?"

"I'm fine," Raven said.

He stared at her for a moment. "I want to know why you were out by the Lewiston Mule Barn during the robbery."

"Are you suggesting I had something to do with the robbery?"

"No. I want to know why you were around the mule barn."

"What do you know about the mule barn?" she asked.

He opened his mouth but made no reply.

"Walt."

"I have been hearing talk lately."

"So, you know about the dog fighting?"

He did not reply.

"Walt!" she said, raising her voice. "They mistreat those dogs. Dog fighting is illegal."

"Actually, it's not," he said feebly.

"Well, it should be," she said. "Those dogs are chained to posts. They're covered in scars and open sores and the little dogs—the ones they use to bait the fighters—well I hate to think what they suffer."

"Wait," he said with wide eyes. "How do you know all that? You were there, weren't you? You went to the fight."

Raven kept her eyes down, glancing briefly at Min Lee who got up and moved to the sink.

"Is that why you are limping?" he asked. "Did something happen?"

When Raven did not reply he turned to Min Lee. "Min Lee, tell me what happened."

Min Lee just looked at Raven. "You need to tell him," she said. "He'll find out soon enough."

So, she did.

43

"Mr. Goldsmith will see you now," the secretary said.

Raven stood, smoothed her dress, and self-consciously touched her hair. The call had come to the house shortly before lunch from the attorneys, Silverstein and Goldsmith, to appear at their office in an old mansion on Chicago's North Side.

"Miss Griffith," Mr. Goldsmith was already standing when Raven entered the office. "Thank you for coming in on such short notice."

He was a small, trim man with dark, slicked back hair and wire-rimmed glasses. He motioned for her to sit in a chair opposite his desk and then took his own seat. His office was not at all what she expected. Instead of dark paneling and walls lined with dusty law books, she looked around at a spacious office with baby blue walls and a high ceiling. A large window to her right looked out into the canopy of a chestnut tree that supported a platform bird feeder. It was covered in birds of all sorts.

Mr. Goldsmith cleared his throat and nodded over Raven's shoulder. Raven turned and was surprised to see a young woman sitting in the back of the room with an open notebook on her lap. She was presumably there to witness the proceedings.

Mr. Goldsmith opened a folder that had been sitting on his desk and asked, "Do you know why we have called you here?"

"I presume it has something to do with Katherine's estate."

"I do represent the estate of Mrs. Katherine Ruebottom," he began. "Mrs. Ruebottom, as you probably know, has no heirs or descendants, and she has instructed us to give all of her tangible personal properties, including her residence, to you." He paused, perhaps because of the surprise that registered on Raven's face.

"As you are no doubt aware, her fortune is considerable and there are several conditions that must be met. Her Will specifies that you occupy her residence, that you keep Min Lee employed—the stipulations and salary are detailed here—and that you continue to work for the welfare of the animals of Chicago."

Raven sat in stunned silence. She had expected something, just because she knew that Katherine liked her—but this? It was almost too much to take in, and it made her feel guilty to have so much when those she cared about had so little.

"Miss Griffith?"

"Yes," she replied. "Yes, of course. I will comply with all of her wishes."

Mr. Goldsmith nodded his head and continued. "We are, naturally, authorized to monitor your activities to ensure that you remain in compliance." He got up and walked around the desk with some papers, which he had her sign. After his assistant had signed as a witness and he had stuffed copies in an envelope he shook her hand, congratulated her, and walked her to the door.

Outside, Min Lee stood leaning against the car reading the newspaper. When Raven emerged, she folded the paper and asked, "Well, how did it go?"

Raven leaned against the car alongside Min Lee, folded her arms, and told her the story.

"I feel so guilty," Raven said.

"Why?"

"Why me?" said Raven. "Why not leave it all to you?"

"You know why," Min Lee replied. "Because I told her not to. I don't want the responsibility."

They sat in silence for a moment, leaning against the car.

"When my mother died," Raven said finally. "I felt she had abandoned me. I resented the fact that I was left to cook and clean for my father and my brother. Now, I'm ashamed to say, I feel abandoned again. Katherine is dead, Jo is in jail, and Walt—well, I don't know what to think about him."

"You're in love with him." Min Lee said it as a fact.

Raven did not reply.

"Death is natural and something to be embraced," Min Lee continued. "Look at all the times you have put your own life in danger."

"I didn't fear death. I didn't even think about it. I always felt that it wouldn't happen to me."

"I suppose that's better than living in fear of it," said Min Lee, "but it can't be good for your health."

Raven looked at her and laughed for the first time in days.

"Confucius said, *If we don't know life, how can we know death?*" said Min Lee. "Think about the dogs. They're going to die, but they don't fear death."

"I know," said Raven, "but I fear it for them."

"You fear their absence when you should be enjoying their presence. You need to embrace this life." After a pause, she continued, "Do you remember our late-night discussion on the back porch a few weeks ago?"

"Vaguely."

"You said you have always had a way with animals, but you felt it was a hopeless calling. I reminded you that you must pursue it—and you have succeeded admirably."

"How so?"

"You have stepped into a world dominated by men—often cruel men—and stood up for the animals, sometimes at considerable cost to your own health and safety. I admire you for that."

"You admire me?" said Raven, turning to Min Lee. "You are one of the most competent women I have ever met. You taught me how to defend myself, how to behave like a lady. I'm the one who should be admiring you. Maybe it is time we both put our past behind us and get to work. It's what Katherine would have wanted."

"Then I guess I had better take Madame home," Min Lee said when Raven was finished.

They both laughed and got into the car. They would not be laughing much longer.

44

T hat woman," said Jo's accuser, pointing a shaky finger at her, "is a murderer."

The courtroom fell silent, and all eyes shifted to the subject of this woman's scorn. Josephine Washington sat stoically at the table with head up but eyes down, her lawyer shuffling papers beside her. She had been transferred to the Cook County Courthouse for the trial after spending nearly a week in the dungeon-like basement of the South Precinct. From where Raven sat on the front row of the visitor section between Min Lee and Harry Fischer, Jo's attorney appeared anxious as he repeatedly glanced back toward the doors of the courtroom.

"She stabbed my Bill for no reason," Mildred Truman went on, "and left him to bleed out on the kitchen floor like a hog at the stockyard."

By now, she was crying, just—Raven figured—for good measure. She was a thin woman with bulging eyes and a sharp tongue.

The prosecutor had saved the most dramatic witness, the victim's wife, for last. Raven and the rest of the courtroom had already heard from the first police officer on the scene, the pathologist who had examined the body, and several of Mr. Truman's coworkers who had attested to his upstanding character. It was a strong case and Raven struggled to understand how this sweet young girl could have done such an awful thing and kept it a secret. Her defense lawyer had conceded her guilt as he cross-examined the witnesses, but he had yet to address Jo's accuser. That was about to change.

Raven had secured the services of Johnny Torrio's lawyer Wilson Conroy after Aaron Goldsmith had turned her down. Mr. Conroy was an imposing figure—tall and slender with snow white hair that contrasted with his navy-blue pin-striped suit. He spoke in a loud, dramatic voice and moved around the courtroom with long, confident strides.

"Mrs. Truman," he began his cross examination, "My client is the daughter of your only sister. Is that correct?"

"Yes."

"And you offered to take her in when her parents were killed in the Eastland disaster."

"Yes."

"The sinking of that ship was a terrible tragedy. Did you receive any life insurance money from the shipping company on Miss Washington's behalf?"

Mrs. Truman appeared uncomfortable for the first time and hesitated over the question.

"Mrs. Truman?"

"Yes," she said finally. "We received a thousand dollars."

The attorney paused, giving the jury time to think about her financial gain.

"How did your husband feel about having your niece come to live with you?"

"He didn't want her at first."

"What made him change his mind?"

"When he saw her, and he could see how sad she was—that's when his heart softened."

"His heart softened," he repeated. "Could his heart have softened because he saw how lovely she was?"

"That's ridiculous," she said. "What are you suggesting?"

"Did you and your husband enjoy a good relationship?"

"Of course, we did."

"If that is so, I wonder why he frequented houses of prostitution."

Mrs. Truman's cheeks were flushed, and she was at a loss for words. Mr. Conroy finally seemed to warm to his task, as a rumble swept through the courtroom.

The judge banged his gavel. "Mr. Truman is not on trial here," he reminded the attorney.

As the judge was speaking, the doors at the back of the courtroom squeaked open and all eyes turned to the intrusion. A small thin man with close-set eyes and a pointed nose walked in holding the arms of two nervous looking women.

"I have no further questions, your Honor," Conroy said.

He resumed his seat next to Jo, Mrs. Truman was excused, and the prosecution rested its case. It was time for Wilson Conroy to begin the defense.

"The Defense calls Miss Ruby Tilden," Conroy began.

Ruby Tilden, one of the women who had just arrived, appeared to be a prostitute with her flashy clothes and long auburn hair. As her testimony unfolded, the court discovered that she was a former prostitute who ran her own den of iniquity known, simply as *Ruby's*. It was located near the stockyards where William Truman worked on the killing floor. According to Ruby, he stopped in on a regular basis on his way home from work.

"Did Mr. Truman have any special proclivities?" Conroy asked her at one point.

"Proclivities?" Ruby asked.

"Did he have any special likes or dislikes?"

"He liked 'em young, and he liked it rough."

"Rough?"

"He liked to choke the girls a bit. Paid extra for it."

"How rough was he?"

"He gave one of my girls a black eye. After that I had to reel him in."

"And how did you do that?"

"I had my bouncer kick his ass."

The courtroom erupted in laughter and the judge banged his gavel.

Raven felt hopeful for the first time as the image of a belligerent bully emerged. She glanced at Min Lee, who gave her a confident nod and then toward Harry, who simple appeared mesmerized by the proceedings.

The other woman was even more damning. Emma Ossman had been the Truman's maid prior to Mr. Truman's murder. Their relationship was based on intimidation rather than money. She testified that he had cornered her several times, placed his hands on her private parts, and choked her on one occasion, prompting her to quit her job.

For his final witness, Mr. Conroy called Josephine Washington to the stand. Raven found her testimony difficult to listen to. She lived with her Aunt Mildred and Uncle Bill for a little over three years after her parents died. At first, she was grateful to have a place to live, but that began to change during her second year with them when Uncle Bill began to make improper advances. Raven did the math and figured that would be about the time that Jo was becoming a woman.

"What sort of improper advances?" Conroy pressed.

Jo wrung her hands and looked around at all the strangers in the room.

"Miss Washington?"

"It started with him placing his hand on my... my bottom..."

"Liar," shouted Mrs. Truman.

Raven felt Harry stiffen, and she placed a hand on his arm.

"That'll be enough of that," said the Judge with a bang of his gavel.

"Pretty soon, he was sneaking into my bedroom at night."

Jo paused and began to weep.

"Did he ever...?" Conroy let the question hang in the air.

Jo just nodded in the affirmative.

"Tell us about that final evening."

"We were in the kitchen late one night," Jo said so softly that the judge admonished her to speak up. "I couldn't sleep so I went for some warm milk. He was there, sitting at the table with a bottle at hand. He appeared to be drunk. As I stood at the sink, he got up and came up behind me. He pressed himself into me and reached around to grab both of my ..."

An audible gasp went up from the courtroom.

"There was a knife on the counter in front of me." She hesitated, appearing to regain her composure. "I fought back the only way I knew how."

"Good for you," mumbled Harry.

"She's lying," shouted Mrs. Truman as she jumped to her feet. "She seduced my Bill. She killed him for no reason."

The courtroom erupted in pandemonium. The Judge banged his gavel furiously and had the bailiff remove Mrs. Truman from the room. The trial wrapped up quickly from that point. There were closing arguments, and the Judge gave instructions to the jury before they retired to deliberate.

Raven tried to imagine herself being assaulted by having some loathsome man putting his hands on her. It was, in some way, worse than her own experience of having a man tie her up in a building and try to burn it down with her in it. Her attacker had wanted to kill her, but his touch had been violent, not intimate.

The Jury needed less than an hour to determine that Jo was not guilty of murder.

After the judge had banged his gavel and forced everyone to stand so he could exit the courtroom, Raven, Min Lee, and Harry made their way to Jo and gave her a hug.

Mr. Conroy offered her his hand, and she thanked him.

"It was actually a pleasure," he said as he gathered his papers. He looked at Jo and continued, "I don't often get to defend innocent young women. My clients are usually a bit more challenging if you know what I mean."

Since he worked for Johnny Torrio, Raven could only imagine.

After Conroy walked out, she turned to Jo and asked, "Are you ready to come home?"

"I don't know," Jo replied looking at the floor.

"What's wrong?"

"I killed a man," she said. "I lied to you two and to Katherine."

"You didn't lie to us," said Min Lee. "You simply failed to disclose. There's a big difference."

"It was self-defense," said Harry.

When Jo didn't respond, Raven asked, "Is there anything you have really lied about?"

"No."

"Then we need you to come home."

"We?"

"Yes, we," she said. "Min Lee and me—and the dogs. We're your family now. Let's get your things and get out of here."

45

The change in her life was almost too much to absorb. Raven had never sought wealth and power and had never even imagined the twin responsibilities of managing Katherine Ruebottom's household and running the Association. But here she was on a Saturday morning sitting at Lou's old desk, fielding calls and dispatching people to rescue animals—even though the Association's board members were still seeking someone to hire as Lou's permanent replacement. Madge was meeting with the auditors, preparing the financial statements that she and Raven had reviewed for presentation to the Board at their annual meeting in a few weeks. She wanted to do a good job despite their apparent lack of confidence.

Raven had sent Jo to deliver a couple of dogs to their new adoptive families and had just finished helping a husband and wife select a dog for their little boy. Bexley, the big black shaggy dog, was finally going to a good home. Now, only Bea, the female German shepherd, remained from the group she had rescued from the research compound.

The ringing of the telephone on her desk made her jump.

"Hello."

"Is this Raven Griffith?" asked a man's voice.

"Yes."

"Officer Walter Miller asked me to call you. He needs you over at the Lewiston Mule Barn. Do you know where that is?"

"Who is this?"

The man hung up.

Why would Walt have someone else call her? Why not call himself? She called the police station but was told that Officer Walt Miller is out. She called his home, but no one answered. Everyone was out of the office, so she would need to lock up and go see for herself. She grabbed her purse, checked her gun, and walked downstairs. She was startled, however, by a man standing at the door. He was short and nicely dressed, right up to the gray fedora on his head. He had a hand in his pocked that appeared to hold a gun.

"You're coming with us," said the man with the gun. He grabbed her purse and nodded over his shoulder toward a police car at the curb. Its back door stood open. Captain Yancey glared at her from the passenger's seat.

She thought about fighting but decided to keep her silence. She allowed them to place her in handcuffs and would bide her time. She would take her chances at the police station with Walt, Sergeant O'Malley, and Alice Clement in the building.

Unfortunately, the police car drove up LaSalle but failed to turn right on Chicago Avenue. They were not going to police headquarters. Raven was puzzled when the car turned right on Delaware Place and concerned when they turned into the alley and stopped behind the Lewiston Mule Barn.

Yancey entered the mule barn for a few minutes, returned to the car, and told his driver to get Raven out. As the officer took out his key to remove her handcuffs, Sweeney yanked her away and said, "Leave those on. I don't want her to get any ideas."

As his men each grabbed an arm, Yancey moved to face her and said, "Watch her. She's a demon."

"You'll never get away with this," Raven said.

"Shut up," Yancey growled. He punched her so hard her knees sagged, forcing the two men to drag her the rest of the way into the barn.

Raven's eye began to swell shut and she bled from a small cut on her cheek, but she was slowly regaining her senses. "Why are you doing this?" She asked Yancey, ashamed to sound so pleading.

Yancey's man removed the handcuffs and threw them to Yancey. He then tied her wrists together around a post.

"That should be obvious," he snarled. "I can't have you out there telling the world what you know."

As he was talking, the door to the barn opened and light flooded the room. After the door closed, Raven gasped and Yancey smiled at her dismay. His man had returned with a five-gallon gas can and, judging by the way he carried it, it was full.

She pulled at her bindings and screamed, "No."

Yancey's smile turned into a twisted grin.

Fear gripped Raven. She began to sweat, and her breathing became ragged. Her clouded vision caused her to see a different barn—a barn of her childhood where another evil man had tied her up. She was only sixteen years old, and the fire was all around her. Her clothes caught fire, and she was sure to die because nobody knew she was there. Rondell Boyd had somehow come to her rescue. The fear of being burned alive had remained with Raven since that day.

Yancey's man walked calmly around the walls of the barn, pouring gasoline as he went. When he walked down the hall, pouring the fuel toward Raven.

"Help!" Raven screamed. She was wide-eyed and feeling panic as she tugged at her bindings.

"Shut up," Yancey said. He hit her again on her swollen cheek, but it was so numb, she barely felt it. "No one can hear you, anyway."

He walked toward the door, turned back to face Raven, and nodded for his men to leave. He pulled a box of matches from his pocket and struck one. He did not smile as he calmly dropped it to the floor and walked out.

An unnatural calm came over her as Raven watched the fire spread. She felt like a mouse in the jaws of the cat. There was no escape, so her body just shut down.

The fire spread in two directions and quickly encircled her. It began to roar as flames leaped up the walls and caught the roof. Smoke filled the room, causing her eyes to water and her throat to contract. Heat seared the skin on her face and hands. She wanted to cry, but she could only cough and struggle to breathe. Suddenly, light cut through the smoke and she remembered a rescue all those years ago. Her mind was a confusion of heat, smoke, and something else—strong hands cutting her bindings, lifting her, and dragging her toward the door.

She breathed in the fresh air and slowly regained consciousness. She was lying on her back, peering at the smoke-filled sky. She looked to her right at the barn, about fifty yards away and fully ablaze. She pushed herself to an elbow and looked around. A large black car was parked nearby, and a familiar figure leaned against it, mesmerized by the burning building. Raven sat up, struggled to her feet, and joined Benny at the car.

"Looks like you got beat up pretty good," he said, referring to her bruised and swollen face.

Passersby converged on the fire and watched helplessly as it consumed the old barn.

"Have you been following me?" Raven asked.

"No," Benny replied. "The Boss has me keeping an eye on Yancey."

"Looks like you lost him."

"Figured the Boss would be mad if I let the Dogcatcher burn up."

"Dogcatcher?"

"That's what he calls you. You're the dogcatcher and he's the Fox."

She tried to smile through her damaged face at the thought of a notorious gangster calling her anything. "Can you give me a lift home?"

She climbed into the front seat with Benny. Her coughing made her chest ache.

"Maybe I should take you to the hospital," he said.

"No" she replied. "I'll be okay. Just take me home."

It was time to begin fighting back.

46

R aven had slept poorly, despite the laudanum Doctor Jackson had given her. He had said her cheek was probably broken, but there was nothing to be done except give it time to heal. Her head felt like she had been kicked by a mule and served as a reminder that the fire had not been some terrible dream.

Min Lee had been furious when she saw Raven's face, and Raven thought she might need to restrain her from going after Captain Yancey. Min Lee was still a bit sullen as she poured Raven a cup of coffee.

"Thank you," Raven said.

When Min Lee did not answer, Raven continued. "Are you going to sulk like this all day?"

"Those men must be stopped," said Min Lee without turning from the preparation of Raven's breakfast.

"Not by you, they don't," Raven said to her back. Lizzie placed her head in Raven's lap, and she stroked the dog's coarse fur.

Min Lee served Raven a bowl of fried rice and scrambled eggs that had been prepared in a large bowl-like pan she called a wok. She poured Raven more coffee and sat down opposite her with her own breakfast and a pot of tea. They ate in comfortable silence for a few moments until the doorbell rang.

Min Lee answered the door and said upon her return, "It's Officer Miller. I seated him in the front parlor."

"Thank you," Raven said as she rose and took her coffee. "For everything."

Min Lee did not respond.

"Good God," exclaimed Walt when he saw Raven. "What happened to you?"

Lizzie wandered in to greet him, then plopped down under the bay window. Raven described the events of the day before and, as she sensed his growing anger, told him, "You and Min Lee need to let me handle this."

As if on cue, Min Lee entered the room and asked Walt, "Would you like some coffee?" When he declined, Min Lee told Raven she was going to run some errands and would be out for the rest of the morning.

"So," Raven said, at last. "What brings you out here?"

"I stopped by to tell you to be careful—that something's up. But I guess I'm too late."

"That's all right." She smiled a crooked smile and said, "I have a plan."

"Would your plan have anything to do with some of your gangster friends?"

"Well," she said, "It certainly won't involve any help from the police."

"Thanks a lot."

"You know what I mean."

They sat in silence until Walt nodded at her cup and said, "I believe I would like some of that coffee."

She got up and motioned for him to follow her to the kitchen where she poured a fresh cup for herself and another cup for him. As they stood at the counter, she noticed he was not using his crutch.

"How's your leg?" she asked.

"It is much better since they loosened the bandage. I hardly notice it, now."

She led him to the table at the window overlooking the garden. "This was Katherine's favorite spot," she said. "She and I spent hours here, talking and watching the dogs."

"What will you do now that she's gone?"

"Oh," she looked up sharply. "I forgot to mention. I'll be staying here. She's given all of this to me."

He let out a whistle as he looked around. "You are a very rich lady."

"It would seem so."

"The gentlemen will be lining up at your door to sweep you off your feet."

"They'll be wasting their time."

"Which part, the lining up or the sweeping?"

"Oh, I might enjoy the lining up part. But I won't be sharing this with anyone. It'll just be me, Min Lee, and Jo."

"And the dogs," he added.

"And the dogs," she laughed.

"A gorgeous young woman like you ought to be thinking about sharing your life with someone."

"Gorgeous?" Her hand went to her damaged face.

He reached across the table and stroked her bruise. "This will pass—and it has little to do with your beauty."

"That may be," she looked into his eyes. "But it seems the best ones are already taken."

Her heart was racing as they gazed into the garden and silence filled the space. "Have you ever had the grand tour of the house?" she asked him.

"I would love to see your new home," he said with a smile.

"Well," she stood and waved her arm, "this is the solarium. Mr. and Mrs. Ruebottom came by their money late in life, and she told me he liked to show off his wealth. You'll see that in all the rooms."

She led the way down the hall to the front of the house.

"The front parlor," she said, "is pretty typical. The bay windows overlooking the street are as much to let us view the world outside as they are to let the world have a glimpse inside the house."

She moved to the fireplace mantle and picked up one of dozens of objects that were crowded onto its surface. "It's all a little over done for my taste. I expect I'll be cleaning house one of these days."

She took him back into the hallway for a peek into the library and dining room before heading upstairs. As they ascended the stair, Walt let out a small gasp when he saw the second-floor hall.

Raven chuckled. "That was my reaction when I first came up here."

She gave him a moment to take in the black marble floors, the ornate white marble balustrade around the stairwell, and the Chinese artwork that lined the walls.

"Where is your bedroom?" Walt asked.

Raven glanced at his face to see if he was having her on, but he merely looked back at her. She walked to her bedroom and when she turned, he was right behind her. They looked at each other for a moment before he bent down and let his lips brush hers. She felt as if she had been seized by a jolt of electricity. She grabbed him around the neck and melted into his arms.

Raven pulled up the sheet to cover her naked breasts. She was entirely comfortable, but for the fact that she was in bed with a man who was married to a woman she considered to be a friend.

"We can't do this," Raven said. When Walt didn't reply she continued. "It's not fair to Gladys."

"You didn't seem so reluctant a few minutes ago," he quipped.

"Yes, well," she hesitated, "I must have been lost in the moment."

"How's your face?" he asked.

"Thanks for reminding me," she said. "It hurts like crazy."

He reached over and stroked her hair, careful not to touch her bruises.

"I'm serious," she said. "I've never felt this way. I've always been able to enjoy myself with men and not worry about any consequences. But after what you have done for me, I can't bear to be the one to wreck your marriage."

He stopped stroking her hair and laid back, folding his arms across his chest. He stared at the far wall for a moment, causing Raven's heart to ache a bit. She was giving Walt back to his wife. Raven felt an ugliness wash over her in the silence of her bedroom.

"I guess now that I've seen you naked," Walt said softly, "I can trust you to keep my secrets."

"Oh, God," she said. "What's wrong?"

He reached over and took her by the hand but did not look at her. "It's about Glad," he began. He was silent for so long that Raven wondered if he was going to continue. "She's…"

Raven glanced at him. His embarrassment was profound. His lip was quivering. She wanted to take him in her arms, but she refrained. What could be so bad? Was this policeman's wife a master criminal—perhaps a serial murderer?

"Glad," he said finally, "prefers the company of other women. She is what is known as a Lesbian."

Raven was stunned. She struggled to understand.

"But," she said hesitantly, "you're married—I mean she's married to you, a man."

"We got married before the war," he explained. "We had not been together very long before I shipped out. In the years I was gone, she met Valerie Taylor, and they developed a relationship. She waited for me, but things were never the same."

"Why don't you just get a divorce?"

"It's not that simple," he said. "We genuinely care for each other. And we need each other for professional appearances—for our careers."

Raven rolled out from under the sheets and straddled him, causing him to wince as she touched his bandaged leg.

"You could move in with me," she said.

He reached up, cradled her face in his hands—careful to avoid her bruises—and kissed her gently. "I'm afraid we're going to have to be content with this."

She had never felt so strongly about a man before. He was everything a woman could hope for, but something in his tone and actions told her it was futile to argue. His hands slid from her face to her breasts and she felt him stir beneath her. She clutched his hands to her and began to rock against him. If this was all she could hope for, she would take her happiness where she could get it—especially now. It would take her mind off her problems with ruthless gangsters and crooked policemen.

47

*H*er interlude with Walt had left her feeling drained—both from the physical exertion and from the revelation that followed. Walt had managed to get out of the house before Min Lee returned and Raven did not want to face anybody either, so she left soon after. As she walked, and the fog cleared from her brain, she decided this was as good a time as any to talk with Johnny Torrio about her problem with the police captain and with Brian Sweeney. She took a chance on him being there and, since Min Lee had the car, caught the streetcar to the Four Deuces. She arrived in time to see Alphonse Capone stuffing two suitcases into the back of Benny's car.

"Going on a trip?" she asked Capone.

"Moving back to New York," Capone said. In reply to her look of surprise, he continued. "I was just out here doing a little job for Mr. Torrio. I've got to get back to my family."

"Maybe you'll come back and see us one day."

"Maybe," he said. He looked closely at her face, then took a hard look at Benny. "You didn't tell us she got beat up this bad."

"It's not as bad as it looks," she said in Benny's defense. "If it wasn't for Benny, I wouldn't be here."

She saw Benny stiffen and turned to see Johnny Torrio emerge from the building, followed by two bodyguards, who took up stations a few feet to either side of the gathering. Both had hands inside their jackets, and both were looking carefully up and down the street.

Torrio walked up to Raven, eyeing her carefully. He held her face by the chin and gently turned it from side to side, looking at her cuts and bruises but saying nothing.

"You want me to stick around, Boss?" Capone said. "I'd be happy to take care of that son of a bitch."

"No," Torrio replied. "I need you to go back to New York and deal with that other matter for me. Get with Frankie Yale as soon as you get off the train."

"But..." Capone began.

"Al," Torrio held up a hand to cut him off. "I'll take care of this. You get going." Torrio nodded to Benny as a signal to get moving.

As they watched the car drive away, Torrio turned to Raven and said, "Come inside." He was through the door before she could move.

He stopped in the hallway and asked, "Have you ever seen our operation?"

"I've only ever been in these rooms." She nodded toward the small office and the adjacent parlor where she had met with Capone.

"Let me show you around," he said.

Most of the first floor was taken up by a large room with a bar at one end and tables in the middle. Before prohibition, Torrio explained, this had been the saloon. The alcohol still flowed here every night, but now it had to be done more discretely. Officials were paid to look the other way and, when that failed, a system of lookouts up and down the street kept them from being discovered.

They started up the stairs, and he turned to one of his bodyguards and said, "When Benny gets back from the train station, tell him to go to the flower shop."

"I have a standing order from Frido's Flowers," he explained to Raven as they ascended the stairs. "I get fresh flowers in here every week to keep the place looking classy."

The stairwell went all the way to the fourth floor. Torrio stopped at each floor to explain the building's layout. The second floor was horse betting, the third floor was the rest of the gambling—poker, roulette, faro, and blackjack, and the fourth floor was where the girls work. He made it sound so respectable, as though he was giving a tour of a sausage factory—here is where the meat is chopped, here is the meat being stuffed into the casings, and the front of the shop is where we sell the product.

He led her back down to the second floor and into a room that appeared to be his office. It was spare, with no window, few furnishings, and a single green-shaded lamp on the desk to light the room.

"Have a seat," he said.

The tour had made her a little uneasy. Gangsters did not give up their secrets easily—and without purpose. What was Torrio up to? Why was he confiding in her?

"So," he said. "What do you think?"

"Impressive."

"How would you like to work here?"

Her expression must have changed, because he threw up his hands and said, "Not like that. Not upstairs."

"Mr. Torrio," she began before he cut her off.

"I could use someone with your grit. A woman who can stand up to the rest of these goons and buffoons. Help me see things from a woman's perspective."

"Mr. Torrio," she repeated.

"Call me Johnny."

"Johnny," she continued. "I appreciate the offer, but I like my job. I just need to get Brian Sweeney and Captain Yancey off my back."

"It would be a lot easier for me to protect you if you came to work for me."

I might as well put a target on my back, she thought but did not say. The thought of working for this dapper, charming man was repugnant. Raven saw how easily Capone had ordered the murder of Sweeney's men, and she had no doubt that Torrio would have done the same. She hoped her feelings were not showing, because this man could just as easily order a hit on her—perhaps even pull the trigger himself, if necessary.

"I really need to get going," she said as she stood. "I just came here to see if you could help me with Brian Sweeney."

"I know," Torrio said. "You won't have to worry about Sweeney much longer."

She paused as his words sunk in. "Thank you, Mr. Torrio."

"Johnny."

"Johnny," she repeated.

"No need to thank me," he said as she turned to leave the room. "You need to understand that this is not for you. He's a business rival and I'm going to take care of business. You have bigger problems than Brian Sweeney. Don't expect me to help you with the police."

"That's my next stop."

"What's your next stop?"

"I'm going to see the Captain."

"What?" He rose from his chair and moved toward the doorway where she stood. "You need to think that through. Yancey is the most dangerous kind of gangster—one with a badge."

"What choice do I have?" she said. "I'm just going to try to reason with him—assure him I won't make trouble and we can just live in peace."

"Guys like Yancey don't do deals unless it benefits them," Torrio said. "He'll try to buy your loyalty. He'll probably want you to go to work for him."

"Like you did," she said, and regretted the impertinent reply.

"Yeah, but he won't take no for an answer, like I did."

48

Y ou've got a lot of nerve coming here," Yancey said. "I can't decide if you're brave or just plain stupid."

She looked around the office. His desk was piled high with papers and the shelves were crowded with framed photographs of Yancey in his uniform days. She was grateful for the glass walls and the gaggle of people outside scrambling around on a Monday morning—most of them police officers, some of them, she hoped, honest. She was seething with anger and hatred but tried her best not to show it. She wished she could put a bullet into his smug face.

"I don't want to spend the rest of my life looking over my shoulder," she said. "What do I need to do to make peace with you?"

"What's it worth to you?" he countered.

"What do you mean?

"A girl with your looks and body. I think you can figure out what I mean."

His gaze drifted down to her chest before his cold, blue eyes bored into hers. The faintest of smiles played across his lips. She knew what her answer had to be but wondered how to tell him that was the last thing that would ever occur—and wondered at the consequences of her actions.

Before she could formulate a reply, he said, "I hear you're pretty friendly with Officer Miller. You might want to think about your answer before you speak."

The threat to Walt made her angry, so she stood up to leave.

"Sit down," he said coldly.

"And if I don't?"

He opened his drawer and brought out something. He placed his hand on his desk and moved it enough that she could see a small revolver underneath. He pulled it back and placed his hand—and the gun—under the desk.

"You're not going to shoot me in front of all these people," she said with more bravado than she felt. In fact, her knees were trembling, so she sat down. "Why do you work for a gangster like Sweeney?"

"I don't work for him," said Yancey. "He works for me."

Raven knew that was true, but this was not the time to let him know. "Why do you work with him at all?"

"We have some common business interests."

"What could you have in common? He's a murdering crook and you're a police officer."

His eyes flickered. She had struck a nerve, so she decided to pick at it. Besides, her hand was now inside her purse and resting comfortably on her pistol.

"He has something on you, hasn't he?"

His face darkened. "Shut up," he said. "You don't know what you're talking about."

"Is it something you did? Maybe something early in your career?" She was stalling for time but also looking for a way out of this mess.

She didn't expect a response and was surprised when he said, "I killed somebody I shouldn't have—a kid who was in the wrong place. Sweeney helped me cover it up."

"When was that?"

"It doesn't matter," he said. "It was a long time ago."

He became quiet but kept his eyes on her.

"Why are you telling me all this?" she asked.

"Good question," he said. "Maybe because I know you'll never tell anyone."

His icy stare gave her chills. She gripped her gun and began to pull it from her purse when someone knocked on the door behind her.

"Not now," he shouted.

Then he looked at her and said, "Take your hand out of that purse—very slowly—and leave the purse on the desk." After she complied, he continued, "I've been dealing with troublemakers like you my whole career." He got up with his hand in his pocket. "Let's go for a little walk."

He put a hand on her shoulder as they walked out of the office and into the hallway. Then he placed his arm around her shoulder as though they were old friends walking down the hall and through a door into the stairwell. He guided her up to the roof of the building. When they emerged into the frigid outdoor air, he released his hold and pushed her toward the edge of the three-story building, openly pointing the gun at her. Snow was falling in heavy, wet flakes, and the breeze was picking up.

She raised her hands as he locked the door to the stairs and directed her to a section of the roof that was not visible from the taller buildings in the area.

"What are you going to do?"

He edged over to the low parapet that surrounded the flat roof and glanced down with a smile. "A fall from this height is going to hurt pretty bad," he said. "It'll look like an accident, or maybe a suicide. I did all I could to talk you down, but you were desperate after I refused your advances."

"You're crazy."

"Get up there." He motioned to the parapet with his gun.

"No."

She should have been afraid, but she was not. She thought about Lou, who was gunned down trying to save her. She thought about Jo, who stood trial for murder when she was only trying to defend herself. She even thought about Sean Malone and his brother Danny. Two kids who had been swept up in the world of gangsters and crooked cops. She had seen enough. If this man was going to murder her, he was going to have to work at it.

"Get up there." He said again. He was growing angry, and he moved toward her, nudging her in the shoulder with his gun. As he did so, she grabbed his gun with her left hand and thrust upward with her right, snapping his elbow in the wrong direction. He dropped his gun, screamed, and sagged at the knees. He grabbed his injured right arm with his left hand. Raven could sense the rage building in him. He lashed out with a foot, trying to kick her off the roof but she seized his leg and allowed his momentum to carry him toward the edge of the roof. His eyes filled with fear as she placed her shoulder under him and, with relative ease, lifted him over the parapet. His scream told her all she needed to know. She did not look over the edge at the results.

Raven sagged against the parapet and looked around. He had chosen his spot well. Nobody could have witnessed what had just happened. She had to move quickly. She picked up his gun and dropped into a ventilation duct. She then unlocked the door to the stairwell and turned back to the rooftop scene. The snowfall had thickened. She could barely make out the edge of the roof where Yancey had disappeared, and her tracks were being erased by the wet snow.

She crept back to the second floor where she peeked out the door to see everyone spilling out of the building. Word about what had happened to the Captain must have had spread. When everyone was gone, she slipped into his office and retrieved her purse, looking carefully around to make sure there was no trace of her presence.

Plenty of people would have seen her in there with him, but they would have also seen her leave the building with him. If anyone asked, she would tell them he was alive the last time she saw him, which was technically true. She left the building and turned in the opposite direction of the crowd that formed around the body on the sidewalk. As she turned the corner and left the area, she was still shaken by what had occurred. But she took comfort in the fact that Captain Yancey would not be bothering her—or anyone else—ever again.

49

There's nothing like the smell of fresh dog poop to get your morning started," said Josephine.

Raven chuckled for the first time in days and leaned on her shovel. The kennel was full. Every cage housed at least two dogs and one cage held a large spotted hog. Lizzie was sprawled on the floor, ignoring the workers who shuffled in and out. Raven felt strange—numb, really. She had killed a man yesterday and did not feel any remorse.

"You know you're the boss now," Jo quipped. "You don't have to be down here."

"The job's only temporary," Raven reminded her. "Besides, I needed to get out of the office."

"It looks like you're feeling better," said Jo.

"I'm starting to," Raven replied. "I just want to get on with my life and stop worrying about gangsters and corrupt policemen."

Jo stopped sweeping to look at Raven. "One of the bad policemen fell off a roof," she said. "That ought to help matters."

"It does," said Raven. "But corrupt policemen are like cockroaches. If you step on one, another one takes his place."

"What are you going to do about Brian Sweeney?"

"Johnny Torrio said he would handle Sweeney," Raven said. "But if I don't hear from somebody soon, I'm going to see Sweeney myself."

"Are you sure that's a good idea?"

"What choice do I have?"

Jo did not respond. She let herself out of the pen she had been sweeping and moved into the next one. Its residents included two large boxers they had been calling Dempsey and Willard after the famous boxing champs.

Raven watched Jo move easily among the two formidable dogs and announced she was going back upstairs. As she opened the door to walk up to her office, however, she was brought up short by Alice Clement with her hand in the air ready to knock. Raven was immediately on the defensive, wondering if the detective wanted to question her about Captain Yancey's death. She invited Alice up to her office and had her new secretary bring them some coffee.

"I see in this morning's newspaper that Captain Yancey fell off the roof of your building," Raven said, deciding to seize the offensive.

"So I understand."

"How did that happen?"

Alice shrugged. "Maybe he jumped. He had thrown in with Brian Sweeney, and Sweeney's operation is being overrun by those Italians. People like Yancey are like a cancer in the Department. Good riddance, I'd say. It's being investigated by the department and the Coroner, but I doubt they'll find anything."

Raven decided to let it go at that.

Alice sipped her coffee and said, "So, you're in charge of all this now?"

"Temporarily," Raven said. "Until they find the right *man* for the job."

Raven allowed Alice to keep looking around the office while she observed the detective over her cup of coffee. She was a small woman—in stature, at least. But she had a manner about her that was confident to the point of being brash.

"I need your help with a case," Alice said, finally.

"Me?"

"It's a murder case that involves dogs—which I believe you know something about." She shifted her gaze from the outer office to Raven. "Are you interested?"

"Of course." Raven leaned forward and placed her arms on her desk.

"It involves a woman by the name of Mildred Moynihan," Alice began. "The Moynihans live in a fancy neighborhood on Schiller Street, just around the corner from your house."

Raven sat up straight. "My house? How do you know where I live?"

"I've been asking around," she said. "Miller gave me a little personal background and O'Malley said you have helped him on a case." She paused and then continued her story. "Anyway, the Moynihans are loaded, but it seems the Misses found herself a new, much younger, man and hubby was in the way. We got the call early this morning. She claims her dogs were attacking her. When her husband came to see what was going on, she shot at the dogs and killed him by accident."

"What about the dogs?"

"They're fine. She claims to be a bad shot."

Raven let it all sink in for a moment, and then asked, "How can I help with this?"

"Why would two dogs just up and attack their owner for no reason?"

"Some dogs are trained to do that. It's just their nature. This dog here," she pointed to Lizzie who was laying just outside the door to the office. "is a good dog, but in the wrong circumstance, I would not want to face her in a fight—much less two of her."

"But the dogs in question aren't like her. They're Labrador retrievers."

"Labs?" Raven repeated.

"Yes," Alice replied. "Big dogs but not, to my mind, vicious killers."

"Far from it," Raven laughed. "They're gun dogs, bred to retrieve birds for hunters. They have a soft mouth and a gentle disposition."

"Would you be willing to testify to that in a court of law?"

"Sure."

"Good," Alice said. She placed the coffee cup on the desk and leaned back. "There is one more thing."

"What is that?" Raven asked, suddenly feeling defensive.

"We have a lot of cases that involve animals," Alice began. "I've dealt with some of them myself. I've proposed to the Police Commission that we start an Animal Welfare Division," she paused, "and there is plenty of support within the ranks."

"And?" asked Raven.

"And," said Alice, "I put your name forward as a candidate to run the division. They're voting on Tuesday night."

"That's tomorrow," said Raven.

"I know. Sorry for the short notice."

"How can you do that?" Raven asked. "You're just a detective."

"I have friends in high places—or rather friends who are the wives of people in high places." Alice took a sip of coffee and continued. "Most of the Commissioners can't stand me, but they know the press loves what I represent. They choose their battles carefully. The only reason they hired me in the first place was to boost their image with constituents who will soon get the vote. Having a woman head-up a division that deals with animal related problems isn't so distasteful to most of those bastards."

"Would I have to give up my work here?"

Alice appeared surprised by the question. "Probably. But it's not so much giving up the work here as it is doing the same work for a different organization—an organization that can actually do something about cruelty to animals."

"Would I be a police officer, like you?"

"No. This is a civilian position. You wouldn't have arrest powers, but you would have a couple of officers under your command."

Raven laughed.

"What's funny?"

"I guess I would be the City Dogcatcher," she said. "Someone recently suggested that's what I already am. He'll probably be amused."

"So, what do you say?"

Raven wasn't sure she wanted to play the game—trying to be a woman in a man's world. The men would be constantly trying to undermine her authority. But she could do a lot of good for the city's animal population. She finally said yes, despite her misgivings.

50

T he Coroner's report came out last night," declared O'Malley. "It was suicide."

"How could they know that?" asked Raven.

"A process of elimination," replied Walt. "There were no marks on him other than those consistent with a fall and there was no sign of anyone else on the roof."

"But why would he do that?" Raven wasn't sure why she felt compelled to press the issue, but she had to know if anyone suspected.

"Everyone in this building knew the Captain was in Brian Sweeney's pocket," said O'Malley. "He probably saw the writing on the wall. Just a few days after Yancey's death, Johnny Torrio started pushing Colosimo out of the way. He's brokering a deal with all the city's major gangs. Our sources tell us they're going to share the Prohibition wealth. Every gang in the city has its own territory—even Sweeney and his boys."

Raven did not respond. She knew that Yancey had been calling the shots, not Sweeney. Even though Torrio was now running things, the thought of Brian Sweeney still being out there gave her a shiver.

"We do have some good news," said Walt. He looked at O'Malley.

"With Yancey out of the way," O'Malley began, "the dogfighting ring has been broken up. The dogs are being held at the police stable."

"What about...?"

"We have Katherine's dogs," Walt cut her off, "and Lou's mean little dog, Max."

Raven smiled. It was almost too much to take in—the dogs rescued, Yancey dead, and O'Malley and Walter recommended for promotion to Lieutenant and Sergeant.

"Where is Alice?" Raven asked. She looked expectantly toward the outer office.

"She's not coming," O'Malley replied.

"Why not?"

"She's upset," O'Malley said.

It suddenly dawned on Raven why Walt had called last night and summoned her to the headquarters so early in the morning—before the news broke.

"I didn't get the job," she said, "did I?"

O'Malley hesitated and glanced at Walt as if expecting support. Walt grew suddenly interested in his shoes.

"They gave it to someone else," said O'Malley.

"Let me guess," she said. "They wanted a man."

"It was a political favor," Walt said bitterly.

"But Alice seemed so sure."

"Alice needs to learn that she can't fight the machine," O'Malley said.

"What about the new dog pound?" Raven asked.

"They approved that," said Walt.

"But they can't decide where to build it," O'Malley continued.

"Politics again?" asked Raven.

No one answered, allowing an awkward silence to smother the room. Raven was mildly upset. She felt rejected, which was ironic considering she had thought about turning down the job. She had received a letter in yesterday's mail offering her Lou's old job as superintendent of the Animal Welfare Association. She had been insulted that the salary was considerably lower than Lou's, something she knew because she had been reviewing their financial records. Her plan had been to tell the association that she had been offered a better job and see if she could leverage a more appropriate salary—even though she did not need the money. It was the principle.

As she glanced at the outer office, she was struck by the number of people that worked for the Chicago Police Department. She saw uniformed officers, plainclothes detectives, and clerks. If she were to work here, she would just be one more cog in a very big machine. She felt her disappointment turning to relief.

"I'd still like to use you on special cases," said O'Malley. "If that's okay with you."

"Sure," she said.

O'Malley stood up, signaling an end to their meeting.

"I'll see you out," Walt said to Raven as they also stood.

He held the door for her and followed Vincent out, closing the door behind him. They were walking down a long hallway toward the stairs when he suddenly grabbed her hand and pulled her into a small unoccupied office. He grabbed the dog by the collar and pulled him inside, as well, and closed the door.

Without a word, he wrapped her in his arms and kissed her. She was too surprised to protest. He reached behind her and turned the lock as she held him tight.

He pressed her against the door and began to hike her skirt but was interrupted by someone trying the door, first by twisting the lock, then by knocking.

"Is someone in there?" a voice said through the door.

She began to giggle, but he placed his hand over her mouth. They adjusted their clothes, and he led her through another door and into an adjoining office where a typist greeted them with a surprised look.

"I was just showing Miss Griffith around the office," Walt explained as they strolled through her workspace with Vincent and back out into the hallway. A man with a mop bucket stood knocking on the door to the office they had just vacated.

"You know," Walt said when they reached the lobby and each took a seat in the reception area, "it's better that you didn't get the job— better for us, I mean."

"I suppose you're right." she smiled at him. "We would probably run out of rooms to hide in."

"Are you okay?" he asked, suddenly turning serious. "You do realize that it was just politics as usual."

"I'll be fine," she said. "Nobody likes being rejected. But I have other opportunities."

Before Walt could respond, the desk sergeant across the room looked up from a phone call and said, "There is a shootout going on right now down in Canaryville!"

Walt jumped up without a word, grabbed Vincent's leash, and ran back inside toward O'Malley's office. Officers scurried everywhere as Raven left the building, worried once again about Walt's safety.

51

After the abrupt end to their meeting, Raven returned to her office and immediately composed a letter to the Association accepting the superintendent's position. On her walk back to the office, she had decided to make a few demands. She wanted to make improvements to their kennel facilities, she wanted to build an equine shelter, and she wanted to open a free clinic for dogs and cats. She also wrote that she would be looking for a new veterinarian and would be promoting Josephine Washington to Small Animal Officer. With the letter sitting in an envelope on her desk, she was gazing out the window when a police officer burst into the room. For a moment she panicked, irrationally thinking he might be bringing some bad news about Walt and the shootout he had been called to an hour ago.

"Are you the department's new dogcatcher?" he asked.

"No, I'm not. What do you want?" She was angry—angry at his abrupt approach and angry at being referred to as a dogcatcher.

"O'Malley sent me," he said. "There's been a shootout on the South Side and the dead guy has his own private zoo—a bear, a couple of monkeys, and the biggest damn snake I've ever seen. He wants you there right now."

"Tell him I'll be there as quick as I can."

Her anger disappeared as she rushed downstairs to grab a net, a catchpole, and Josephine. Raven explained the situation to Jo, who said, "We can't catch a bear with a rope and a pole. We'd better get Harry from the zoo."

Thirty minutes later, after sending Jo to the zoo, Raven stood in a basement three doors down from the house where she had once confronted Brian Sweeney looking at a dead man in a cage with a full-grown bear—probably a male, judging by its size. Harry, Jo, and a couple of workers from the zoo should be on their way bringing ropes and crates. Walt was picking up bullet casings from the floor. The man had been shot while inside the cage—perhaps while he was cleaning and feeding the animal. The bear appeared to be agitated but unharmed.

O'Malley faced her. "Seems like we've been here before," he said. "Only this time it's not some dog, and you're not going to handle it with a piece of cheese and a rope on a pole."

She looked around the room—at the cage with the two monkeys who were silently watching the proceedings, at the glass-fronted box with a huge mottled brown snake inside, and at the bear pacing before her stepping around the dead man at each turn. Then she turned to O'Malley and said, "Why don't you and Officer Miller wait upstairs. Send down the people with the crates when they arrive and let me do my job. I'll call you when we're finished."

He looked at her through squinting eyes, apparently unsure how to react to being ordered around by this young woman. Finally, he motioned to Walt and walked to the stairs. He turned and said, "Hurry it up. I don't want to be here all day."

As they ascended the stairs, Raven said, "Would you please hand me the catchpole?"

"What are you planning to do?" Walt asked.

"I have an idea," Raven replied, "but I need you to leave me alone."

"Not a chance," Walt said.

"Toss down the catch pole and wait at the top of the stairs. I'll call if I need help." When he just stood there, she said more forcefully, "Go. And don't let anyone come down here until I say."

She watched him walk up the stairs and felt bad for being so rude. He handed down the pole and retreated to the top of the stairs.

"Close the door," she said.

When he did so, she sat on a rickety chair opposite the cage and removed the rope from the pole as she watched the bear pace. The animal slowly calmed down and began to watch her.

Nearly ten years ago, when she was just sixteen, a bear much like this one came to her town. It had accidentally killed a man in a wrestling match outside a bar. After the bear was confiscated, the town decided to build a zoo around it and her father was named the zoo's first keeper. She had been introduced to all types of animals, but her time with Zeke the bear had the most impact on her life. She had fed the bear on nights so cold that his food would freeze if he didn't eat it right away. She had attempted to untie the bear from a tree to lead it away from a dangerous house fire, and she had entered its cage with her father to rescue her brother after he had been locked inside by a disgruntled zookeeper. She felt a connection to that bear and wondered if that connection could be transferred to this one.

She watched the bear closely and noticed that it was looking at its overturned water bowl. She rose from her chair, filled a bucket with water from the sink, and carefully unlatched the door to the cage. The bear backed up, pursed its lips, and snorted, but showed no sign of charging at her. It was clear that the bear was accustomed to having its owner enter its cage, so Raven closed the door behind her. Moving very slowly and talking in hushed tones, telling the bear what a good boy he was, she inched over to the water bowl, turned it upright and filled it with water. She backed away and the bear immediately went forward and began lapping the water.

"Is everything okay down there?" said Walt from the top of the stairs.

"Yes," Raven said loud enough to be heard, but so loud as to disturb the bear.

She slipped out of the cage and went back to the sink where a bowl of dog food had been placed. This would have been put into the cage after the owner had finished cleaning. She emptied most of the food onto the counter and carried a small amount back into the cage along the rope that was slung over her shoulder. She wanted to gain the animal's trust with some food but did not want it to gorge itself on a full bowl. That would come later when he was back at the zoo.

She held the bowl of food toward the bear. He inched closer and pulled some into his mouth with his lips. She squatted, remained very still, and touched the beast on his head as he came toward the bowl again. He did not react. This bear was comfortable being handled and had probably been raised around people, like Zeke the wrestling bear.

Unlike dogs, who wear their emotions in their facial expressions and body language, bears are difficult to read. But Raven continued to feed, touch, and then rub the bear. He made no move to back away and even seemed to relish the contact.

She slipped the rope around his neck and front leg, ensuring that if he backed away and tightened the noose, he would not strangle himself. Using gentle pressure on the rope, she eased the bear out of the cage. He resisted a little but seemed to grow more comfortable as she guided him up the stairs.

"Are the zoo people here yet?" she hollered up the stairs.

"They just arrived," said Walt. "They'll be right down with the crate."

"Tell them to wait. We're coming up."

"What?" exclaimed Walt. "Who's coming up?"

As Raven and the bear emerged, Walt jumped back from the basement steps and rushed to open the front door to the house. Raven Griffith emerged onto the porch with a large black bear on a leash, like some great dog. They were both so calm that it must have appeared to all who witnessed the event that they had done this before.

EPILOGUE

Saturday, April 3ʳᵈ

*I*t was all Raven could do to resist hitting Anson Roker with the shovel she was holding. Her best friend growing up had been a Negro girl named Lizzie Harmon—Lizzie, the dog's namesake. And when Raven was a teenager, Rondell Boyd, a Negro man, had pulled her from a burning building and saved her life. Raven's affinity for people of color was deep-seated and genuine, so she had little tolerance for racists.

"He's telling you what to do," Raven told Roker, "because he's in charge of this place."

"I'm too old to start taking orders from a nigger," Roker said.

"You use that term again and your face is going to look like the flat end of this shovel," Raven hissed, pushing the shovel toward his nose.

"Raven," Rondell stepped in between them. "It's okay."

"It's not okay."

"Roker," Rondell continued. "You don't want to mess with her. If you don't want to work here, then clear out."

Roker was part of a team of men sent by the City to help clean up the old Jackson Boulevard Foundry. He was a dumpy, middle-aged man with mutton-chop whiskers and a bad disposition. The other

J. D. Porter

half-dozen men seemed content to let Roker fight their battles and equally ready to go back to work when told.

The two-acre site, a half mile west of Union Station, had been a foundry and smithy for its first hundred years and, when motor vehicles began to come into their own and blacksmiths fell from favor, it found new life as a saloon. Prohibition had put an end to that. The City was happy to donate it to the Animal Welfare Association as its newest operation—the Louis Hanson Equine Shelter. It had been a dream of Lou's and a way for Raven to honor his memory with some of her newfound wealth.

Rondell's plan was for them to gut the interior of the saloon and return it to its original use as a stable and workhouse. It would support a paddock covering more than half an acre which would hold most of the animals and a series of smaller holding stalls and corrals for the animals that needed special care or veterinary treatment.

In the process of demolishing the interior of the saloon, the workers also needed to demolish the outhouses—a job that usually went to Negro crews. Having their roles reversed was just too much for some of them to bear.

Raven let Rondell walk away believing he had had the last word before she turned back to Roker and moved her face close to his. She said in a low voice that the other men could hear, as well, "You'll do what he says and treat him with respect. Do you understand?"

He puffed up a little before his eyes began to shift from side to side and he inched back from her. He looked back at the men behind him and said, "Alright, let's get back to work."

Raven walked over to where Rondell was working on the gate to the barn and leaned against the wall.

"How's the dog working out?" Raven asked. Bea had followed Rondell to where he was working and plopped down behind him, watching the workmen with suspicion. Bea had been living at the kennel—passed over for adoption on numerous occasions—and Raven had a feeling the big German shepherd might be a good addition to Rondell's operation.

"She's a smart dog. She's not mean enough to be a good guard dog, but she's good with the horses and mules. She'll have a place in the stable and I'll let her out at night to walk the grounds." When he finished pounding the nail to fasten the hinge, he turned to Raven and said, "I don't need you coming out here and fighting my battles."

"I know," she replied. "I just have no patience for people like that. I can't help it."

He went back to hammering and said without turning, "Do you still want me and Essie at your dinner this evening?"

"Of course, I do. Why would you ask that?"

"You know why." He stopped his work and turned back to her. "I'm not sure it a good idea for us to be seen in your neighborhood—much less going in the front door."

Raven looked at him for a moment before she replied. "I don't care what people say. You and Essie are my friends. Min Lee will pick you up at six o'clock."

She did not wait for his reply.

"What are we waiting for?" asked Jo. "I'm starving."

"Not what—who," Raven replied. "We're waiting for Min Lee to get back with Rondell and Essie."

The two women sat in the front parlor overlooking the street. Raven had insisted that Jo remain there as Raven flitted in and out, obviously overseeing something in another part of the house. It was after six o'clock and it would be dark soon.

Suddenly Jo sat up in her chair. "What is he doing here?" She was watching Harry Fischer walk up the front steps.

"Oh," Raven said in mock-surprise. "Didn't I mention that I invited Harry to join us?"

Jo jumped up and had the door open before he could knock. Raven could see that they wanted to embrace, but they held hands instead.

Before they could sit back down, Min Lee arrived with their other guests—which included Lou's dog, Max. Rondell and Essie had adopted him after Min Lee convinced Max that women weren't so bad, after all.

After everyone had greeted each other, they went through to the kitchen where the curtains were drawn. and the table was empty.

"Where's dinner?" asked a disappointed Jo, looking at the table.

Raven faced the group and said, "When I received news of my inheritance," she looked around the kitchen, "and it began to sink in what it meant, I was overwhelmed. I'm a simple girl. I've never been responsible for anything like this. But I have some people in my life that can probably help me figure out how to deal with it." She paused. "I wanted to do something special to celebrate our good fortune." With that, she opened the door to the back yard and led them outside.

While Min Lee and Jo had been ordered to remain in the front of the house, the garden had been transformed. Electric lights had been strung in the trees, casting a merry glow on an evening scene that would soon be bathed in the soft light of a full moon. A simple table had been set beneath a temporary arbor in the back corner of the garden. The yellow and white daffodils were tucked under the white early spring blossoms of the dogwood trees along the back wall while the red and pink tulips were a perfect complement to the pink blossoms of the flowering crabapple trees that lined either side of the garden. The scene was completed by Lizzie lying next to the gazebo, Max sitting on the steps to the house, and the two terriers, Gracie and Sophie, sniffing around the tables as if they, too, were waiting for someone to serve their dinner.

"I've had this catered," Raven said to Min Lee, "so you could join us."

The dinner was a special treat for Raven, not because of the food—which was pleasant but not particularly memorable—but because of the company. Min Lee took some good-natured ribbing as her companions compared the food to what she might have prepared.

Jo was smitten by sitting down to dinner next to her beau, and Rondell recounted his day preparing the site of the new equine center. It was the kind of conversation any normal family might have.

After the dishes had been cleared away and coffee had been served, Raven said, "I want to thank you all for being here—for being my friends. I want us to be a family and this dinner is exactly the type of family time I was hoping for."

"You don't need to thank us," said Jo. "We love it here. We love you."

The rest nodded in agreement.

"It looks like someone is late for dinner," said Min Lee.

Everyone turned in the direction she was looking. Walt Miller stood on the back steps of the house with Vincent at his side, wagging his tail.

"The front door was unlocked," he said as Raven approached him on the steps. "I let myself in."

She glanced back at the table where all eyes were on her, so she was careful not to touch him. She did, however, lead him into the kitchen where, away from prying eyes, she was able to embrace and kiss him in private while Lizzie and Vincent sniffed each other. She took him by the hand and led him into the front parlor. She fixed them both a drink, lit herself a cigarette, and the dogs plopped down between them.

"What are you doing here?" she asked.

"Min Lee suggested I stop by."

"Min Lee?"

"She knows about us, you know?" he said.

"You told her?"

"No, I didn't tell her. She just knows things."

Raven sipped her drink and looked out the widow toward the tree-lined street. The new electric streetlights cast a warm glow on the people who strolled along the sidewalk. She had everything she could want—a meaningful job helping animals, a beautiful house, plenty of money, and a back yard full of the best friends a person could ask for. And she had a wonderful lover—albeit a married one. Life was almost perfect—but just, almost.

Her gaze came to rest on a car parked across the street with two men in the front seat. At first glance, the men did not appear to be a threat. But as her thoughts began to sharpen and her eyes began to focus, she locked eyes with the man nearest her. She held his gaze for a moment, then turned back to her conversation with Walt, determined not to be intimidated by Sweeney's man, Finbarr.

ABOUT THE AUTHOR

Figure 1: Jana, Simba, and Author (ca. 1989)

J. D. Porter managed parks, zoos, and museums for over forty years and memorialized that career in his first novel, *The Menagerie: A Zoo Story*.

But dogs are the animals that bookend his life's story. They protected him when he was a child. They shared his home and marriage, helped him raise children, and comforted him in retirement. *The Dogcatcher and The Fox* is for them.

.

Made in United States
Orlando, FL
27 February 2024

44157562R00168